Praise for *G*

'The kind of big-hearted, emotionally br[...] you love fiction . . . *Goodwood* is many [...] tiously constructed mystery, an affectio[...] time and a place, and a darkly lovely con[...] it's a complete revelation, the conjuring up of a sad, beautiful, indelible little world of its own' The Sydney Morning Herald

'Goddamn brilliant. This funny-sad mystery about growing up, missing persons and dark truths about your neighbourhood will gently, gorgeously demolish you' Benjamin Law

'*Goodwood* is gripping, moving, often funny and written with a sure ear for Australian country-town vernacular. Very good.' Mark Colvin (on Twitter)

'Lyrical without being abstruse, colloquial without being contrived. Her characters, while familiar, are nuanced and authentic, and her depiction of small-town life is bang-on in both its endearing and suffocating ways.' *Readings Monthly*

'A little bit *Twin Peaks* and a little bit *Picnic at Hanging Rock*, *Goodwood* is a terrific, thoroughly Australian novel . . .' *Australian Women's Weekly*

'. . . the world Throsby builds around her teenage narrator in this book is so vivid it can occasionally feel more like fact than fiction . . . *Goodwood* is wonderfully lush and well-realised . . . The intrigue slowly builds to the point where the urge to learn the truth about the disappearances becomes overwhelming. The ending does not disappoint.' *The Australian*

'A lyrical, rolling ballad of a small country town hit with a one/two punch of grief and a one/two punch of burgeoning sexuality for the story's narrator, seventeen year old Jean Brown. The characters are rich and myriad, from family and friends, neighbours, shopkeepers and barflies. All are beautifully realised . . . Refrain and reprise are used brilliantly in a composition that's rich in rhythm with a melodic tone conceived from a keen imagination, an observant eye and a fine ear for idiom and the colloquial.' Sydney Arts Guide

'The portrait of small town life is given a deep richness by Throsby, in this her first novel, presenting a very readable, enjoyable, quirky, slightly wry look at the many, many characters you will find in any town, on any given day, pretty much anywhere in the world, let alone Goodwood, somewhere in Australia.' Blue Wolf Reviews

'a chilling, evocative and buzzed-about debut' *Who Magazine*

'*Goodwood* is a sharp, well written and charming novel . . . Although the book can be dark in nature . . . there is a multitude of colour underlying the paragraphs.' The AU Review

'. . . so much truth, so much aching and pain by humour . . . What a wonderful book. I can see the Australian novelist continuum from Patrick White and Thea Astley in her explicit representation of the character of Australians in regional towns. Others have compared Throsby with Tim Winton. I hope she is writing another book.' Lindy Morrison in Loud Mouth

'[*Goodwood* is] very, *very* readable. I devoured it in a couple of sittings . . . thoughtful and authentic . . . these portraits were outstandingly done. Top reading indeed.' Fair Dinkum Crime

'The first half of Throsby's book promises a delayed sort of coming of age story about the ties we share amongst the people living amongst us, the inescapable interconnectivity of small townships and the way a death or vanishing sends ripples through a community. But it is equally an insight into the personal goings-on and formative queries of protagonist Jean, who must process the central mystery while also calibrating her sense of reality and emerging bisexuality . . . If you put *Goodwood* side-by-side with some of the more obvious choices of queer youth canon, it offers an alternative to the masculinist narratives that have dominated Australian queer fiction.' *Kill Your Darlings*

Holly Throsby is a songwriter, musician and novelist from Sydney, Australia. She has released five solo albums, a collection of original children's songs, an album as part of the band Seeker Lover Keeper, and has been nominated for four ARIAs. Holly's debut novel *Goodwood* (2016) was a critically acclaimed bestseller, shortlisted for the Indie and ABIA awards, as well as the Davitt and Ned Kelly awards.

Dear Alice,
Hope you enjoy
this as much
I. Thank you for
your book :)
FB challenge 2019
♡ Eloise

Also by Holly Throsby

Goodwood

CEDAR VALLEY

HOLLY THROSBY

ALLEN&UNWIN
SYDNEY · MELBOURNE · AUCKLAND · LONDON

First published in 2018

Allen & Unwin
83 Alexander Street
Crows Nest NSW 2065
Australia
Phone: (61 2) 8425 0100
Email: info@allenandunwin.com
Web: www.allenandunwin.com

 A catalogue record for this
book is available from the
National Library of Australia

ISBN 978 1 76063 056 0

Set in 13.9/19 pt Perpetua Std by Bookhouse, Sydney
Printed and bound in Australia by Griffin Press

10 9 8 7 6 5 4 3 2 1

For Alvy

1

Benny Miller was not the only person to arrive as a stranger in Cedar Valley on the first day of summer in 1993.

A man arrived, too—a calm-faced man in a brown wool suit and a wide-striped tie, clothing too warm for the weather. He strolled down Valley Road, past the hairdresser and a small cafe. A warm wind stirred, carrying with it the faint smell of pies and horses, and the man paused for just a moment before he sat down. Benny Miller would have driven right past him in her station wagon on that bright and brimming day.

Here she was, this young woman Benny Miller, all of twenty-one. She pulled off Valley Road, concentrating on the directions she had committed to mind. A curved street lay before her and Benny eased along it, veering left at the end, two hands steady on the wheel. Wiyanga Crescent, when she reached it, was narrow and short, a cul-de-sac surrounded by bush. She stopped at a weatherboard cottage, double-checking the number on the letterbox, and pulled her car into a bricked driveway covered in leaves.

Benny Miller got out and stood straight as a pole. She stretched her long arms and took a moment to look around. Low-slung houses were set apart widely and neat grassy footpaths were lined with flowering trees. Boats and camper trailers sat in faded carports. Cicadas sang in the damp air. Full of apprehension, Benny blinked at the street and then turned to stare at the modest green cottage: her new home.

•

On that same day—the first of December—the man in the suit arrived too. He made his way along Valley Road, arousing little attention, and he sat down directly on the footpath in front of Cedar Valley Curios & Old Wares.

Curios, as it was known to locals, was a big old shop, as cavernous as a barn. It had a large glass frontage with gold-leaf signage and antiques arranged in the window. Cora Franks, the proprietor, saw the well-dressed man as he sat down and leaned his back against the glass. And if she hadn't been deep in conversation with Therese Johnson (about the extramarital affairs of Ed Johnson), then Cora would have got up straight away and said, 'Excuse me, sir, but that isn't the best place to sit—there's a bench for that purpose just along in front of the Coiffure.' But Therese was so upset, on the verge of tears, and Cora didn't think it a good time to interrupt.

Eventually, Therese left and an out-of-town-looking lady came in and asked to see some of the watches that Cora kept in the display cabinet. Then Mary Anne arrived and Cora got to chatting. Later, she organised the books on the back shelves, and she tried on some new blouses that had come in as part of a deceased estate, and by that time it was almost five and she had forgotten about the man on the footpath altogether.

•

Just a few streets away, Benny Miller had gone to the metal letterbox outside the cottage, opened the lid and fetched the key from inside, just as she'd been instructed. She walked along the path through the long grass at the front of the house and went up the steps to the verandah. The whole look of the place was nicer than she had imagined—the weatherboards, the stained-glass windows, the steep slant of the roof—although she hadn't really known what to expect on the drive.

Benny had never been to Cedar Valley before, nor to many other places either. She'd been born and raised in Sydney and was yet to travel—except for a primary school excursion to Canberra and a high school excursion to Jindabyne, both of which had been cold. Her childhood home was a terrace house in Rozelle, with a view of the power station. Her most recent home, up till this morning, was a terrace house in Glebe, a few doors along from the cinema. She'd shared it with three friends she met at university. They were good friends, good people. But Benny had always been wary of friends in some deep-down way and, despite their goodness, she had maintained a careful distance, perceptible only to herself. She was so grateful—almost guiltily so—when they had helped her load her car for the drive to Cedar Valley, waving and yelling their goodbyes as she pulled out of the carport and honked her horn, laughing.

But of course the laughing hadn't lasted. By the time the outer suburbs of Sydney had become unfamiliar, a spring of sadness had welled in Benny's chest, along with an ordinary old fear of the unknown that she did her stoic best to ignore.

Why had Benny Miller come to Cedar Valley? Well that was simple enough. Benny had come on account of Odette Fisher, her mother's old friend. Odette owned this pale green cottage and had said that Benny could stay there as long as she wanted. The offer had drawn Benny like a magnet. She had quit her job at the pub, handed in her final assignments and sat her exams. Then she had sat in her room in Glebe, listening to Harry Nilsson, packing her clothes into an open suitcase, and imagining her new life in a small town with its lonely sophistication.

The fact that Benny had never actually *met* Odette did not deter her. She had thought about her a great deal. And she knew her face so well from the photographs. Odette and Benny's mother were the closest of friends. Benny had keenly collected pictures of them together and kept them in a cardboard box, along with her other treasures. Not a month went by when she didn't look at them, these pictures of her mother, and of her mother with Odette, in various poses: sitting at a bar, standing in front of an old car, leaning against a long wooden fence, their faces fresh and free.

And then Odette's letter had arrived to sit on Frank Miller's kitchen table like a prize.

'It's from Odette Fisher,' said Frank, Benny's father. 'Her name's written on the back.'

He let out a nervous laugh and kept his eyes on the tin of cedar polish he was applying to a dining chair.

'Your, ah . . . your mum's friend, Odette Fisher,' he said to the chair.

The letter was addressed formally to Benita Miller, and Benny took it eagerly to read it in the car.

'Dear Benny,' it said. 'I am Odette Fisher, an old friend of your mother. I write to say how very sorry I am, Benny, to hear the news. I haven't seen Vivian in some years but of course I'm heartbroken. Please, if you need anything would you let me know? I'm sure Vivian would want me to check in on you, and I feel awful that we have never met. Perhaps you would consider visiting me where I live in Cedar Valley, approximately two and a half hours from Sydney. It would be so nice to get to know you a little. If you would ever like to talk, do call me on this number anytime.'

A telephone number was written below in black pen.

Benny sat in the driver's seat and held the letter, and then she read it again. Afterwards, she drove back to her house in Glebe, fetched her box of photographs down from the top shelf of her cupboard and sifted through them to find the photos she knew were of Odette.

Then she sat on the bed and lay the pictures in a neat row on the quilt.

There was Odette Fisher.

And next to her, there was Benny's mother.

A cold feeling came over Benny, like stepping into snow, and then the old familiar stirrings of yearning and shame. But on that day, something new followed. Perhaps it was something close to excitement—a bustling in her chest. *It would be so nice to get to know you a little.* Benny shut her eyes and balanced, as if on a rope, between strange divergent feelings. Then she lay back on the bed, stared at the ceiling, and decided that she would call Odette Fisher, just as soon as she'd worked out what she wanted to say. And when she did call, it was in that brief and oddly comfortable conversation that Odette had made the offer: of her accommodation; her company. Benny could feel the warmth in the older woman's voice coming down the phone line. How easy it was to talk with this woman, Odette Fisher.

'That house has been sitting there empty all year, Benny. I'd be happy to have someone in it. And you could come visit me as much as you like. I'm just a ten-minute drive out of town up the mountain. I'd so love to have you around.'

So here she was—Benny Miller in Cedar Valley—standing in her high-waisted jeans and T-shirt on the unfamiliar verandah with a key in her hand, while the well-dressed man on Valley Road was sitting on the footpath.

•

In one report, he was seen to extend his arm out and then above his head, elegantly, 'like a dancer'; in another he rested his chin against his chest, and then turned his head slowly from side to side, as if stretching the muscles in his neck. There was nothing unsavoury about the look of him. No indication of drunkenness or insanity. He was handsome enough, with kindly eyes, and in 'perfectly good condition', according to Janet Avery, who nursed at Valley Road Family Medical and was quoted later in the newspaper. Everyone who walked past the seated man that afternoon reported his healthy appearance as much as his calm and contented expression.

He just stretched and sat, and stared a little, and sat some more, and at some point—after a good while sitting on the footpath up against the big glass window under the gold leaf letters—he died.

2

A person could come at Cedar Valley from several directions. From the north or south, it was just a few moments off the coastal highway, via a charming stretch of road where cows looked on from a large paddock and horses mingled under a clump of trees near a fence. Towards the east, small roads beat a meandering path that eventually found the ocean. Sparkling beaches lined the coast with sand as white as teeth.

But if you came in via the big motorway, which was off to the west, it was a treacherous descent down the bushy mountain on a mosquito-coil of a road. It wound in and out in the speckled shade and moss grew along the edges of the bitumen. Occasional white posts were the only thing to stop a car from skidding through the thick ferns and off over the edge of the mountain.

This was the way Benny had come in that morning, her ears popping with the altitude, and her old car rattling at an angle around the tight curves. Benny sat stiffly, gripping the wheel, and she had taken the advice of every road sign, especially the ones that called for a speed limit of twenty-five kilometres per hour. At one point she realised she was barely breathing, such was the intensity of her concentration. It was the steepest road she had ever encountered, and the bends were the sharpest. By the time she had reached the bottom, a small rim of sweat sat along the back of her neck.

In Benny's station wagon, along with Benny, were most of her worldly belongings. She'd purchased two suitcases from the Vinnies on Glebe Point Road and filled them full of clothes. Tapes and books were stuffed into old beer cartons and plastic bags. In the footwells were some small furnishings (a reading lamp, a bedside table). She had stored her larger items in Frank Miller's garage, while he chewed his fingernails and admitted nothing of his true feelings.

Benny's most important possession—her box of photographs and personal treasures—sat on the passenger seat beside her.

At the bottom of the mountain, greatly relieved, Benny let herself look about at the tall gum trees that grew thickly all around. Their trunks were cream, or brown, or grey and gradually they gave way to open space. Paddocks lined with wire fences. Some sheep on a tufty hill. Farmhouses with machinery beside them and old tin sheds. She saw a boat in a driveway, under a tarpaulin, and short white birds with long bent necks.

Soon enough Benny came upon a bridge that stood like a sentry before the town of Cedar Valley. It was old and grand, with tall sandstone towers that caught the light in a particular way and seemed to glow. In a moment, Benny was driving over it, and she saw how high it was over the brown water. She slowed the car to a crawl, rolling the window down and hearing, for the first time, the sound of a rushing river.

All of this would have happened just moments before the well-dressed man sat down on Valley Road. And it infuriated Benny ever after that she couldn't remember seeing him as she came in, but of course she didn't, she was too busy looking around at the main road of the town. She drove past a post office, a pizzeria, a hardware store, a bookstore, and she felt good about the general feel of the place and the look of the people. A man in a brimmed hat and a flannel shirt was reading a newspaper in a neat park. Benny saw how wide the main street was—it was immensely wide—and she took in the handsome brick shopfronts with verandahs above them. There was a crowd of people outside a shop called Fran's World Famous Pies, and a big pub sat on a broad corner, painted pink and yellow and green. A truck rattled past, filling her car with an unfamiliar aroma that Benny would soon recognise as horses.

But Benny didn't see a man in a well-made suit, and she didn't notice the gold leaf letters that spelt out CEDAR VALLEY CURIOS & OLD WARES either. Small street trees were planted along that section of Valley Road, and there was a particularly low awning that obscured easy vision from passing cars.

Benny merely drove by, turned left at the grocery store, past the weedy vacant lot, and soon found the pale green house, the key in the letterbox.

She unlocked the door and stood for a moment in the living room that smelled of dust and closed windows. There was a slow-combustion fireplace in the corner and a pile of logs and newspapers in a basket beside it. Odette had told her the house was furnished, and it surely was: long couches with large cushions, a coffee table, an armchair, everything tasteful and old. There was a wooden sideboard with a record player on it, and paintings in antique frames on the walls.

Benny went along the hallway to the kitchen, put her bag on the table and read a note Odette had left on the bench. It said she'd been over yesterday to turn the fridge on and that she'd left some milk and cheese in it. Benny saw fresh bread on the counter, some peaches, and dirt-smudged eggs in a bowl.

Possum may still be living in the shed, he sleeps in the washbasin on the shelf. Python lives in the roof—don't worry, he can't get into the house.

Benny read this and glanced up at the ceiling worriedly. Then she unlatched the double doors that opened out onto a little deck, and she sat down on the slats and ate a peach.

The garden was overgrown with trees and weeds and vines, and the shed at the back was an old slanted thing with a corrugated-iron roof and a door hanging off one hinge. Behind it was bush, dense high gum trees with cicadas singing in them and bird calls she didn't recognise.

Benny contemplated the wild garden and thought of sending a letter to Jules to tell him where she was and what she was doing, but as soon as the thought occurred to her, she knew she most probably wouldn't.

Instead, she went back inside and decided on the front bedroom, which was smaller than the middle one, but she liked the picture window facing the street. She made a few trips to the car, bringing in her suitcases and boxes, and she unpacked her sheets and made the bed. A quilt was folded on the seat of the picture window so she spread it out on top and thought the bed looked nice. She opened her box of treasures, setting her collection of interesting rocks and stones in a neat line along the bedhead. Then she pulled out her favourite photo of her mother and put the silver frame on the bedside table.

Benny Miller sat still in the quiet room and stared at the picture.

'Hi, Mum,' she said. 'I miss you.'

The walls were cream and the room was quiet. Benny's mum—whose name was Vivian Alice Moon—smiled back from the photo.

'I miss you too, Benny,' said Benny aloud to herself, as if it were her mother talking, and she lay back on the coloured quilt.

Benny was not much of a crier.

She was more given to quiet rumination, or spells of busied distraction, buoying herself with some activity or another, finding relief in her capabilities, keeping herself afloat with a valiant kind of independence.

But being so far from home—perhaps that's what it was—the newness of it snuck up on her. She pulled her knees up to her chest, squeezed her eyes closed and, though she did everything she could to hold it in, out it came, the hot tears and sound. Benny lay on her side and made a cocoon of her body there on the bed, curling herself up as small as she could as if trying to disappear. She wept softly at first. Then she creaked open, like the door of an old shed, and she sobbed with all the elemental sadness that a person can only feel when their mother has newly died.

3

Cora Franks generally shut Curios at four-thirty, but on that day it was a while after. She'd got stuck into the book organising and decided to make new signs for her sections: *Romance*, *Crime/Horror*, *Action*, *Fiction*, *Cooking* and *Misc*. The signs were good, she thought, since she'd used a ruler under the letters to make the bottom edges straight, and she'd made them out of fluoro cardboard, so they stood out from the front of the shop if you were looking back towards the bookcases.

What stood out when you looked at the front of the shop, though, now that Cora was on her way towards the door, was the silhouette of the man in the suit, who had sat down there—how long ago now? A long time. What on earth was he still doing there? Begging? Cora Franks shook her head in annoyance and stepped out the front door, closing it behind her, and while she was in the process of locking it she began speaking, very sternly, to the suited gentleman on the ground.

'Excuse me, *sir*. That is not the best place to sit.'

The man stared calmly forward. His eyes were fixed on the chemist across the road. They were blue—his eyes—or they were grey; it was hard to tell in the five o'clock light.

'Sir?' said Cora, looking across at him now.

She finished locking up and shuffled on her brief legs the three or so metres to where he was sitting.

He was leaning back so his head was propped against the glass. His legs were straight out in front of him and his feet, in polished shoes, splayed out to either side. Looking at him front on, the gold lettering of *Old Wares* appeared to go right through him like a stake, impaling him sideways. His body covered most of the W. He looked so peaceful it seemed almost a shame to disturb him—and he had such a likeable face. Cora was already feeling bad for thinking ill of him. He was the kind of man who made you feel safe just to look at, like a gentlemanly hero from an old movie. He would know the way out of a difficult situation, a man like that. And what a nice suit it was, a properly authentic vintage suit.

'Sir?' she said again, more gently.

'Not one for conversation, is he?' said Lil Chapman, who had wandered out from the quilting shop next door to have a cigarette. 'I've seen you sitting there most of the afternoon, doing your stretches. You like to stretch, do you? Are you from out of town?' This last part was said slowly in a loud voice, as if he were either a moron or lacking basic knowledge of the English language. Lil Chapman, her hair faded and her cheeks creased with age, looked up to the sky and blew out a line of smoke.

Cora just stared downwards. Perhaps she went a little pale.

'Sir? *Please!*' she said, urgently this time, and waved her hand in front of his face.

The man did not blink. His chest, under a wide-striped tie that looked moderately expensive, was perfectly still.

'Lil,' said Cora, 'I think we'd better call someone.'

4

B enny Miller had stayed on the bed awhile, inert, staring out the picture window, and then she'd got up and looked around the house.

She opened every cupboard in the bathroom and inspected the scant contents: a bag of cotton buds, an old loofah, oatmeal soap, some Gumption. The wardrobes in all the bedrooms were empty, except for coathangers and spare blankets. The third bedroom, at the back, had a single bed and an old easel in the corner. There was no television, no tape player, and the record player didn't work. But Benny did find a small radio and an old jaffle iron in one of the kitchen cupboards, and she made a cheese jaffle. She ate at the outdoor setting on the small wooden deck.

Benny had plugged the radio in and found a local station but outside she couldn't hear it above the cicadas. The air teemed with their tremendous singing. And every so often a sound like a branch breaking off a tree came from the bush behind the shed—*crack!*—and loud rustling would follow. Benny wondered what creatures dwelt in that bush, and she was surprised to find these noises—the rich aliveness of them—quite calming.

•

Cora Franks, meanwhile, was not calm. She opened Curios again, her hand shaking as she inserted the key in the lock, and went directly to the telephone to call someone. Cora couldn't decide if she should request an ambulance or a policeman, so she dialled triple-o and asked for both.

'A man has died,' she said. 'A man is dead on the street!'

The operator, a dour woman, responded in an untroubled voice with a series of rehearsed questions. Had the man been checked for signs of life? Were there dangers present to other persons? Had the man met with foul play?

'Yes, we checked him, kind of,' said Cora. And, 'Oh. Well—hold on and I'll have a look.'

There was no sign of danger or foul play as far as Cora could see. But now that these things had been mentioned, Cora began to wonder. She looked around for intimations of violence or an impending threat, and was a little disappointed to report that she couldn't see evidence of either. No discarded weapon, no trail of blood. Not even a lonely *drop* of blood. Just a man leaning against her window, who looked perfectly fine, apart from being dead.

Lil wandered in wanly and she listened as Cora was describing the scene, even managing to get in a comment about the weather (it was getting a little windy) and lamenting the fact that death had taken this particular man, who clearly had an old-world sense of style.

'He must've been on his way in to buy something,' said Cora, as the thought occurred to her.

The operator remained unmoved.

'Nerves of steel, have you?' Cora asked as the conversation drew to its natural close.

'It's been a long day,' said the operator, and Cora hung up.

Then she and Lil, arms folded, waited on the footpath beside the man, as if guarding him from potential predators, while a small crowd gathered.

'He's passed,' said Cora to the congregation while the dead man stared at the shops opposite. 'We've checked him,' she added reassuringly. 'He's very dead.'

The wind was picking up a little, Cora had been right about that, and across the road, on a high verandah, washing flapped around in the breeze.

With numb detachment, Lil Chapman noted that the dead man's eyes were a kind of 'pea green'.

Cora said, 'Imagine just being dead like that with your eyes open? Everyone can just look right inside.'

And Janet Avery, the nurse, commended his healthful appearance. 'I walked past him at lunch and thought how good he looked,' she said to Keith Hand, who ran Cedar Valley Brake & Clutch up on the corner. 'I thought: there is a man who has good blood pressure. He looks a bit like Kerry, don't you think? Tall Kerry from the RTA?'

Keith tilted his head and looked at the dead man. 'I guess he could be a cousin of Kerry.'

'Does Kerry have a cousin?' asked Maureen Robinson, who worked across the road at the chemist. 'Should we call the RTA?'

Several shopkeepers stood around then and began discussing the strangeness of the scene. The out-of-town-looking lady who Cora had served earlier appeared again and hovered by a tree. Indeed, the small flock who'd assembled only served to attract more—many of them tourists—and there were about twenty-five people in total when the police arrived.

Constable Gus Franklin and Constable James Hall—both in uniform, Franklin's a little tight around the torso—were first on the scene. They'd strode the brief distance from the police station. Not long after, the ambulance arrived, followed directly by a fire truck. The ambulance officers got out and walked over steadily, as if there wasn't a day in their lives that they didn't see a dead man on a footpath. They knelt down beside him and administered some basic checks. The female officer consulted her watch and made a note of the time.

'He's passed,' Cora said to the officer.

'Shuffled off,' said Lil.

'He's been here all afternoon,' said Janet.

The female ambulance officer looked back at Janet, puzzled. 'And you only just called?'

'Yes, he's long gone, love,' said Lil to the officer, by way of explanation, her thin hair blowing about in the wind.

Then Janet added, to clarify, 'Oh no, I didn't call.'

The ambos exchanged glances before standing up and speaking to the policemen in low voices. There was nothing that could be done for the man, that much was obvious. There was no point in producing a defibrillator or rushing him off at high speed to the nearest hospital in Clarke.

Someone went back to the ambulance to collect a white sheet. The firemen, having established the futility of their attendance, crossed the wide road to buy pies. Therese Johnson, who seemed slightly put out by the disruption to her afternoon, stood impatiently near a street tree, her arms folded. And Betsy Dell, of ample breast, talked loudly about the nature of heart attacks.

'I'd say that's what's got him,' said Betsy, who owned the grocery store and whose husband had died in '91. 'That's what gets them,' she said, nodding, and Janet said, 'Oh, Betsy,' in commiseration. Then, when Betsy had returned to the store, Janet announced to the crowd: 'I think it was more likely an aneurysm.'

Cora Franks, a bundle of nerves who hadn't stopped talking to anyone who'd listen, took a moment to examine the man again, in case a closer look could help her to solve the mystery of him. She hunched down and edged forward, her silver necklaces clinking together, the proximity of herself to the dead man making her wonderfully anxious. Then, just as Cora was beginning to feel a twinge of recognition (did she know this man?), a gust of wind swept across the footpath with such force that it ruffled the tops of the dead man's trousers, giving the appearance that his legs were moving.

Well.

Cora Franks squealed like a schoolgirl and reared back in terror. 'Oh, for God's sake!' she said, grabbing Lil by the arm and then falling about laughing at herself. '*Ha ha ha*. Good heavens!' said Cora. 'I thought he moved.'

5

B enny Miller locked the door of the pale green house, and walked with the twilight towards the main road of the town.

It was coming on to a warm evening, if a little windy, and Benny wanted to acquaint herself with her new surroundings, to look at every shopfront and see what was on offer. She passed a fibro house with garden gnomes on the lawn and an old man sitting on a little concrete porch. He raised an arm and waved, as if Benny were an old friend, and she waved back and smiled to herself as she continued on.

At the corner of Valley Road, Benny considered her options. To the left was a florist called Tender Thoughts and a police station in an old sandstone building. Opposite that was the park. A Driver Reviver van was positioned alongside the rose garden and Benny could see two women packing up polystyrene cups and biscuit tins from a collapsible table. The big pink pub was the Royal Tavern, and coloured lights hung along the wooden fence of the beer garden. Benny crossed the wide road and read the dinner specials on a sandwich board. A handwritten sign was stuck up inside the window, advertising a job. She decided on going there for hot chips and a beer later, after her walk.

In the grocery store, Benny wandered up and down the short aisles, trying to work out what she most immediately needed. She had only a few hundred dollars saved and would have to make it last. She bought bananas, a small box of Weet-Bix, a can of tuna and a packet of ground coffee. Benny paid the woman at the till, who had sparse blonde hair and an enormous bosom.

'Hooroo, love', said the woman as Benny was leaving. And then: 'There's been a bit of an incident down the road, if you're heading that way.'

'Oh, okay,' said Benny as she left, and it was such a nice evening, even with the wind, and Benny liked the town very much already. It had a sense of history to it—she could see that in the old brick buildings, their lofty grandness—and the air smelled clear and different. A hairdresser called the Old Paris Coiffure seemed to have very little to do with Paris, apart from an image of the Eiffel Tower on the sign. A restaurant next to it offered Chinese, Thai and Australian cuisine. Beyond that was a small cafe, dark and closed.

Benny was busy looking in through all the shop windows and it wasn't until she'd passed the cafe that she saw the commotion ahead: a crowd of people gathered around. Benny noticed them, the people, before she saw the ambulance and the fire truck.

Well, this was a lot more dramatic than she'd expected. She passed a quilting shop and came up upon the backs of a small crowd, with everyone leaning in and gaping at something. There must have been thirty people there, speaking among themselves.

Benny nudged her way in and looked—and she was just in time to see the man in the brown suit slumped slightly against the window of the antique store, his eyes fixed on some destination across the street. Without thinking, Benny followed the man's gaze to see what he was staring at. She guessed it to be the Cedar Valley Pharmacy, a little chemist across the way that looked like any other chemist, except it was in a stately brick building, and some clothes were hanging on the verandah above it, several white shirts blowing in the wind.

Benny looked back to the man and stood and watched him until she knew he was dead. She knew it by his stillness: his chest that didn't breathe and his eyes that didn't blink.

An ambulance officer draped a sheet over him and then went back to the van to fetch a stretcher. Two policemen wandered over to the ambulance and held a short conference there, around the stretcher, and when they'd finished they went across to the dead man and gently lifted the sheet, just enough to slip a hand under and pat the areas where one would expect a pocket: the sides of his trousers; the outside of his jacket. Lifting the sheet higher still, they squinted at the face, trying to stoke some sense of recognition. Apparently finding none, the men patted a little more thoroughly around the outside of the clothing, and one dared to put a cautious hand inside the jacket for a quick check. Empty-handed, they restored the sheet to its former position and turned to the small crowd.

'Did anyone here see this man earlier today?' asked the big policeman. 'Before he became, uh, deceased?'

Huddles formed, the big policeman began to take notes, and the other officer jogged back across to the station, returning shortly with a camera. He aimed it at the sheet and the surrounding area and clicked away. Then the ambulance officers helped to lift the sheet strategically so photos could be taken of the body, the face, the attire.

Once the photographs had been taken, the policemen stood around and took more notes, and the ambulance officers rolled the stretcher over to the dead man.

Benny Miller was fascinated by all of it.

Standing there among the crowd, she took in every detail, her shopping bag at her feet.

What a peculiar thing to see, she thought, as the wind blew along the pavement, rustling the branches of the little street trees. A particularly strong gust lifted the sheet covering the man in the suit and revealed a shiny black shoe. The sides and the sole were so clean and unscuffed, it was like he hadn't walked a step in it. And it was when the lanky policeman came over and straightened the sheet so it covered the shoe again that Benny's mind went suddenly, unexpectedly, to her mother.

Vivian Alice Moon.

Oh how the mind has a mind of its own. Benny tried to push the thoughts away, but of course she couldn't. In an instant, the sense of Vivian Moon was so strong that Benny closed her eyes and a dreadful vision appeared, of Vivian under the sheet, slumped there against the window, her hair so lovely and gold.

Benny scolded herself silently; how ridiculous she could be. And yet the vision persisted: an awful sense that her mother had merged with the sad form under the white sheet. That her mother was the man, and the man was her mother.

Vivian's death, so fresh and recent, had come as such a shock that Benny had not allowed herself to wonder much about it. Certain details were too difficult for her to contemplate. Like how still Vivian Moon would have been. How unblinking. Did her foot splay to one side? Did her head slump forward? Benny swayed a little there on the footpath, filled with unease, voices chatting away around her, and she wondered, did her mother suffer?

'Well I don't know about you, but I'll be needing a brandy,' said the very loud voice of a short woman in half-moon glasses, and Benny came back to her surroundings.

The ambos had lifted the man onto the stretcher, and the stretcher had gone into the back of the ambulance. The policemen were speaking to each other in quiet voices. Once the ambulance had departed, the townspeople went their separate ways and the loud woman ushered a handful of other women into the antique store. Benny watched through the big window as they pulled chairs into a small circle, deep inside the shop, and she saw the woman switch an extra lamp on and fetch glasses from a cabinet. She poured brandy from a crystal decanter in the soft light, waving her free arm about as if relating some kind of dramatic narrative.

Benny's thoughts of Vivian passed. She picked up her shopping bag and watched for a moment longer through the window of the antique store, charmed by the community of it—all the ladies debriefing with their brandy—and then she turned and walked back towards the green cottage.

It was almost dark. Benny had lost her appetite for hot chips and was no longer thirsty and the sky was a vast thing above her, clear of clouds, and she could see the first of the low evening stars. There were lights on in weatherboard houses and the sound of televisions and the cidadas had stopped and now there were crickets. Benny walked quickly and began to pulse with excitement at what she had seen.

Back in the cottage, she changed directly into her bed shirt and got into her new and unfamiliar bed. Then she lay sleepless well into the night, looking out the window at the black trees moving about with the wind. She thought endlessly about the man in the suit, about her mother, and she listened to the ungodly sliding sound coming from the ceiling, like someone dragging a sack of potatoes, intermittently, across a rough surface.

If anyone had told Benny Miller that she would see her first dead body on the main road of a small country town, of all unlikely places, she would have scoffed in disbelief. And if anyone had told her that a single python in a roof space could have made such a heaving racket, she would not have believed that either.

6

The following morning Benny roused early with the yellow sun that came in the picture window. Loud birds squawked from the surrounding trees, and others squawked from off in the distance. Benny lay still in the bed and smiled listening to them, this rich chorus of birds, of which kookaburras were the only ones she could identify. Those morning birds were loud enough to wake the whole town.

Odette had told her to come over in the morning, so Benny got up presently, dressed, and ate Weet-Bix in the garden. Wary of appearing too eager, it was a great disappointment when, having done this, she checked the clock on the stove and found it was barely seven. She went back to the bedroom and read several chapters of a new novel she'd bought herself as a rare treat before she left, about a man who had an arduous life and moved to Newfoundland. Benny appreciated his predicament, but she found it unusually difficult to concentrate. She put the book down eventually and unpacked the remainder of her clothes into the wardrobe and the chest of drawers.

It was just before nine when she got into her car. She sat, warming the engine, studying the map Odette had left on the kitchen dresser. A red texta line drew the way and Benny followed it with her finger, familiarising herself with the turns. Then she reversed out, the map on the passenger seat beside her, drove to the corner, turned right and continued past the grocery store and along Valley Road.

As she passed the big antique store called Cedar Valley Curios & Old Wares, Benny slowed down. She wasn't sure what she was expecting to see, but there was no sign of the events of the previous evening. No policemen were gathering evidence, no area had been cordoned off, and many of the shops on Valley Road were yet to open. She carried on through the town, over the bridge, and up the steep hill into the scrubby bush.

Taking note of the odometer, Benny counted three kilometres before an unsealed road manifested on the left, indicated by an honesty box with a handwritten sign that said LIMES ETC. Benny drove along it until she arrived at the fencepost with horseshoes on it, and she rattled over the cattle grid and up to the house.

Odette Fisher, having heard the car, was standing on the steps of the verandah in an oversized shirt, cotton shorts and ugg boots, smiling a broad smile and waving with one arm high above her head—a big wide wave, like signalling to someone at sea.

In her collection of photographs Benny had two favourite pictures of Odette Fisher and her great friend Vivian Moon. In one, which looked to have been taken in a wide-open field, Vivian was sitting up on a wooden fence and Odette was standing next to her, both women smiling. Benny loved Odette's smile almost as much as she loved her mother's—the way it took over her whole face and made her shut her eyes a little so they squinted. The photo was black-and-white and on the back someone had written *1971* in pen. Odette and Vivian were both wearing bell-bottom jeans and tight knitted jumpers.

In the other photo, there they were in a bar, elbows on the table, leaning in and posing. Odette's smile was less broad and more conspiratorial, and Vivian was alluring, in a low-cut top and with a cigarette in one hand. A little wisp of smoke curled out the side of her mouth. Both women were halfway through their drinks and the table was crowded with empty glasses.

Benny liked the first photo better, but the second was somehow transfixing. She could not count the number of times she'd looked at it, stared at it, got lost in it. She didn't know who took the photo, or where it was taken. But those women—those two glamorous women, looking out. Benny wanted so much to know what they were talking about, and to be a part of the conversation.

And now here was Odette, as a much older woman, walking down the drive as Benny got out of the car.

'*Benny*,' said Odette with feeling. 'You're here.'

She put her arms out and drew Benny in to hug her. The stillness of the morning and the bright light of it disappeared as Benny allowed her face to rest on Odette's shoulder for a blessed moment. Time came to a merciful halt. How lovely it was to be held by a person like this, of such reassuring strength. Benny closed her eyes and felt—in an instant—protected. Like finding shelter from the rain.

And then time started up again.

Odette, gripping her firmly by the shoulders, pushed Benny out into the day, so she could get a good look at her.

Benny blinked. She had next to no expression, save for bewilderment at the embrace and how nice it had felt. Odette was a little heavier than in the photos, with creases next to her eyes and mouth, but her wide, intelligent face was still so familiar. Her hair was grey now, in a loose bun, and something in her posture suggested a long life of physical activity.

Odette surveyed Benny then; she looked all over Benny's face, down to her feet and back up again. Her intensity was exhilarating and Benny had the sense of something very unfamiliar. Someone is *seeing* me, she thought. Someone is looking at me and seeing me: this powerful woman in the ugg boots.

A cow mooed nearby and Benny smiled nervously, looking beyond Odette to the barbed-wire fencing along a paddock, a hammock strung up between two trees, big wooden garden boxes covered in netting. She noticed a dog next to Odette too, a thin kelpie. The dog stared up at the older woman, as if awaiting instruction, and Odette stared at Benny.

'Oh, Benny', said Odette, with sad kindness. 'You look just like her.'

Benny, overwhelmed, felt such a rush of gratitude. 'It's very nice to meet you,' she said.

7

The Cedar Valley police station was a single-storey sandstone building opposite the park. It was a 'historic' building, as were so many in the town, with a hipped roof and windows topped with arches. A neatly clipped hedge went around the front and sides of the premises and made the whole thing look like a scene from an English village.

There were only a handful of officers working in Cedar Valley and its surrounding towns on any given day. On a normal morning, a lone police car would be parked out the front of the station, waiting for something illegal to happen. That year, the most common complaint was theft, which was how it generally was. It seemed that people loved to steal things from the paddocks and sheds of Cedar Valley. Farm machinery, spare parts, fuel, sheep. Every so often a house would be burgled or something would catch fire. On a particularly fast day, a small cannabis plantation was found by a bushwalker on a property near the riverbank and three arrests were made.

But December 2nd 1993—the day after an unknown man had died of unknown circumstances on Valley Road—bristled with minor intrigue from the outset and only got more interesting as it went along.

Detective Sergeant Anthony Simmons—an impressively tall and solid man—sat in his small office with its cheap furnishings and a mediocre view of the war memorial. A photograph of his wife and two daughters, mannered in their posing, sat in a brass frame on his desk. Noise from the common area (the ring of a telephone, a boiling kettle) spilled into the room, and a fan revolved on the ceiling, providing little relief for a man so prone to easy sweating.

'I just got in now, Mrs Franks, and I'm telling you I don't know anything about him. I was up in Clarke all day yesterday, I didn't get home till late. You should be talking to Constable Franklin or Constable Hall.' This was what Simmons was saying, perhaps a little curtly, to Cora Franks.

'But since you're here and they're not,' said Cora.

Simmons smiled thinly. It was true—Franklin and Hall were over at the courthouse talking to the clerk, informing him that an unidentified male had died on Valley Road yesterday in a somewhat mysterious manner, an odd-sounding case that Simmons had been made aware of only half an hour previous.

Cora Franks, festooned with cameo brooches, indicated her impatience, and Simmons pushed his chair out rather abruptly, strode out of the office to Hall's desk in the common area, and returned moments later with a slim folder of papers. He sifted through them while Cora sat watching.

'You made a statement last night,' he said, looking at one of the papers.

'Yes, and you see I told James that the man sat down outside the shop at twelve-thirty, but now I think perhaps it was later. I went over it with the girls last night and we decided it was later.'

'Did you now?' said Simmons.

'Yes we did, Tony,' said Cora.

Simmons stared back at Cora. He patted his chest. Cora gazed across at him blankly. Simmons raised an arm and waved it around to indicate the scant officialdom of the room.

'I mean Sergeant,' said Cora.

'Detective Sergeant', said Detective Sergeant Anthony Simmons.

'Isn't that fancy,' said Cora.

Simmons sighed. He was relatively new to Cedar Valley in the sense of living there, but he was not new to Cora Franks. Cora was in a book club with his mother, Elsie Simmons, and their book club had been meeting for twenty-seven years. Book club took priority over everything else: weddings, funerals, anniversaries, the birthdays of their children. In Elsie

Simmons's life, and in Cora's, few things were as important as book club, despite the fact that some of the members found it difficult to finish the books, and so for every fourth meeting they travelled to Clarke and saw a movie instead.

Simmons was from Clarke. He had been born in Clarke and gone to school in Clarke and then later he worked in Clarke, making his way through the ranks from probationary constable upwards. He liked Clarke very much. It was a big town to the north—'the commercial centre of the Gather Region'—and it had everything a person could need: four pubs, a shopping plaza, government services, several schools, many churches and the best pineapple pork in the world. Simmons had been very content there, king of the castle, and the thought of moving would never have occurred to him if it wasn't for his mother, Elsie Simmons, who was ageing rather dramatically in Cedar Valley and requiring of assistance.

Elsie Simmons, his mother, said, 'You mustn't move down here for me. I'm fine.'

Jenny Simmons, his wife, said, 'She's dying, Tony. Apply for the transfer. We'll rent for a few years before the girls start school.'

He applied for the transfer, and they were renting, and unfortunately the girls were still too young to start school. Detective Sergeant Tony Simmons, who had only recently acquired the distinction of 'detective', was now a somewhat reluctant resident of the town of Cedar Valley and held a mild contempt for what he considered the insignificance of the township.

'I've been wondering if he was coming in to buy something,' said Cora Franks. 'Given his obvious taste for antique clothing.'

'He probably was,' said Simmons uncaringly, and he recalled what Gussy Franklin had mentioned earlier, on his way out the door to the courthouse: that the dead man was dressed up in a full vintage suit, on the first day of summer. He'd probably expired from heat exhaustion. And Gussy Franklin had said that when they searched him for ID, he had nothing. No wallet. No bank cards or licence. No cash. Simmons had only been half listening when the boys were telling him about it from the doorway, and Jimmy Hall's eyes always popped out like that, so Simmons couldn't tell if he'd been normal or excited.

'So you told Constable Hall the man sat down at twelve-thirty. What time do you think he sat down now?' asked Simmons.

'Closer to one,' said Cora. 'Because Therese was on her lunch break, you see. She was very upset—about a private matter—and so we weren't paying attention to the time. But let's say one. You can tell James that.'

'I will alert Constable Hall,' said Simmons.

Cora paused, as if considering her next statement. 'And I also think, now that the shock's worn off, that there were some very unfamiliar faces around yesterday. If you know what I mean.'

'I don't,' said Simmons.

'Well,' said Cora, 'I was talking with Lil and, as we understand it, it's not unusual for a person who has done something illegal to kind of hang around. You know: at the scene of the crime. So they can see their handiwork.'

Simmons grinned, his teeth showing. 'No one said this was a crime scene,' he said. 'Did you ladies read something scary at book club?'

'Tony, don't be condescending,' said Cora. 'There was a dead man on the street! If it wasn't a crime scene then what was it?'

'Just a scene,' said Simmons, and he rose to signal an end to the conversation.

Cora stood up and went over to the doorway, clutching her handbag. 'So you'll keep me up to date then? Seeing as I'm the one who's found him.'

'Mrs Franks, as I understand it he was sitting on the main road in plain sight.'

'Yes, but I'm the one who found he was dead,' said Cora Franks.

Simmons stared at the woman.

'I'll be hearing from you then,' said Cora. 'And I'm not your maths teacher, Tony. Call me Cora.'

8

Odette Fisher swept back her arm, indicating the door of her dark-wooded farmhouse, and said, 'Come on in,' so Benny, Odette and the thin dog went in.

The house was bright inside and jazz music was playing from a record player. Odette moved around the space with ease. 'I'll put the kettle on,' she said as she walked across a Persian rug and into the open kitchen area, where cast-iron pots hung against a wall.

Benny looked up at the lofty, rafted ceiling and saw a patch of blue through a high skylight. She looked down and saw the dog staring back at her, and she noticed the grey hairs that sprouted around its mouth and eyes. A fireplace in the far corner had a small dark window on the front and a long black chimney pipe that extended upwards from the top, and hundreds of books lined the walls on long wooden shelves. Odette, standing by the stove, lit the gas under the kettle and talked away, but Benny was so taken by the loveliness of the house that she barely heard the words. Odette had to ask her twice if the cottage was okay before Benny said oh yes, that it was. She thanked Odette for the food she had left and told her she'd chosen the front room with the picture window.

'I hope the python's not too noisy,' said Odette. 'A friend of mine stayed in the cottage for all of last year and I think he grew kind of fond of it in the end. It eats the rats, you see, which is always helpful.'

Odette fetched a tin off a shelf and opened it up and began spooning tealeaves into a teapot. The dog hovered, watching Benny, and Benny reached down and patted its head—it closed its eyes and lifted its chin when she did that—and she felt very inexperienced all of a sudden, very green, like a new shoot of grass in a big old field.

Odette talked so easily—her voice deep and educated—about the things you get used to, living in the country, and Benny stood there self-consciously, as straight as the chimney pipe. She glanced around the room and saw that interesting artefacts were everywhere: ornaments, pottery, religious-looking icons, an ancient upright piano. There was art on the walls, too—paintings—and photographs in frames, some of them of colourful landscapes and others black-and-white, with people in them. She wondered if any of Odette's photographs were of Vivian Moon.

'I just got off the phone,' Odette was saying. 'What a day for you to arrive! Did you hear we had a man die on Valley Road?'

'Oh yes,' said Benny.

'Well, that's not something that usually happens,' said Odette. 'I just spoke to my friend Maureen, and before that to Annie. People like to talk in the valley. It's very reverberant, you'll notice that.'

'I saw him,' said Benny.

Odette put the spoon down.

'You saw him?'

'Just before they put the sheet over. I went for a walk to look at the shops.'

'Benny, that must've given you a fright.'

And in some strange way it had—given Benny a fright—but in such a peculiar and indirect fashion, bringing up such gruesome thoughts of Vivian. Benny couldn't have explained it even if she'd wanted to. 'He had very shiny shoes,' she said instead.

Odette smiled. She returned the tea tin to the shelf and set two mugs on the benchtop.

'Funny how that stuck out to everyone so much,' she said. 'What he was wearing. More than that he was dead.'

The dog left Benny's side and settled stiffly on a rug, and Odette raised a hand towards the couches and told Benny to make herself comfortable, so Benny wandered over to a brown couch and sat down, and the dog rolled over onto its long side and let out a groan.

Benny watched Odette moving around the kitchen. She didn't want to miss anything. The wide windows above the

43

bench looked out over the grass and fence and paddock and bush. What a wonderful thing, she thought, to have a view across a paddock from the kitchen.

'He really looked quite peaceful,' she said.

Odette lifted the kettle and poured steaming water into a teapot, keeping half an eye on the unassuming young woman sitting in her lounge room.

'Aren't you funny,' she said, and she brought the mugs over, set them on the coffee table, and then went back for the teapot.

Benny sat on the couch and wondered what she could add to the conversation, wanting very much to say something charming or clever. She wondered if it was morbid to go on about the dead man, but she had thought so much about him since the previous evening. Her mother, the dead man—how could she explain her sense of the two of them? How she felt it oddly fortuitous, the way she had arrived there yesterday and wandered up the road and seen him. As if there was a lesson in it, or a sign. Benny was sure of that. And she was sure, too, of how she felt there in Odette's living room: which was suspended, in some liminal space between disparate feelings. Benny had never felt so at home and yet so nervous at the same time.

Odette brought over the mugs, and then she brought over the teapot and milk and sat down on a velvet armchair opposite. She poured tea for them both and settled back, holding her cup, and told Benny that this was going to keep the town busy for a while. Everyone was wondering who he was, and no one seemed to understand how he came to be dead. Maureen Robinson, Odette's friend who worked at the chemist, said the man in the suit had looked perfectly healthy. 'I can't imagine it's normal to just sit down and die, but there you go,' said Odette. 'And I can't believe you saw him. Your first day in town and that's what you see.'

Benny poured some milk into her tea, picked up her cup and leaned back in her chair too, trying to appear as relaxed as Odette did. Then, when the elegant woman began asking questions, Benny found herself talking about her studies (an arts degree at Sydney University), and her share house in Glebe. Odette was generous in her questions, and very focused, and soon Benny was speaking a little of her interests (books, music, geology). They talked and, all the while, Benny was yearning to make a good impression, hoping that Odette Fisher would like her.

The dog got up and went to the door and scratched at it, so Odette went over and let it out, leaving the door open then, and when she returned she seemed to take the opportunity of the lull in conversation. She looked quite serious when she said, 'Benny, I am so sorry.' And then—slowly, warmly—'I am just so sorry about your mum.'

Benny's mind went still and she looked down at her teacup and its milky contents.

Odette hesitated. She cleared her throat. 'I'm sorry if that makes you upset, for me to mention it.'

'It's okay,' said Benny, and the older woman and the younger woman sat there opposite each other, while the sound of unfamiliar birds came in through the open door.

'Benny, do you mind me asking, what was she like, more recently? Vivian—was she in good spirits?'

Benny was confused as she sat there on the couch. What did Odette mean? How could Benny have any idea about her mother's spirits, before her death?

'I wouldn't know,' she said.

And then it was Odette's turn to appear confused. 'I'm sorry,' she said. 'I guess that's a difficult question to answer.'

'It's just that I didn't know—' said Benny, and the phone began to ring over near the kitchen, startling them both.

Odette swiped the air with a hand and said, 'I don't need to get that,' and the two of them sat there awkwardly for the extent of the ringing, Odette with a puzzled look on her face, and then she shook her head, as if silently dismissing some preposterous notion.

'Well, I guess no one really knows anyone, do they?' she said kindly.

Benny sat uneasy on the couch. 'Yes, but I haven't seen her,' she said, and her face flushed then with shame. 'I haven't—I *hadn't*—seen her in years. I really didn't know her at all.'

9

In his office in the Cedar Valley police station, Detective Sergeant Simmons said, 'Gussy! Jimmy! Sit rep!' to the open door and a moment later Franklin appeared, and then Hall.

'That was Clarke Base,' said Tony Simmons, indicating the telephone.

'What'd they say?' asked Hall.

'They said you should sit down and tell me more about what happened yesterday,' said Simmons with a wonderfully fake smile.

So Constable Gussy Franklin, a wardrobe in a uniform with a somewhat offhand manner to him, and Constable James Hall—the opposite, a weed—sat down.

It amazed Simmons that Gussy Franklin got around so effortlessly, given his proportions. His was an enormous man, always a little pink in the face and with no discernible neck. But he had a languid kind of casualness about him that made him a popular person to drink with, if a slightly lacklustre policeman, and Simmons found his presence oddly affirming.

Hall, on the other hand, thin-hipped, with a sunken chest, struck Simmons as a man who felt he was of very little consequence in the world. Perhaps he had, at some point, set about overcompensating with an earnest diligence that matched his eyes, which popped out a bit too far from his face and gave him a look of constant surprise. Jenny Simmons reckoned Hall was far too eager for any woman to take him seriously—and he did seem bereft of female attention. James Hall once told Tony Simmons, after a few beers (which he did not handle well), that he'd been dacked in high school on a near continuous basis, and Simmons—who had been known to dack in his time—had laughed his head off at the bar.

Now Simmons stared at Hall and then at Franklin, and he said, 'This is your one, boys. Yeah? But why don't you enlighten me. Tell it all over again from the start.'

Gussy Franklin, in his amiable fashion, took the lead. Yesterday had started off pretty normal. The boys had been doing paperwork all morning. The other officers from the area were out on various matters—there'd been a heck of a car accident on the coast road, traffic was backed up for hours—and someone had pinched two hunting rifles from Nigel Haling, who had a small farm next to the river. At lunchtime, Hall went down the street for a pie and Franklin ate a delicious ham on rye on the bench outside, next to the hedge. Franklin had been married one year and his wife still made his sandwiches.

'That's nice for you, Gussy,' said Simmons.

'It was, mate,' said Franklin. 'And that's when I saw Les come past and he said there was a bit of a weirdo down the road.'

'Ah, lovely,' said Simmons. 'Les.'

'Yeah, I know.' Franklin did a quick roll of his eyes. 'Les said the guy was doing something funny with his arms—weird kind of stretching and whatnot. Les did a little impression of him. He said, "I think he's had a few. You should see his outfit." And then, later on, we got the call that we had a dead 'un. And that's when we went across to have a look.'

There they'd found quite a scene: a small crowd of locals gathered, and Cora Franks carrying on like a pork chop. Everyone was standing around a dead man in a brown suit on the footpath outside Curios. He was just sitting there with his eyes wide open. He didn't even look that dead, really; he could've been lost in thought if you'd only glanced in his direction.

Franklin and Hall found the whole thing most unusual.

'It was odd as a sock, boss,' said Gussy Franklin.

So Franklin stood around, taking the temperature, and Hall returned to the station to fetch the camera. He took a roll and a half of shots, everything down to the neatly tied, near-new laces on the dead man's shiny shoes.

The ambulance officers couldn't offer an opinion as to cause of death. It looked natural, they said, but it didn't feel it, and they weren't sure why that was. He was young, perhaps that was it. The man looked to be in his mid-fifties at the most. And he was so composed, no signs of distress or discomfort. He hadn't vomited or bled; he hadn't even collapsed. He was slightly slumped, sure, but surprisingly upright for being so dead.

Plus, there was the groomed look of him—recently shaved and his hair brushed back neatly. His fingernails were filed and clean. Hall had logged all this diligently in his notepad, the tidy appearance and the clothing, so oddly formal: brown trousers, a white shirt, a wide-striped tie, a pullover and a jacket. He would certainly have been warm. But more to the point, he looked like he'd stepped into Cedar Valley from another era, let alone another town. Everything about him looked antique. And wasn't that a funny place for a man like that to sit: in front of an antique store?

The boys had done a quick canvass, but they'd need to get more statements. The ambos were good enough to drive the body to the morgue at Clarke Base, and Franklin and Hall had met them there. Then Dr Ping Williams, the government medical officer, had strolled in wearing her white lab coat and thick-rimmed glasses, a tiny woman who spoke so softly Gussy Franklin had had to bend his hulking body down to hear her, while Hall stood nearby taking prints.

Finally, Franklin logged all the property the dead man had in his pockets: cigarettes, a box of matches, half a pack of Juicy Fruit gum, a bus ticket, a train ticket, and three combs. That was it. No ID, no wallet, no bags, no money, no wedding ring, nothing that gave any indication as to who on earth this gentleman might be.

'Cold to touch, was he?' asked Simmons.

'Dead for at least an hour before we got there,' said Hall.

'Did you give him a whiff, Jimmy?'

'I did, boss,' said Hall. 'You know me. He didn't smell like booze, though. Or even cigarettes actually, even though he had cigarettes.'

'What kind of man carries combs?' asked Franklin.

'A poofter,' said Simmons, and he and Franklin snorted.

'Judging by the outfit, too,' said Franklin. 'A real fancy pants.'

Hall moved in his chair uncomfortably, and Simmons grinned. Then he frowned—Detective Sergeant Simmons, so mercurial—and he looked down at the property book in which Gus Franklin had listed the dead man's belongings.

'A bus ticket.'

'I'm waiting for a call back from the company,' said Hall.

'Very good,' said Simmons.

'What did Clarke Base say?' asked Hall.

'Well, look,' said Simmons, who had called Ping Williams specifically to check in on their dead man. 'I just called on something else and Ping mentioned your dead 'un. She reckons it's a weird one.'

Hall blinked with anticipation. Simmons—who was slightly irritated by the fact that he'd been having a very long lunch with some of the Clarke boys at Panda Garden yesterday, chatting away over too many Crown Lagers, and had missed the whole episode—was pleased to have regained the upper hand in regards to pertinent information.

'Get this,' he said, with a twinkle in his eye.

The boys leaned in.

'This is what Ping says, right? You know the fancy suit?'

The boys nodded.

'Well. Every label—are you listening?—every label from every piece of clothing he was wearing—trousers, jumper, underwear, everything—every label has been *very carefully removed*.'

Hall looked surprised, not that this was unusual for him.

Franklin stared at Simmons, mystified. 'What does that mean?' he asked.

Simmons laughed and shook his head. 'I have no fucking idea,' he said.

10

It had always seemed to Benny Miller that Vivian Alice Moon was like sand that slipped through her fingers. As a child she had sensed this, on the fringes of her mind. And as she had grown older, Benny had spent much fruitless time trying to hold on to some fragment of her mother, even one tiny grain. But, of course, the holding only led to spilling. Confusion and doubt always won. And any idea of Vivian Moon as one thing—her singular mother—only gave way to multitudes.

Now, sitting across from Odette Fisher in the farmhouse, Benny was so puzzled. Why would Odette ask her such a question? How would Benny know anything about Vivian at all?

The fact of it was this: Benny had never lived with her mother, not even for one year as a baby. According to Frank Miller, Benny was five months old when Vivian packed up her things and left them. Why? Well, Frank Miller was always hesitant to say. 'Your mother loves you, Ben. She didn't leave because she doesn't love you.' That was what he would offer. But that didn't explain anything at all, it didn't make the leaving any better, and it didn't make sense to Benny when Frank would say nothing more, evading her questions in such a way that she eventually learned not to ask.

So young Benny would lie in her bed and ceaselessly wonder: What's so wrong with me that she didn't take me with her? What's so wrong with me that she won't come for me now?

Benny Miller was convinced, in some deep core of herself, that all of it was due to some terrible fault of her own, and as a child she would go about in her quiet grief. She busied herself with her collections, fastidiously arranging stickers in an album, cicada shells on a sill, and silently blaming herself. And then she'd sit stupefied when Vivian would sometimes arrive on a rare visit, swanning in unannounced, full of glorious warmth.

Frank, in the kitchen, quiet and reproachful, then disappearing out the back for long spells, smoking a joint perhaps, on the seat near the barbecue.

Vivian, as familiar with the house as if she'd just returned home from a routine errand, would explode into flattery. 'Benny, my baby. I've missed you! Aren't you so big?' And the smell of her was like nothing else in this world, the aching smell of her, and the way her long hair fell in Benny's face when she hung her head over the pillow to say goodnight.

Later, she would become involved in some hushed conversation with Frank—tense whispers behind a closed door—and by morning she'd be gone.

Vivian Alice Moon, when she left, drained all the light from the world.

But what did Benny really know for certain?

Well, not much at all; the vague, milky impressions of a child. A mother—fleeting, chaotic, sometimes apologetic—alighting occasionally, until she stopped doing even that.

Meanwhile, Frank Miller, who did not seem to have access to many words, was a well-meaning neglector. Some nights he would go out when Benny was still too young to be left alone, and he would not come home until she was too fretful to go to sleep. On Saturdays he would drive around Sydney, stopping to look in old furniture shops for bargains. The trips would last hours, and Benny would tire of going in and watching him searching around anxiously, looking for something of value, haggling with the shopkeepers. Lonesome and bored, she would wait in the car. Finally he would give up and be irritated about it, and they'd drive home again, where he'd grill fish fingers and mash a boiled potato in a bowl with salt and butter and Benny would eat quietly while he watched the television.

On one occasion, Benny cried on account of having to vomit—she had food poisoning—and Frank couldn't cope with that in the slightest. He looked at the bathroom floor and said, 'Oh, Ben, oh, Ben,' in a distant way, and chewed his fingernails while she suffered there.

Frank chewed his fingernails whenever something difficult arose, so at any mention of Vivian he would nibble away. In the end, the only facts that Benny knew for certain were these: that Vivian Moon was born in Adelaide and had grown up in the suburb of Brighton. Her mother, Nola Moon, had been a secretary of some kind and her father, Clive, a chemist. Every Christmas, Nola and Clive sent Benny twenty dollars enclosed in a card. On her eighteenth birthday it was fifty dollars, but that was from Nola alone, Clive having died. They were sweet people, if the cards were anything to go by, but apparently not fond of visitors or travel. They had other grandchildren in Adelaide, Benny was told, and a lot on their plate, and she didn't think much about them apart from how best to spend the twenty dollars.

Vivian left South Australia in 1961. She would have been nineteen. She moved to Sydney and studied at Sydney University. Benny had no idea where she lived, or what she did, and then there was a yawning gap of unexplained time until 1969, when she met Frank Miller at the Newcastle on George Street and he must have done something to impress her. Who knows what she saw in him, a man who cared so much about old furniture. But Benny had the photos and she could see he'd once been handsome. Perhaps his reticence had seemed like a puzzle in need of solving, but it wasn't long before Vivian took off for the first time—this before Benny was born.

'Ah, you know. Europe,' Frank said when Benny asked where Vivian had gone.

But all of a sudden, she came back again, to Frank—as mysteriously as she had left—and she pushed Benny out into the world in November of 1972.

What happened after that? If only Benny knew.

'She could be very evasive,' said old Irene Miller, Frank's mother, of Vivian Moon one very hot day. 'But smart. And didn't she let you know it.'

Benny, a teenager by then in denim short shorts, nudged for more, and Irene, fanning herself with a women's magazine in the living room, never could hide her disapproval. 'I'll say this about Vivian: some of us choose to stay, you know. And we don't complain.'

Then Irene ordered Benny to fetch her some water— everything was so impossible because of her arthritis—and Benny went reluctantly to the sink and never did like her grandmother, Irene.

Now here was Odette Fisher, sitting across from her, and already Benny liked her very much. She had been prepared to like her, poised to, but when she met her—just that morning—she was almost overwhelmed to find that she really, truly did.

'I had no idea,' Odette was saying in response to this revelation that Benny had not seen Vivian, had not *known* her. 'I thought . . .' She trailed off and stalled, perhaps considering how to continue. Benny could see that she was mystified, and yet concerned not to say the wrong thing to this poor girl who, as it happened, had not known her own dead mother.

'I must have got the wrong impression,' said Odette finally, and she forced a smile. And then, 'You know, I should show you around. Why don't we go outside?'

So they went outside.

Odette ushered Benny through the door and onto the front verandah. There was a rocking chair with a knitted blanket on it facing the paddock. They went down the steps and Odette led the way to a small enclosure up the hill. To the left, Benny saw two brown cows beyond the fence, and she noticed the sound of her own boots walking in the tough, thick grass.

'Those are my house cows. Retired house cows. I'll introduce you later. And this is Bessel.' Odette gestured to the dog. 'He can be a bit forward.'

Excited by hearing his own name, Bessel turned and reared upwards, standing on his hind legs for a moment to let out a brief woof.

Inside the enclosure—a wire structure with a wooden frame—were chickens. Benny watched their heads jerk back and forth awkwardly as they pecked at the dirt and straw, and saw they were mostly brown and speckled. Two of them rushed towards Odette and made excited sounds.

'These are my girls,' said Odette, smiling at Benny. 'Have you known many hens before?'

Benny said she hadn't.

'These two are very gregarious,' said Odette, pulling leaves from a plant in the grass and feeding it to them though the wire.

Bessel considered the chickens momentarily and then took his leave to pee against a fencepost. Odette and Benny stood side by side, looking at the hens in silence. Eventually Odette put her arm around Benny's shoulder and squeezed it in a reassuring way before taking her arm away again.

Benny thought that was one of the nicer feelings she had ever felt.

'So,' said Odette. 'Why don't you tell me more about this dead man.'

11

The bus from Clarke to Cedar Valley followed a direct route down the coastal highway and made very few stops in between. There were some dear little towns in the region, inland across the river or up around the mountain, but the bus ignored those. They were too out of the way. It had a limited job to do and the job was this: to begin at the train station in Clarke; to make five stops in Clarke; to pause one last time at the very edge of Clarke; and then to plough along the fifty-minute slog to Cedar Valley, stopping at Barrang and Galarra only, and hoping very much, as dusk came, that the kangaroos and wombats would stay clear of the road.

There were two bus stops in Cedar Valley, one on each side of Valley Road. The bus set down its passengers, welcomed new ones, and continued on to Solent Inlet, where it terminated, turned around, and did the whole blessed trip in reverse.

Simmons was not usually one to catch the bus, nor to consider the bus, but today the bus was of great interest. In the past ten minutes he had learned more than he'd ever need to know about the Gather Region Bus Service—a fleet of ten vehicles operated by the Neville family, who were based in Clarke. Simmons had been more than happy to take the call when Doreen Neville herself phoned the station with information about the driver who'd been rostered on the previous day. It was Mark. And when Simmons had explained that he needed more than just a first name, Doreen was delighted to give him a brief history of the Neville family's deep connection with the transport needs of the region, and reveal the number of their coaches that boasted a four-star rating (it was six). And then she digressed.

'You said Simmons? And you're a policeman. Would you be Neville Simmons's son?'

Simmons felt a familiar tightness in his stomach. 'Yes, ma'am, I am,' he said.

'Oh, well, goodness me,' said Doreen. 'I always remember meeting Neville for the first time because we shared a name, in a roundabout sort of way. He was the best mayor we've ever had, and I'm not just saying that.'

'Thank you,' Simmons forced himself to say. 'And now, Mrs Neville, what's Mark's surname?'

'Who?'

'The driver. Mark.'

'Oh, yes, love. Mark Foy. Like the department store. No relation.'

She gave Simmons a telephone number and he wrote it down and thanked Doreen Neville. Then he left the station, passing the neat hedge that pleasantly reminded a person of the mother country, and walked across to the bus stop.

Simmons ran his finger down a column of the timetable stuck to the wall of the shelter. He knew the dead man had been in the possession of a ticket for the 11.44 am bus from Clarke station and, on a weekday, according to the timetable, the 11.44 am bus from Clarke station arrived in Cedar Valley at 12.52 pm. Simmons looked down the street to the antique shop and checked his watch. Then he walked in what he considered to be a regular pace. It took forty-eight seconds to get to the front window of Cedar Valley Curios and Old Wares.

Simmons stood outside the shop and looked around. There was no indication that anything unusual had happened here only yesterday. He could see Cora Franks inside, her back to the window, right down the rear of the shop near the bookshelves. The Quilting Bee sat to the right, and the real estate agent to the left.

Simmons scanned the pavement, and he looked up to examine the underside of the awning. A wasps' nest was perched up in the corner.

Then Simmons sat down on the ground, in the spot that the man had been sitting, and he leaned his back against the glass and looked out at the street. There were some cars parked over to the right, outside the hairdresser. There was a line of them down to the left, too, near the video store. But the little street trees on this particular section of the footpath were planted in a bed that extended out into the wide roadway, making an area where cars could not park, and allowing a good view across the street even from a low, seated position.

Simmons sat and he looked—just as the man had looked— in an attempt to ascertain what the unknown man had been looking at.

The Cedar Valley Pharmacy was the main thing he could see.

That and Fran's World Famous Pies, which had a little crowd out front, and Fran, who was a roundish thing, generally with an apron on her. There she was, standing on the footpath, chatting with her customers.

There was a phone box, and a bench, and then the shop on the other side of the chemist was empty, newspaper lining the windows. Identical street trees on the opposite footpath made it difficult to get a clear line of sight to the bookstore or the Cedar Valley Public Hall.

Simmons could see Maureen Robinson at the counter of the chemist, serving, and he glanced up and saw some washing hanging over the railing of the upstairs verandah and wondered, briefly, who lived up there above the pharmacy.

He nodded, making mental notes. Then he found that standing up again was painful and sadly ungraceful, and a noise of exertion came out as he straightened. Simmons put his hands on his hips, saw Cora making her way towards the front of the shop, and before she could reach him he turned and walked the forty-eight seconds back to the station, eyeing off the boys as he went through the common room. They had brought Les in to make a statement.

'Gentlemen,' said Simmons.

Les, with his silly hoary grin, said, 'Arrest me, copper!'— something he was so fond of saying.

Simmons ignored Les entirely.

'Jimmy, I got the number,' Simmons told him. 'I'm gonna call the driver.'

'Sure, boss,' said Jimmy Hall.

So Simmons, with an ache in his lower back and a disgruntled feeling that never quite left him, went to his cheaply furnished office and dialled the home number of Mark Foy, driver of the four-star coaches of the Gather Region Bus Service.

12

Odette Fisher, at the wide stove in the farmhouse, cooked an omelette with eggs from her own chickens and Benny watched the whole process like a student might.

Benny had never fetched fresh eggs from a henhouse before, and Odette had allowed her to do it, laughing at how Benny was so cautious, as if the eggs would combust or the chickens would protest. They hadn't, and in fact Odette had scooped up a brown hen and held it against the curve of her chest, petting it firmly with her palm.

Odette cooked with very little fuss about her—whisking the eggs and some chives with a fork until they had an even texture. She poured the mixture into a heavy pan that was hot and full of melted butter and she used the fork to whisk it more, in the pan, chatting away to Benny at the same time. Then she shook the whole thing vigorously so the sloppy contents all went to one side, making a half moon of eggs, and all of a sudden she was folding it over with the fork to form a neat parcel, and titling the pan so the omelette slid onto a waiting plate.

Afterwards, they ate outside at a wooden table behind the house, near where the bush started. The view took in the whole paddock as it sloped gently down one edge of the mountain, citrus trees on this side of the fence, and a big open shed which had Odette's car in it, and tools hanging along the walls.

Benny found the omelette and accompanying salad to be particularly delicious. She thought about the way Frank Miller cooked eggs, and how the yolk would be too hard or the white too soft or, if scrambled, pieces of shell would surprise her. For a moment, she wished Frank Miller was someone altogether different. But she put the thought aside and she and Odette talked about the dead man, and it was a relief not to be focused on Vivian.

Benny described the scene outside Curios again and Odette listened intently, interrupting several times to ask questions. What was so special about this suit? Had he keeled all the way over? Then, at the end of Benny's recount, Odette leaned back in her chair and went, 'Huh,' as if the whole thing was curious in a particular way she hadn't expected.

'This is a delicious omelette,' said Benny.

'Oh, you're easy to please,' said Odette. 'You'll have to come over to eat more often,' and she smiled serenely. Then she served herself some salad and talked about Cedar Valley, and she gave a little of her history with it, and of her friends who lived in town, and Benny began to assemble a vague outline of Odette's life in her mind. She formed a few quick impressions, like the fact that Odette wasn't fond of Clarke, the large regional town to the north where they had more amenities and bigger shops. Clarke had very little character. But Cedar Valley was a lovely place. Apart from the daily ebb of tourists, and a few volatile people who lived permanently in the caravan park, there was a great sense of community in the township.

Sometimes Odette missed living in the cottage in town, where people would pop in all the time and there was a different kind of energy.

'Some of my friends think I must get so lonely, living out here like a shag on a rock,' said Odette, and she laughed in a way that made Benny wonder if Odette was lonely or not.

The two brown cows had moved up the paddock, nearer to the chicken coop, and Benny could see them from where she sat. One ate at the grass with no interruption, and the other spent a while stamping a hoof into the dirt, and three white birds with yellow beaks stood close to them, like friends. Odette explained that house cows were too much work. These two had only four functional teats between them anyhow and had been out to pasture for close to nine years. They liked a scratch behind the ear and to lick your boots, and the smaller one would be eighteen years old next February, even older than Bessel. Benny found the slow bulky presence of the cows to be an unexpected comfort.

'They're advertising a job at the pub in town,' said Benny, when Odette had finished speaking about the cows.

'Tom is? At the Royal?'

'The big pink pub,' said Benny. 'I thought I'd apply.'

Odette sat back, seeming slightly surprised. 'Well, good for you,' she said, and she told Benny that the man who ran the Royal was Tom Boyd, and that he was a good man. Tom's wife was Odette's friend, Annie, and Benny might see a bit of her. Tom and Annie had a big house on land just out of town and two girls.

'I think that's a wonderful idea, Benny, to get a job while you're here. You seem very capable. And if there's one thing you want it's financial independence. It's the key to your freedom. Now, when you go in and talk to Tom, tell him I sent you. Tell him you're family,' Odette said.

Benny felt a soft heat rise in her cheeks. *Family.* The way Odette had said it, so offhandedly, like it was of such little consequence—and her insistence that Benny could use it too, this word 'family', in relation to Odette Fisher and herself.

Odette ate some remaining bits of salad and then put her fork down, as if preoccupied with something.

'You know, when you were telling me about the man who died—it's so strange. It reminds me of a thing that happened a long time ago.'

'What thing?' said Benny, too quickly. 'What is it?'

Odette let out a little laugh, startled by Benny's enthusiasm.

'Oh, it's silly. It's a very old case, but quite famous, I think. A man was found dead in a similar kind of way, that's what reminded me of it.'

Benny waited for Odette to say more, but perhaps Benny had appeared too curious, or perhaps Odette had spoken up and then wished she hadn't, because she put one plate on top of the other and stood up.

'It's nothing,' she said. 'I can't really remember the details. I feel silly even saying it, it was a hundred years ago.'

13

Cora Franks was exhausted. She hadn't slept well. She was kept up by thoughts of the dead man in the suit and Fred had not been a receptive listener when she woke him in the night to discuss it. He rolled over and said, 'Cor, this one can wait till morning.'

'But what if he was murdered?' whispered Cora in the darkness.

Fred Franks groaned.

'Do you think he was murdered, Freddy?'

'How could anyone have possibly murdered him?' whispered Fred, his voice muffled against his pillow. And then: 'Why are we whispering?'

'Yes, but Janet said he looked so healthy,' whispered Cora.

'I don't think you can see a heart attack from the outside,' said Fred.

'Janet said it was more likely an aneurysm.'

'So why are we talking about murder?'

Cora rolled over, irritated, and stared at the sliver of moonlight on the carpet.

'We can talk about murder in the morning,' said Fred.

But when morning came Fred had gone off fishing and Cora was positively bursting with an odd mix of excitement and distress. Why was it that some part of her was so pleased about the whole thing? Why was it that just an inch of her hoped he *had* been murdered? Was she a monster?

The only thing that made her think otherwise was a persistent fantasy: that she had saved the man at the eleventh hour by administering mouth-to-mouth resuscitation and the whole town had cheered. She liked this fantasy, which she had cultivated when she couldn't sleep at one in the morning, and again at around three. But the fantasy kept being interrupted with a certain gladness that a man had died against her shop window, a quiet revelling in the intrigue it had created around her and her establishment.

How monstrous she was.

I am a ghastly person, thought Cora Franks, and she took a sip of weak tea.

•

That afternoon, Therese Johnson stayed a bit too long at Curios. She kept reaching for another bag of Lan-choo and filling her cup up again, going on about Ed Johnson and how she knew it for certain this time because he'd come home from the Royal smelling of some graceless perfume—musk—and Therese would never dream of wearing musk.

'It was an awful fragrance. The kind that really elbows its way into a room and gives you a headache,' said Therese, her red hair set as it always was: about half a foot all the way around her head, giving her the appearance of a pharaoh. Therese had been such an attractive and cosmopolitan woman in her time and yet, while vestiges of her beauty remained, Cora struggled increasingly to see them.

'How ghastly,' said Cora, about the musk, and Therese, and herself. 'But, Therese, you mustn't jump to conclusions. Remember the last time? He had a very good explanation.'

Cora didn't believe a word she had just said, but what was she supposed to say? Ed Johnson was a shit. Everyone knew that. But he was Therese's shit, and Therese loved him, and she seemed mostly willing to ignore his indiscretions until a rogue fragrance made them all too difficult to deny.

'Last time? *Which* last time? Oh, for God's sake . . .'

Therese whimpered into a tissue and Cora said, 'Now, really, when you don't know for certain, it's best just to ask him and see what he says.'

Again, rubbish. But Cora was tired. And while it was always interesting to hear of someone having an affair, it was getting a bit old with Ed, and she really wanted Therese to leave.

And how was it that Therese could show such a heartless disinterest in the man who had died? How could she sit and talk exclusively about Ed at such a time, when a human life had been so mysteriously extinguished just outside the door?

'I do need to finish that watch cabinet' said Cora and, after a further half-hour of pained monologue, Therese rose and announced that she was doing foils for Barbie Robinson at two-thirty.

It wasn't long after that Cora did a very uncharacteristic thing and closed the shop early.

'You right, Cor?' asked Lil from the doorway of the quilting store. She was dressed down in a lilac tracksuit, a cigarette in her bony hand.

'A bit under the weather,' said Cora.

'I feel a bit off myself,' said Lil. 'Fred home?'

'Should be,' said Cora. 'I'll be right.'

'You hear anything more?' Lil indicated the big window where the dead man had died.

'Tony said they're waiting to hear from the hospital. Or the morgue? They're waiting to hear from the person who checks the body.'

'Golly,' said Lil. 'I just keep on thinking about him! He was just so *dead*, wasn't he, Cor?' She took an urgent drag of her cigarette.

'He was,' said Cora, and she gave Lil a wave before walking the short distance home in the afternoon sun, feeling not the best. She checked the letterbox then continued down the path to her front door, let herself in, and found Freddy Franks sitting on the couch reading a fishing magazine.

'You're home early,' said Fred.

'Did you go to the lake?' asked Cora.

'I did. I got a couple of flathead.'

'Oh good, I didn't feel like those chops,' said Cora, and she went straight to the bedroom.

She changed into her house clothes and spent a while in front of the vanity, brushing her hair with her favourite soft-bristled brush. That always relaxed her. Later, at the kitchen table, she wrote a few cheques and addressed the envelopes. Long, slow thoughts about the dead man plagued her—and she went over her own awfulness, and got lost again in her resuscitating fantasy. And it was about then, as she hovered over the dead man's face in her mind's eye, her lips parted and ready to blow, that the faint nag of recognition came again. His face. Had she seen it before? She closed her eyes tightly and pictured him. How he'd been so motionless, staring off into the middle distance.

No.

No, she had never seen him before. She didn't think she had. And yet she had this strange feeling.

But before she could decide one way or another, she was distracted by something out the window above the sink: that old Volvo was pulling in to the driveway next door.

Cora got up and peered out the window and saw a young woman get out of the car. A girl, really. She looked almost too young to be driving. She stood up, straight as a rake, then entered the green house.

Cora went to the fridge, and got the flathead and set it on the bench. Fred had filleted it carefully, leaving the skin and the wings on, and Cora liked it when he did that.

'Who's Ed getting his leg over this time?' she said to Fred from the kitchen.

Ha ha ha, went Fred's sleepy laugh. 'Does Therese have a hunch, does she?'

'Is it the one from Solent or the one from Clarke?' asked Cora.

Fred came to stand in the doorway. His white hair was thick and wavy and his face was brown from fishing. He was such an easy person, Fred. He had this oddly uncomplicated relationship with the world. It was a friend to him. He didn't struggle with his position in relation to other people, and Cora had no idea what that kind of existence might feel like. How did Fred aquire his natural simplicity? This was something Cora had long wished to learn.

'It's not funny,' she said, fetching some garlic from a wooden bowl.

'I know,' said Fred. 'Bloody Ed. He thinks he's Christmas.'

'Which one?'

'A different one. It's Linda this time. The one from the chicken factory.'

'*Her?*' Cora pictured the red-faced woman called Linda— so tawdry—her bra straps hopelessly visible from under her tank tops. She was from out of town but she drank at the Royal like a local. And she was married herself, as far as Cora knew, and Cora knew a great deal. 'Well he's certainly lowered his standards,' she said.

'Yeah well, Ed's an opportunist. I guess he saw an opportunity,' said Fred. 'I've got to change the gas bottle. And then we can talk about murder.' And he walked out the back towards the barbecue.

Cora went back to the fish. She rested it on a plate and began making a marinade, slicing a clove of garlic and imagining Ed, in one of the rooms above the Royal, having his way with Chicken Linda before heading downstairs for another game of pool.

Then the front door opened again on Odette Fisher's cottage next door and Cora looked out her kitchen window and saw the young woman walk down the driveway and turn towards the shops. She had a nice figure, Cora thought. Lovely posture. Maybe she was a dancer, or some kind of gymnast. And not that it should come as a surprise, given her relation, but goodness gracious, she really did bear a striking resemblance to the young Vivian Moon.

14

Mark Foy's phone rang out. The monotonous sound of the dial tone, like a bored bird, went on for an age before culminating abruptly in an engaged signal. Apparently Mark Foy did not own an answering machine.

Simmons waited a while and dialled the number again, propelled by his own interest and, an hour later, irritated, he gave up and told Franklin to call.

'It just rings out,' yelled Franklin through the open door.

Then Franklin stepped out and Simmons got curious again at around four, and finally Mark Foy picked up and said, 'Hello?' in the casual voice of a bus driver.

'Mark Foy?' asked Simmons.

'Speaking,' said Mark Foy.

Simmons smiled. He introduced himself—still enjoying the sound of the word 'detective' in his title. Then he proceeded to ask Mark Foy if he recalled a well-dressed passenger taking the bus the day before, and if he'd be willing to give a formal statement.

Sure, Mark Foy remembered the gentleman in the brown suit and striped tie. He'd been sitting at the bus stop outside the train station at Clarke, like something from an old movie.

'Yeah, I thought, "Who's this guy think he is? Humphrey Bogart?"' And then Mark Foy laughed down the telephone.

Simmons was silent.

'I mean, sorry—Doreen said he's died.'

'He has,' said Simmons.

'Yeah, bugger,' said Mark Foy, and he explained to Simmons how the gentleman had boarded the bus and bought a single ticket. He was pleasant enough, though a man of few words; he said nothing but the name of his destination —'Cedar Valley'—and then he shuffled along and sat at the back of the bus. Mark Foy then picked up several more passengers, including Des Cohen, who also barracked for the Steelers, and Des sat in the spot closest to the driver's seat and they talked about footy for a fair stretch. Mark was a bit distracted by that conversation, as he told Simmons. The bloke in the suit sat right up the back and, come Cedar Valley, he got off.

Simmons asked if the man had any luggage with him, or bags of any kind, and Mark Foy said he didn't. Simmons asked if anyone sat with the man or if he interacted with other people on the bus. Mark Foy said he didn't. Simmons asked if anyone else got off at Cedar Valley, and Mark thought about that for a few beats before saying, no, he was pretty sure it was just the man in the suit.

'What kind of voice did he have? Did he sound like he was from the city?'

'I don't know. Like I said he didn't really say anything.'

'Do you remember what kind of money he gave you? A five? A ten?'

'Um . . .' Mark Foy seemed to be thinking about this. 'Oh yeah, he had the exact change. That's always nice, isn't it?'

Simmons wrote this down. 'Anything else you can think of? Anything unusual?'

'Well, yeah,' said Mark. 'I thought he must be hot.'

Simmons made a noise of agreement and thanked Mark Foy for his time. Then he hung up and was reading over the notes he had taken—his handwriting so oddly childlike—when Franklin appeared at the door.

'Kerry from the Clarke RTA does not have a male cousin who's missing, and his brother is accounted for,' said Franklin, grinning.

'I'll sleep better tonight then,' said Simmons.

Franklin put his hands on his very wide hips. 'Les had nothing.'

'How surprising.'

'I mailed the prints off to Parramatta.'

'Very good.'

'They were hard to get. The prints. Jimmy struggled.'

'Why's that?'

'Stiff fingers,' said Franklin, and the two men considered that quietly before Franklin added, 'The paper ran a mention of him though,' and he held up the newspaper so Simmons could see it.

Simmons beckoned him in with his hand, and Franklin opened the paper to page two and set it on the desk. MAN DIES ON VALLEY ROAD read a small headline, with a few sentences reporting that an 'unknown man' had died of 'unknown causes' outside Curios & Old Wares in Cedar Valley.

Simmons read the article quickly then he closed the paper and said to Franklin, 'Well good for him, he's famous. Can you turn the fan up on your way out?'

Gussy Franklin obliged.

The hot air moved around, ever so slightly.

Simmons opened the bottom drawer of his desk, where he kept his sweat towel and his painkillers. He retrieved the towel, bent over in his chair, and wiped his torso under his shirt. It was so unappealing when the sweat announced itself in wet patches on the material. He wiped his face and neck, too, before putting the towel back and slamming the drawer shut. Then he leaned back and collected his thoughts about the gentleman in the suit, who was proving far more difficult to identify than Simmons had expected.

Who was this man?

Hall had been at it all morning and had so far established that the dead man had caught the 7.23 am train from Central Station in Sydney and got off at Clarke. No one working at Central remembered him, but that was no surprise to anyone. It was a busy station.

So, what did he do in Clarke? Did he meet someone? Did he buy something? Did anyone even see him? At this point all Simmons knew was that at 11.05 am the man was sitting at the Clarke Station bus stop resembling Humphrey Bogart. He boarded the bus, with no bags. He had exact change—so he knew already how much the bus ticket would cost; Simmons found that interesting—and he'd had no other money on him once he'd bought that ticket.

All of this was peculiar.

Why would a man come to Cedar Valley with no bags and no money?

Simmons considered this and made a clicking sound with his mouth—*tock, tock, tock*. He glanced at the phone and wondered if he'd hear anything about cause of death before the end of the day. He should visit his mother after work. Elsie Simmons. His heart popped a bit when he thought of her recent fragility.

Simmons looked down at his small pile of notes and a photocopy of the fingerprints of the unknown gentleman. He must have known someone in Cedar Valley. Why else would he come here with no means even to buy a pie, let alone leave again?

And if he had no bags, surely he must have had a wallet at some point. So, what if he was *relieved* of his wallet in some way? What if he dropped it?

If he got off the bus in Cedar Valley and walked directly to Curios, or even if he strolled there slowly, he would have sat down at approximately five to one. This fitted well with what Cora Franks had said. But surely more people must have seen him. Cedar Valley was small, but it was no ghost town. There were people about all the time on Valley Road.

They needed to put out a call for more information.

Simmons stood up and walked out of his office, a determined feeling rising in his chest.

'Call the bus company back,' he said. 'Ask for lost property and see if anyone found a wallet on the bus. Maybe he dropped it and no one's put it together.'

Franklin nodded.

'I'm gonna walk back and see if I can't see a wallet fallen somewhere in the gutter. Or bloody *something*. Jimmy, you're coming with me.'

And so Constable James Hall, eyes like tiny saucers, and Detective Sergeant Anthony Simmons walked back across the road to the bus stop, and then very slowly down to Curios, with their eyes and their noses to the ground.

15

The Royal Tavern was a big old building on the corner of Valley Road and Gould Street and was painted pink like the chest of a galah. The frames of the windows, of which there were many—tall and spread along both levels—were yellow. The doors, dormers and the entirety of the second storey's wraparound verandah: a pale peppermint green.

Benny Miller stood on the footpath looking upwards, admiring the colour scheme. She stared at the stone numbers under the eaves, commemorating the year of construction, 1859. An old sign for VB hung in the window, and next to that the handwritten note advertising a vacant position. *All rounder required*, it said, and Benny Miller walked up a stone step and through the main doors of the pub with all the confidence she could muster and the words of Odette Fisher in her head: *Talk to Tom and tell him you're family.*

Music was playing when she walked inside—something by Slim Dusty—and the sound of it was good; it reminded her of Frank Miller in a welcome way. A few men were sitting up at the bar, and two women were perched on stools at a high table under a window. Afternoon light poured in, golden on the floorboards, and a pool table sat centrally, with coloured balls set up in a neat triangle. Olden-days photos of Valley Road were hung on the walls.

Benny approached the bar slowly, trying to suppress the discomfort that came from being a stranger in a bar such as this, full of locals who were well acquainted with one other. A grey-haired man was pouring a beer into a tilted glass and talking to a fellow in a terry-towelling hat, and Benny stood rigid between two stools and waited. She looked around and saw all kinds of memorabilia stuck on the walls and arranged on shelves. Postcards, Polaroid photos, old toys and figurines, a taxidermied possum. And money; there must have been a hundred bills from all different countries, tacked up in neat rows.

'What're you having?' the man behind the bar asked in Benny's direction, his voice as deep as a valley.

'I'm here about the job,' Benny said.

'Ah, brilliant,' said the man. 'Come have a seat.'

Benny followed him along to the far end of the bar and sat on a stool, while the grey-haired man leaned his elbows on the bar mat and said, 'I'm Tom.'

How old was this man? Benny couldn't tell. He must have been over fifty, with his thick grey hair cropped very short.

His skin was tough and tanned, and grey stubble covered his cheeks.

Benny introduced herself and explained that she was new to the town. She had experience as a bartender, she told him, and had worked part time for almost two years at a pub in Sydney; before that she'd waitressed in a cafe. Benny offered the name of the pub—it was the British Lion—and the name of the publican, who had liked Benny well enough, and Tom wrote this information down on the back of a coaster. He asked her where in town she was living and she told him—on Wiyanga Crescent—and she remembered her instructions from Odette.

'Odette Fisher told me to come by and see you about the job—' she said '—because I'm . . . family.'

The sentence had come out strangely stilted. Benny had been too eager and then she'd faltered at the end of it and tripped on the last word.

'Odette?' asked Tom in his gravel voice. 'Are you her . . .' He paused as if sizing up Benny's age and appearance, trying to guess the relation.

'Oh. Well, I mean—' And Benny stopped mid-sentence, blushing. What kind of family was she supposed to be? Why had she just announced it like that with no further plan?

Tom looked at her, waiting, and then said, 'Well, tell Odette I said hello.'

Benny looked down at the damp bar mat, and Tom carried on, untroubled, explaining the opening hours and shift times, the pay. All the information was coming out rather quickly, Tom still holding the coaster on which he'd written *British Lion, Glebe*, and Benny realised then that he was never going to look up the telephone number and call.

'We'll do a two-week trial,' said Tom. 'See if we like each other.'

'Okay,' said Benny, and she felt very pleased.

'Okay then, Benny,' said Tom, friendly and concise, and he told her to come back at ten the next morning so he could show her how things worked, and she could do a shift straight after, if she liked. Then he wrote down her roster on another coaster, including a day shift on Sundays because they'd started a new lunch special and it was proving popular.

'Ed over there runs the bistro, when he feels like it,' said Tom, and the man called Ed, a few stools along, turned his head around.

Tom raised his voice a little. 'This here's Benny,' he said. 'For the job.'

Ed tilted his schooner glass at her with an unnerving kind of confidence and looked Benny up and down.

'You're hired,' said Ed, grinning before he turned around again, and Benny thought he had eyes like a snake might. They were little leaden eyes, both vacant and hungry at the same time.

'See you at ten then,' said Tom Boyd.

Benny stood up. She looked down at Tom's black T-shirt and saw it had a drawing of the pub on it and *Bistro, Gaming, Free beer tomorrow!* under the logo. Benny wondered if she'd get to wear a T-shirt, too, and she hoped she would. In fact, what she really wanted was to sit down right then on a stool, order a middy of beer and drink it at the bar with these local people. But, no. Benny Miller, often at the expense of her own enjoyment, was ever vigilant not to appear too eager.

Instead she said, 'Yes, ten o'clock,' and she held her hand over the bar for Tom to shake it.

Tom Boyd, slightly amused by the formality of the gesture, took her hand and shook it firmly, and Benny found his rough skin to be as warm as sun.

Then she turned around and left, walking straight out of the big pink galah of a building and back down Valley Road towards the shops.

16

No matter how hard Simmons and Hall had looked for it, there was no wallet in the gutters of Valley Road. Torchlight revealed no wallet in any drain. An unsavoury search of two bins found no wallet, emptied and discarded, in either. And it wasn't among the dry leaves under the hedge by the bus stop, nor—according to the lost property service at the Gather Region Bus Service—on the actual bus either.

Adding to their growing frustration, along with there being no wallet, there were no new other clues either. Nothing physical, at least. A lone identification card, a money clip, even an extra comb—all of this would have been something. A person at the bus stop who had managed a conversation with the man and was waiting there to share it—now that would have been fantastic. But Simmons and Hall, during their laborious search of the short distance between bus stop and window, found nothing.

They reconvened at the police station for a situation report shortly before beer time.

Constable Gus Franklin had spent a good while during the afternoon going shop to shop, asking questions. It wasn't possible that anyone on Valley Road hadn't heard about the dead man, he knew that for certain. But perhaps what the people of Cedar Valley didn't understand was this: that at a time when the police had next to no information—when it was barely possible to know any *less* about the gentleman in question—then anything further, even if it seemed insignificant, could be inordinately helpful.

Franklin returned with a few nuggets.

First, Terri, the young assistant to Therese Johnson at the Old Paris Coiffure, had seen the man get off the bus. Terri didn't like to take her break too close to the salon—Therese had a tendency to monitor her—so she was sitting on the bench up next to the hedge at the bus stop, having a cigarette and looking through a magazine. She saw the man and noticed his suit, and though Terri was a hesitant young woman, she was not without ideas. She told Franklin that the man had alighted, kept his eyes down, and walked directly towards Curios. She already knew he was going there, there was not a doubt in her mind she said, 'because obviously he was an antique-y sort of guy'.

Second, Barbie Robinson, on her way to visit her sister Maureen, who worked at the chemist, had seen the man sit down. She was walking by, about to cross the street, and she saw him arrive at the front of Curios. She said he peered briefly in the window and she, too, had assumed he would go in. But instead he turned around to face the road—or the shops opposite?—and then, with what seemed to be a sense of purpose, he sat down gracefully on the footpath. She found it a strange place to sit, considering there was a bench a few doors up outside the Coiffure. But there was something about the way he did it—the intentionality of it—that somehow made it not strange at all. Barbie had thought, 'Oh well, I guess he knows what he's doing,' and she'd gone across to see Maureen, sensing that the man was 'kind of watching me, maybe', as she went on her way.

Finally, Lil Chapman, who ran the Quilting Bee, had decided to remember that she had in fact seen someone approach the man and perhaps engage in some form of conversation. Lil had forgotten this entirely in the fog of his death, but now she miraculously recalled it. A woman had come across from the other side of the street. She'd walked straight up to the man, and then crouched down in front of him. She spoke to him, Lil was sure of it now. But Lil was inside the window of the shop, changing the quilt display, so she couldn't hear the words, nor see if the man had replied. The woman just crouched and spoke, and not too long after she had straightened, still looking at the seated gentleman, and then she went back across the street and away. Or perhaps she went down towards the video store, Lil couldn't be certain about the direction.

'What did the woman look like?' asked Franklin.

'Not local,' said Lil.

'Not local how?'

'Like a city woman; she looked like she came from money,' said Lil, who was a country woman who did not come from money.

When pressed, Lil's more detailed description of the woman was this: early fifties, blonde bobbed hair, white or cream clothing, attractive, and perhaps she wore gold jewellery. And then, reflecting on it: 'She looked like she'd just had her hair done. Actually, you know, if I had to say, I'd say she looked a bit like Nikki from *The Young and the Restless*.'

Franklin raised his eyebrows and somewhat reluctantly wrote this down.

Six other people gave new statements too, but no one had anything relevant to add. Impressions of the man seemed now to vary. He was either calm, drunk, odd, healthy, contented or possibly a dancer. But no one had thought it a good idea to talk to him—to ask him what he was doing or if he was okay. No one, apparently, except for a rich blonde woman who resembled an American soap star.

Detective Sergeant Simmons, standing behind his chair for a quick stretch of his always-aching back, sat down again with a thump. 'Okay then,' he said.

'This one's a real corker,' said Hall.

'So we now have him speaking to a city woman. Or a city woman speaking to *him*. Is Lil Chapman telling stories?' asked Simmons.

'Nah, I don't think so,' said Franklin. 'I think she's just . . .'

'Imaginative?' said Simmons.

'Flustered,' said Franklin.

'Well, it seems like he didn't talk to anyone else. Or go anywhere else, apart from straight to Curios. And then he seems pretty sure of himself to sit down there. Then maybe this woman talks to him, but not for long. And then she's off.' Simmons was looking at the ceiling now with his hands clasped behind his head. 'And then, yeah. At some point—after he dances his arms around like a good little fairy—he carks it.'

Hall, who often tried too hard at male camaraderie, boomed out a laugh.

Simmons looked down at the pile of statements, which had now grown in size. He would just have one schooner and then go see Elsie Simmons, maybe take her something for tea. 'No news from Clarke Base?' he asked, almost as an afterthought.

Franklin shook his thick head. 'They're getting to him. They have a bit of a backlog, apparently, with that crash on the coast road.'

'So when will we have cause?' asked Simmons.

'In the morning,' said Franklin. 'First thing.'

Simmons smiled and whistled and said, 'Well I don't know about you boys, but I'm on the edge of my seat. What do you reckon, Gussy, shall we get a beverage?'

17

It was six-thirty when Benny Miller woke the next morning, nestled on the long couch in the living room of the pale green cottage.

The python had dragged itself around loudly in the night, and Benny had gone in and out of dreams with the noise of it. She had rolled around in irritation, reorganising her restless body and silently cursing the ceiling. At some point, she had issued a drowsy protest by getting up, taking the quilt and a pillow, and retreating to the lounge room. She slept heavily on the couch then—it was soft and comfortable—until the dawn birds began their chorus, and a rooster joined them from somewhere nearby, and then the cicadas too.

Benny got up and made coffee in the stovetop pot she found in a low cupboard. She sat and drank it sleepily at the outdoor setting, where occasional mosquitoes hovered. The bush rang with noise while she thought about Odette Fisher.

Odette had invited Benny over for dinner that night, and Benny couldn't wait to go. And this morning she was to be at the Royal Tavern at 10 am and she would see Tom Boyd again, and now Benny found herself thinking of him. She had seen how his big hand had gripped a small pen with gentle intensity and she smiled at the memory of it. He had reminded her of Jules Cowrie, his dusky skin and the way his veins made long ridges along the tops of his hands. But Jules was just a young man, the same age as Benny, and Benny was not sure how she would describe what Jules was to her now. He had been her boyfriend for two years before he decided to switch universities and move to Canberra. And he'd said so earnestly, so many times, 'Come with me, Ben. Come along with me.'

But she hadn't.

And over the past six months she had answered fewer and fewer of his letters.

Benny went inside to the kitchen and made toast and put butter and sliced banana on it. She found a jar of cinnamon among a shelf of dried herbs and spices in the dresser and she sprinkled some on top. Then she went back outside and ate her breakfast and it tasted good. She pushed Jules Cowrie from her mind and returned to thinking about Odette.

Odette Fisher had said so many things the day before that had caused Benny to contemplate, and of course she had longed for Odette to say more. Every mention of the name Vivian Moon had made Benny ripple with anticipation. She wished to know so much, but a cold, empty feeling always accompanied the knowing and, as always, Benny was divided between two conflicting impulses: wanting to look and needing to look away.

What had Odette been referring to when she said the dead man in the suit had reminded her of something that happened a long time ago? The older woman had a way of making it clear when she wanted to stop a line of conversation on its heels. But the discussion swirled around in Benny now, along with another thought—one that filled her with great discomfort: was Odette Fisher only spending this time with Benny, being so kind to her, out of some misplaced obligation to a dead friend? Benny closed her eyes firmly at the thought of that—as if to hide from the humiliation of it—and hoped that it wasn't so.

The sound of someone watering came over the paling fence next door.

Benny opened her eyes again and looked around at the wild garden, where mint was wilting in the dry earth, and without thinking she got up and untangled a crumpled hose and began to water her garden, too. Vines and weeds and shrubs grew deep by the fence, and Benny watered and felt good while she was doing that, she enjoyed the task of it. She had always found some kind of solace in responsibility.

The old shed sat aslant at the end of the yard, with the bush tall behind it, and Benny rolled the hose back onto its wire mount and wandered down the mossy brick path.

Perhaps there would be tools in there that she could use to tend to the garden—she thought this as she pushed the old door. It creaked open on its one hinge and a smell like damp concrete and soil came out.

On the left as Benny entered were tools, just as she'd expected: a rake, a shovel, some trowels and a rusty push mower. They were all propped against the wall next to a ladder, and on the floor was a bag of straw mulch and a stack of empty pots. Paint tins and snail pellets sat on a shelf, and an old washbasin had a towel folded inside it. Benny remembered Odette's note and guessed that this was where the possum slept.

At the back of the shed, along the length of the wall, were three metal shelves full of dusty relics. She broke a spider web as she went across, her bare feet on the rough floor, and she looked around with some curiosity at a crate of ceramic tiles, old wind chimes, a floor fan, a pile of gardening magazines.

Above all that, on the top shelf, were three cardboard cartons. Benny looked up at them. They were too high for her to see inside, so she reached up and gripped one and slid it off the edge of the shelf towards her, hoping it wouldn't be too heavy for her to catch. It wasn't. She set it down and found it full of old utensils, jars and tins, a few tea towels wrapped around some glassware.

She put that box back and, with little thought as to the impropriety of her prying, pulled down another.

It was full of papers—receipts, bills, recipes written on index cards, a wall calendar from 1980. Benny took a cursory look through the top few layers and saw they were Odette's. She recognised the writing on the index cards, and she saw the name on the bills: Odette Fisher, 5 Wiyanga Crescent. She closed the box again, then lifted it back up onto the high shelf.

At that point it registered dimly with Benny that what she was doing was not respectful. She didn't know what had come over her. She would never have dreamed of looking in Frank Miller's drawers or hunting through his cupboards. But she had no interest in Frank Miller, she realised—no interest in him at all. That was the thing of it. And she certainly had none in Irene Miller. You couldn't have paid Benny to open a drawer at her grandmother's grim house in Lane Cove, where even the hallway smelled sickly and sour.

But Odette Fisher—she was different, compelling. Benny wanted to know so much about her. And, while she knew it wasn't right to poke around in Odette's boxes, she couldn't seem to help it.

So Benny pulled the third box down, finding it much heavier; her arms strained as she held it and lowered it to the floor. The top, covered with silt, was closed, and when she opened it dust floated about in the air. Benny looked down and saw books. The box was full of books and she sunk with disappointment.

What was she expecting to find in there? What possible interesting thing would Odette hide in an old shed in a house she didn't live in anymore? Benny felt foolish, embarrassed by her intrusion, and it was with only vague interest that she picked up the first few books and looked at the ones below. *Lolita, Catch 22*, novels by John Updike, Edna O'Brien, J.P. Donleavy. Benny had read some of these books, others she had planned to read, and she reached in and pulled out more. Volumes of poetry, collections of essays, travel guides and phrasebooks, a *Roget's Thesaurus*. She thought about the long bookshelves lining the walls of Odette's farmhouse and guessed they were full, leaving no room for these, and she silently admired Odette's obvious thirst for literature.

Holding a copy of *The Magus*, Benny flipped through the thin, yellowed pages, arriving at the first page by accident. A name was written in pen at the top right-hand corner, and she quickly saw that this was different handwriting and not Odette's name at all.

Benny stared at the name a long time.

Then she took several more books from the box and checked the first pages of each of them. They didn't all have a name written inside, but most of them did, and the name— written in many different pens—was always the same. It was Vivian Moon.

18

Detective Sergeant Simmons was up early, too. His eyes opened and no sooner had he become aware of being awake than his legs swung out from under the quilt and he was sitting upright and alert on the edge of the bed. Jenny Simmons was snoozing beside him, facing the wall, the sheet over the hills of her body. Simmons put a hand on her hip, patted her gently as a good morning, and a drowsy moan came out of Jenny that gave him a rare feeling of contentment.

This was when his house was most lovely and Tony Simmons felt a fondness for it: when everyone else was asleep.

Simmons had got home the night before when the girls were too tired to be tolerable, and Jenny was in one of her moods because of his lateness. Simmons had been in one of his moods, too, after seeing Elsie Simmons. How frail she was. So much so that she didn't get up to see him out; she only sat there in her armchair and had unusual difficulty reading the newspaper.

'It's these floaters in my eyes,' she said. 'I'm going to have to cancel the paper.'

Tony squirmed inside. Where had she gone, his mother? Where had his vital, robust mother gone?

He had microwaved her a Lean Cuisine and set it on the side table, and she'd been so grateful. But these days—when she was tired like that, unable to sit down with a book like she used to—she seemed so thwarted and bereft.

Simmons sat on the edge of the bed now, in his own home, and his back hurt in the place it always hurt, and he thought about Elsie Simmons and felt something close to misery. Then he got up and showered and dressed and ate the same breakfast he had eaten since he was a child: Weet-Bix and milk. He made his instant coffee and drank it standing up in the kitchen while the girls watched cartoons and Jenny stomped around making lunches with an absent kind of irritation.

Simmons didn't ask her what was wrong. He didn't offer to help her. He didn't interact with his daughters or wash up his Weet-Bix bowl or his coffee mug. He left his pyjama pants and T-shirt on the floor of the bathroom, his used dental floss dangling over the side of the sink, and left for work.

Thankfully, when he stepped inside the Cedar Valley police station a little after eight, he found the satisfying distraction of the job, and a fax from Dr Ping Williams at Clarke Base Hospital morgue spilling out of the fax machine and onto the floor.

Simmons tore it off and spread it out across his desk so it fell off over the side. He spent a little while running his finger down the page, looking for sections of particular interest. He was still standing over it when Hall arrived and stuck his head in. He smelled faintly of aftershave; Simmons caught a waft of sandalwood and something floral.

'Morning, boss,' said Jimmy Hall with forced brightness.

'Jimmy, I think this is getting *very* interesting,' said Simmons, whose mood was beginning to lift towards good spirits.

'I thought it was already pretty interesting,' said Hall, as he came in and sat down, weedy in the chair. 'Is that the post-mortem?'

Simmons kept on reading. He ran his finger along as he went and mouthed some of the words. Then he looked up, realising that Constable James Hall had sat down, and he thought Jimmy looked pretty tired really, but he didn't care enough to ask. Instead he said, 'Let's get going with a statement to the press. Where are the photos you took? We'll need to get a sketch done from the photos.'

'I just picked them up. There'll be a few more on the next roll, too. Stevie needed the little camera when we got back here so I took the Canon to Clarke Base and got a few ID shots at the morgue. They'll be better of the face. I'm heading to Clarke now have a sniff around the train station.'

'Off you go,' said Simmons, and went back to the fax.

Hall stayed sitting in the chair, looking at the fax and then at Simmons, expecting something more.

'I said off you go, Jimmy,' said Simmons, fake-smiling, and Hall, appearing stung by the tone of it, said, 'Oh, right,' and left.

Then Simmons picked up the phone and dialled the number for the morgue at Clarke Base and got on to Dr Ping Williams, the woman who had performed the post-mortem examination on the unknown gentleman.

'Hello, Anthony,' she said, in a cool whisper of a voice.

Simmons said, 'Looks like we've got a weird one, hey?'

And Ping Williams whispered, 'Oh yes,' before taking a small feathery breath and delivering all she had to say.

This death was not, Ping Williams explained, caused by any of the usual suspects. The man in the suit, had not suffered a stroke, or an aneurysm, or a heart attack. In fact, his heart was in particularly good condition, normal in every way—'quite tough and firm,' said Ping—he was in top physical condition, 'really rather fit'.

Simmons wondered how his own heart would fare if Ping Williams were to remove it right then and examine it under an unforgiving lamp.

Dr Williams went on for a while about the general appearance of the body and its organs. The word 'congested' was used several times. Small vessels in the brain were congested. The pharynx was congested. So were the stomach, the lungs and the kidneys. And this was to say nothing of the spleen, which was enormous by usual standards, about three times its normal size—all of which made Ping Williams strongly consider an acute gastric haemorrhage. 'There's blood in the stomach, you see? Blood mixed with the food.'

'I see,' said Simmons, who at that point did not entirely see.

According to Dr Williams's calculations, the man's last meal would have been three or four hours before his death, but it was difficult to be sure of this. Anxiety can halt digestion—Simmons had not known that—so if this man had been anxious about something, his stomach might well have taken its time.

Was he anxious? Simmons considered this. How could he really know? All he could think of was how many people in town had made a point of saying that the man seemed noticably calm.

'It's such a conflict of findings, you see?' said Ping Williams.

And what she meant by that was this: the man had a normal-looking heart. Normal in every way. Yet the further she looked into it, the more likely it seemed that heart failure was the cause of death. The last straw, as it were. But what had caused such a healthy heart to fail?

Simmons became confused. 'But you say it wasn't a heart attack?' he said.

'Yes, but something stopped the blood from being pushed along, because of the cyanosis, you see?' said Ping in her lovely soft voice—a voice that could make a phrase like 'because of the cyanosis' sound like a line from a lyric poem.

'Right,' said Simmons.

'The pupils, too, as I said in my report, they're smaller than I would expect and unusual in appearance. Some drugs can do that. And I suppose the main thing that I am saying,' she went on, 'is that I am convinced that this was not a natural death.'

'*Right*,' said Simmons, finally feeling like the conversation was reaching its desired destination. 'Because you've written here . . .' He looked down at the fax, at the word that had caught his attention.

'Yes,' said Ping. 'I believe the cause of death to be some kind of irritant poison.'

'Poison,' repeated Simmons, because he was rather excited about the word.

'That's correct,' said Ping Williams. 'I believe it was poison.'

And Simmons just laughed out loud at that, a short high-pitched laugh, most unprofessional, and the inappropriateness of it was not lost on Dr Ping Williams.

'I can assure you this was not funny for the deceased,' she said.

'I'm sorry, I must be tired,' said Simmons.

'Shall I continue, Detective?'

And Simmons said, 'Yes, I'm good.'

But there was something rather not good about Ping Williams's assertion that the man had died from poison. And the problem—and this was quite a sizable problem—was that, despite searching for traces of this apparent poison in all the hidden pockets of a human body where poison might secrete itself, she couldn't actually find any.

'And I'm astounded that I can't,' she whispered. 'I was sure that I would. But I've ordered further analysis on some of the organs, and of course blood and urine, so we still may find it.'

Simmons remembered the last time he was at the morgue. He pictured a row of the man's organs lined up in glass jars and then recoiled at the thought.

'But you see, the *absence* of poison in my finding leads me to think that this was not a common poison. I would have thought a barbiturate, a soluble hypnotic, and that still may be consistent. Some poisons decompose very quickly after death, you see? Certain barbiturates just don't come up in analysis. But that is extremely rare, Detective. And how a normal person would have obtained such a poison, I just don't know.' Ping paused for a moment before adding, 'Unless he was a chemist himself.'

Simmons nodded, wrote down *Chemist?* in blue pen—it looked like the writing of a six-year-old—and he said to Ping, 'We'll look into that.'

Ping Williams said, 'It's a very perplexing finding. I detect no mark from a hypodermic needle, so I suggest he ingested it—whatever it was—and I have been compiling a list of possibilities. But whether he ingested it deliberately or not I can't say. We know he didn't vomit. Did anyone suggest that he convulsed?'

'Ah, convulsions—no,' said Simmons. 'Calm, apparently. People said he looked peaceful.' And he laughed again, nervously.

'Baffling,' whispered Ping Williams.

'It is,' said Simmons.

'And along with the lack of identification, and the labels being removed from his clothing . . .' said Ping.

They were silent for a moment, then Ping Williams gave a tiny cough—a cough like a cloud bursting—and Simmons had a sudden thought. 'So he'd eaten?'

'Yes, Detective, he had.'

Looking back at the fax, Simmons searched for the appropriate section, with the receiver cradled between his chin and his moist shoulder.

'A pasty?' he said, finding the part he was looking for.

'Yes,' whispered Ping Williams. 'His last meal was a pasty—or perhaps a pie.'

19

Benny was sitting cross-legged in the shed among the piles of books, a collection of short stories by Flannery O'Connor in her hand, when she heard a woman's voice saying, 'Hello?' very loudly from someplace in the garden.

Benny, alarmed, began picking up books in a panic and shoving them back into the box. She plonked the thesaurus on top, most ungracefully, and pressed the cardboard flaps closed. Then she hoisted the box back up onto the shelf with some difficulty.

'Hello?' said the voice again. It was a yell, really—a woman yelling.

Benny said, 'Coming,' to the garden and she emerged from the shed and squinted into the still-early morning.

At the back of the house, to the right side, there was a gate, and over the gate Benny could see the top of a head. She went up the path through the garden quickly and unlatched the gate, opening it to reveal a stocky woman in a silk shirt.

'Oh, there you are. Hello. I just thought I'd introduce myself. I knocked at the front door, but . . .'

Benny, flustered, looked at the woman and was puzzled for a moment before she remembered where she'd seen her before. It was the woman from the night the man had died on the street—the loud one who'd poured brandy for the ladies in the antique store

'Sorry, I was just in the shed,' said Benny.

'I'm Cora,' said the woman. 'From next door.' She raised a short arm and gestured at the big old house next door. It was a brick house with big windows, and Benny could still hear someone hosing in the yard.

'That's Fred in the yard, he's just watering. Say hello, Fred!'

A man's voice, just audible above the sound of the hose, said, 'Hello.'

'Hello,' said Benny to the fence.

'I brought you a couple of things,' said Cora as she came in through the gate. 'Shall I pop them inside?' She walked across the low deck, rather ahead of Benny, and went in through the double doors to the kitchen, and Benny followed along in her bed shirt.

'Oh, you're not dressed,' said Cora offhandedly. 'But now I do know that you're Benny.'

'Yes, I am,' said Benny, as Cora put a cake on the counter and then opened the fridge and put a plastic container with something yellow in it inside.

'That's carrot—' she pointed to the cake '—and there's some curried egg for sandwiches. My son lives in Sydney now and I don't have anyone to make sandwiches for.'

'Oh,' said Benny. 'Thank you.'

Then she stood back as Cora surveyed the kitchen critically. She watched as Cora went to the dresser drawer and took out a stiff placemat and a coaster and carried these over to the dining table and, with a proprietorial air about her, put the placemat under a plate of half-eaten toast Benny had left there the night before, and a coaster under the glass of water that was set beside it.

'You don't want to damage the table,' said Cora.

Benny said nothing. That she did not want to damage the table was true. And that she did not care much for the attitude of this woman—Cora—was true also.

'You don't say much, do you?' said Cora. 'But Odette has told me all about you and we're happy you're here. It's nice to see the light on. The last fellow who lived here was one of Odette's artist friends. I liked the paintings—big kind of abstract faces and stuff like that—but the house just always smelled of paint! He was a funny old thing. Even quieter than you.'

Then Cora looked at Benny, and her expression softened. It seemed for a moment like she was on the verge of saying something meaningful, even personal. Benny leaned against the counter, in her very little clothing, feeling uneasy and hoping for this woman to leave.

'Well,' said Cora. She straightened up, as if coming out of a dream, and gave Benny a once-over. 'You look like you could do with some cake.'

And then she headed down the hall towards the front door, opened it and stepped onto the verandah.

'I'll get Fred to come over with the mower,' she said, giving the lawn a cursory look.

'Oh,' Benny said, about to protest but deciding against it. The sheer force of this woman, Cora, was something Benny could not be bothered to resist, so she said, 'Okay,' by which time Cora was back on her own property and, with a quick wave at Benny, was hurrying up the steps and inside.

•

Cora Franks went through her house to the back door, sparkling with nerves.

Freddy Franks was putting the hose away and she beckoned to him to come inside, so he put the hose down and walked into the house.

'Is she nice?' asked Fred.

'Shhh', said Cora, and she led him in from the doorway.

Freddy laughed, and Cora frowned at him until he stopped.

'Oh dear,' said Fred, smiling.

'Well, she's shy,' said Cora in an excited whisper, leaning in to Fred. 'Painfully. And very young. She's like a child really. And my God, Freddy, you should see her. It's uncanny! She is the absolute spitting image of her mother.'

20

Gussy Franklin's hulk of a body perched on the bench outside the police station, where he was taking a short break with a cheese sandwich.

It was a hot morning, and Franklin sat staring off beyond the hedge towards the war memorial, a statue of a single solider atop a tall column at the end of the rose garden. He was chewing and staring when Simmons strolled out with a manila folder in his hand

'I would have offered you half, mate,' said Franklin, who would not have offered anyone half.

'Bullshit,' said Simmons as he leaned against the low brick wall that went around the verandah like a battlement. He put his folder down beside him, folded his arms and told Gussy Franklin how he'd just had an interesting little chat with Ping Williams. He spoke in a low voice—as if they might be overheard—and Franklin, sitting with his tree-trunk legs spread as wide as they would go, leaned in to listen.

Simmons, very pleased with himself and his rather surprising information, explained the nature of Ping William's theory.

'Poison,' said Franklin.

'Correct,' said Simmons.

Franklin raised his eyebrows in disbelief. 'Well, fuck,' he said and laughed.

'Exactly,' said Simmons, and he really did love to tell things to Gussy Franklin. He was a great audience, much more personable than Hall. Simmons squinted over his shoulder into the bright sun—light was gleaming on the war memorial—and then he shifted along the wall for more shade.

On discussing it further, they both agreed that poison was a compelling finding, that was for certain. Simmons wasn't sure what he was expecting, but he sure was not expecting that, and Franklin wasn't either. The only problem—and it was a fairly large one—was that Ping Williams couldn't actually find any trace of this supposed poison. Simmons went to some effort to explain this: how Ping was certain there'd been poison, but that there wasn't any to be found, and how some poisons decompose in the body very quickly, so you just can't detect them, or masking agents can be used to conceal them.

Franklin gave a whistle, one that went from a high note down to a low one and then stopped.

Simmons went on. Regardless of the science, this poison theory was the GMO's conclusion. And while it was a slightly tenuous one, given the lack of evidence, Ping Williams was an expert and a professional and no one had ever seen her get fanciful for even one moment. 'The woman barely talks out of her mouth, let alone her arse,' said Simmons. She was precise and thorough. And the main thing to remember was that there was certainly no *other* cause of death apparent. You had the blood in the stomach, the congestion of the organs, the something-or-other that had caused the healthy heart to fail. Ping Williams was ordering further analysis of the organs—a row of clear glass jars full of tissue and fluids—but at this point she had concluded, and may well continue to conclude, that the dead man had died from a mysterious and extremely rare poison.

'So we're treating it as suspicious?' asked Franklin.

'Oh, shit, yes. We're treating it as *bloody* suspicious,' said Simmons.

Gussy Franklin nodded, thinking, and took another bite of his sandwich. It was marvellous how much he could fit in his mouth at one time. He chewed with little difficulty and swallowed.

'But maybe it's just a suicide,' he said.

Simmons nodded. 'Maybe,' he said. 'Maybe. But it's not *just* a suicide, is it. If he administered some kind of undetectable poison to himself and then sat down on a public street in his silly suit? Why on earth would he do that?'

'I don't know,' said Franklin. He finished his sandwich and considered it. 'But probably no one else removed the labels from his clothes. You don't just snip away at some guy's undies tag without him noticing. And probably no one took his wallet. So obviously he didn't want us to know who he was.'

Simmons, his arms folded, nodded again, and Franklin waited a beat before he continued.

'Like, he's come in by bus,' he said quietly. 'He's not known by anyone and he hasn't met anyone. He's died there without wanting to talk to anyone—except maybe this blonde woman who looks like someone out of *Days of Our Lives*. And he's got nothing on him but these few items.'

'*Young and the Restless*,' Simmons said.

A bus went past along Valley Road, *Gather Region Bus Service* written along the side. Simmons turned his head and watched as it disappeared from view, disturbing a flock of cockatoos on the verge as it went.

He turned back to Franklin. 'But then why's he carrying those items at all?' he said. 'Why's he have his cigarettes and his combs and bloody Juicy Fruit and why's he keep his tickets?'

'Well—why any of it?' said Franklin, and Simmons laughed loudly at that, because of the deep and subtle truth of it, he laughed.

'Jimmy's in Clarke,' Simmons said. 'I've got a Clarke cop, a mate, meeting him at the train station, for continuity up there. Those boys know it better. I want to see what he gets. I'm thinking about that little pie cart next to Clarke train station.'

'You hungry, boss?'

'Always,' said Simmons, and he told Franklin to get on with putting together a statement, something basic to release to the press—all the local channels. Someone had to be missing a man in a brown suit.

Franklin stood up and scrunched his paper sandwich bag into a ball. 'I'll write it up, boss,' he said, and he wandered back inside.

Simmons stayed leaning against the wall for a time. It was going to get hotter, he could feel it, and he was going to need his towel. Across from the station, at the park, people were standing around the Driver Reviver van, drinking from polystyrene cups. There was an old woman who, from this distance, looked a bit like his mother.

Simmons had such a funny feeling about this case. This unknown man. It was something he couldn't quite put his finger on, but it was not unpleasant. His mind ticked over and he wiped a little sweat off the back of his neck.

From the folder beside him, he pulled out a photo Hall had taken at the morgue. How grey the dead man's face was. He flipped though several pictures, framed like grim portraits. The unknown man, captured from various positions as he leaned against the wall of Cora Franks's shop, his eyes open, his expression neutral, dead as a doornail in his shiny shoes.

Simmons smiled, he was quite amused, and he had the strangest sense that someone was playing a game.

21

It took a good while for Benny Miller to settle on an outfit for her first shift at the Royal Tavern. She rummaged through the drawers in her new bedroom, pulling out various T-shirts, some button-downs she'd bought at the markets, a pair of maroon corduroy trousers. She tried on a black skirt and found it too formal. She tried a flannelette shirt and found it too casual. In the end, she settled on blue jeans, a navy T-shirt and her boots. She braided her hair in the pink-tiled bathroom, sitting on the edge of the bath.

Benny walked to town slowly via a different route. She turned right early and followed a long street where several houses had caravans parked in their driveways, and hydrangeas grew against weatherboard walls. Lost in thought about her morning discovery—why were Vivian's books in the shed?—she temporarily lost her bearings when she got to Valley Road, at the south end, opposite a big petrol station and mechanical repair. Benny stood for a moment and oriented herself, then she headed north along the main street, stopping to look in the camping supply store and then going into Hargraves Books, where a man sat behind the counter reading *Twenty Thousand Leagues Under the Sea*.

As always, there were people out front of Fran's World Famous Pies and Benny stopped there too, to inspect it. A faded article taped in the front window spoke to the high quality of the traditional steak pie in particular, and commended the atmosphere of the store itself, which had 'all the ambiance of a bygone era'. Benny peered in the big window and had to agree that it did. Dark wooden shelving went along one side, full of chutneys and sauces, and the counter area opposite—a long glass pie-warming cabinet illuminated with soft light—glowed with pies.

Across the road at the bakery, Benny decided on buying something to take with her later to Odette's house for dessert, but it was difficult to choose. The cakes looked ridiculous, decorated with whipped cream and glazed fruits, and like nothing Odette would ever eat. Next to the lamingtons and tarts were some chocolate biscuits, and they seemed to Benny to be the most unassuming, and therefore best, option. She and Odette could have them with cups of tea. So she bought four, and then continued on—past Curios where a closed sign hung in the window—to the Royal Tavern.

When she entered, Tom Boyd was behind the bar, bent over a notebook, writing numbers in columns.

'Good morning, Benny,' he said, looking up, and she liked the way he emphasised her name in that sentence, as if he was particularly glad to see her. And it occurred to Benny properly then just how handsome this older man was.

'Hello,' she said, and then paused slightly, unsure of how to address him.

'You can call me Tom,' said Tom, who seemed to be a man blessed with natural intuition. 'You could call me Thomas Henry Boyd, if you'd prefer, but it'd be lengthy.'

'I'm sure I'll be too busy pouring beers to use that many words,' said Benny.

Tom Boyd had a laugh at that—a laconic laugh—and Benny settled down on a stool while Tom explained to her the type of pub this was.

The Royal Tavern was a community pub. It was the communication hub of the Valley, he said, where everyone found out everything important—or mostly unimportant, as it were—that was going on in the town. The pub had a steady flow of customers. Almost all the local groups used the bistro for their monthly meetings: the fishing club, the river swimming club, the Quilting Bees, the mixed singing group, the gardening club, two book clubs and Shop Night. Lots of tourists stopped in on their way north or south, and many stayed for a meal, but it was the locals who kept the pub alive, and the regulars, rusted-on and faithful, in particular.

'So many clubs,' said Benny.

'Well there's more, actually, but the golf club meets at the golf club and the tennis club meets at the tennis club and the CWA meets at the CWA. I think the bushwalking club just has a little sit down with their thermoses midway along the trail.' Tom smiled.

Benny looked around the bar—this community pub—and noticed things she'd missed the day before. A pair of Dunlop Volleys nailed to the wall, a floral tea set, a framed photo of Jeff Fenech, an Aboriginal flag that looked hand-sewn.

'You'll want to talk to people here. Listen to people. We care for them. Right now I have Gary and Ern doing three shifts a week each and I need another for over the holidays. I haven't had a girl work at the bar before, so this is a bit of an experiment. Try to ignore Ed. But if something feels not right you tell me about it quick smart.'

Benny nodded. 'I'll make conversation, and if I'm harassed I'll express it,' she said.

'That's the spirit,' said Tom. 'You look like you can handle yourself pretty well.'

Tom was an unruffled kind of person. Benny could see that his arms were strong and that his hands were working hands: they had nicks on them like he'd been applying tools to wood. Benny thought that if some calamity were to occur—a flood, a cyclone, a bushfire—Tom Boyd would be the kind of dependable person you'd want to have around.

Tom explained the general duties Benny was to perform. Pouring beers, cleaning the ashtrays, wiping down the spirits bottles when they got sticky, cutting the lemons for the mixed drinks, refilling the fridges and topping up the snacks selection—all things Benny knew how to do well already.

'Come around,' he said, and Benny got off her stool and went behind the bar. He lifted the trapdoor to the cellar, and she followed him down the steep steps.

'Can you change a keg?' he asked. 'I can always do it if it you can't.'

'I can do it,' said Benny.

Tom nodded. 'Good,' he said. He showed her the coolroom and the area where the spent kegs went and the storeroom with extra chips and nut packets and the red wines. He handed her a string bag of lemons to take back upstairs and said, 'You got all that?'

'I got it,' said Benny, who was doing her best to commit everything he said to memory, so she would be a good worker, someone who listened and cared for her customers, someone who would remain in this man's employ.

Then Tom went back up the steep steps and Benny followed, and he climbed up on a stool to switch on the fairy lights strung along the top of the bar.

'Do I get a T-shirt?' she asked him, holding the lemons.

'Sure you do, Benny,' he said, hopping down from the stool. 'It'll swim on you, but you can have one.' And he

122

left her there to cut lemon wedges on a small plastic board while he wandered around opening the side doors and the big windows that looked out onto Valley Road.

22

Cora Franks opened the shop that morning the way she always did. She unlocked the door and wedged it open with the cast-iron dachshund she used as a doorstop. She wandered past the multitude of items that were spread in a rather unwieldy fashion throughout the deep, wide room. Leather couches, provincial chairs, vases and candlestick holders, framed botanicals. On the tables and available dresser tops there were dinner sets, ornate ashtrays and metal tool-boxes. A kangaroo skin was draped casually over a footstool, and a rusted rabbit trap hung above a chamber pot.

After checking that things were in a good position and hadn't been moved about by customers, Cora headed to her counter, which was situated on the right-hand side of the store, around about the middle. It was a long tasteful counter, half of it a glass-topped cabinet, full of brooches and jewellery and ornamental spoons, and the other half an old cedar benchtop that Cora polished regularly to make shine.

She switched on the ceiling lights, lamps, the radio and the kettle, and did a quick wipe-down of the display cabinets, tidying up various sections that needed tidying—there was always so much to do—and finally she settled behind the counter on an elegant yet lumbar-supporting stool, with a cup of tea and an arrowroot biscuit, and turned her attention to the *Gather Region Advocate*.

Today, footfalls sounded a little too soon into her morning ritual. Cora heard them and kept her eyes on the newsprint—an article about a car accident on the coast road. She stared at the photo of the poor crumpled sedan, and hoped that whoever was walking into the shop would be a stranger she wouldn't need to talk to.

What an unusual thing for Cora Franks to hope—but she was beginning to realise that, just recently, something had shifted inside her. In fact, as she sat there, it was occurring to her more strongly that, since the dead man had been found right outside that big front window, she had been overtaken by an odd feeling. It was a foreign feeling, and the feeling was this: she wanted to be alone.

Everything about this was uncommon to Cora. She had never understood why Fred spent so much time off fishing at the lake. It was a solitary drive there and then nothing but watery monotony when he arrived. 'I like to be alone with my thoughts,' he would say when she asked him, and Cora used to scoff and think, how dismal. How *boring*.

But now she didn't feel that way at all.

All of a sudden she imagined herself floating in Fred's boat on the lake. What an absurd notion! Perhaps there'd be long-legged birds there and the reflection of clouds on the water. Cora almost laughed at herself, craving a thing that was so unlike her. But she felt now this unexpected desire to stop having so many conversations that just went on and on about next to nothing all day—as entertaining as she had always found them—and to just sit quietly and truly consider her life: the contents of it, the feeling of it, and which bits of it mattered. And it wasn't only *her* life she wanted to consider. What about the life of the dead man, who she had found? A man whose existence had floated away right there on the footpath. Just as hers could at any moment, just as Fred's could, or anyone's.

But lo and behold, she looked up from the paper and there was Therese, with her stiff hair—what mysterious thing was in hairspray that it could make hair act so unlike hair?

'I asked him,' said Therese. 'You said to ask him, so I asked him.' She leaned against the polished wood with a comb in her hand.

'Why are you carrying that comb?' asked Cora.

Therese looked down at the comb as if she had never seen it before in her life.

'Oh,' she said. 'I must've forgotten to put it down.'

'Well, what did he say?' asked Cora, who now knew full well that Ed Johnson was getting his leg over Linda from the chicken factory.

'He says he's not doing anything with anyone,' said Therese coyly, as if it was just the most foolish suggestion on earth that Ed would run around on her with another woman. 'He says I need to stop worrying so much. And he's taking me to the Riverside for a steak next weekend.' Therese smiled and did a very good performance of 'silly-old-me' as she said this.

Cora took a sip of tea and felt like an awful person. And at the same time, she felt that Therese was an awful person, too. And this was to say nothing of Ed Johnson.

'Well, there you go,' said Cora with a strained smile.

'I feel embarrassed now even to have thought it. He says there's always some out-of-town woman wearing bad perfume at the bar, and I'm sure they all breathe all over him.' Therese laughed. 'And speaking of—did you know Tom has a new girl working at the bar? A young thing, apparently. I haven't seen her yet . . .' Therese trailed off. She wandered over to Cora's little tea-making area and made herself a cup of tea, and then Terri came in the front door with her leather hairdresser's belt on, silver scissor handles all in a row.

'Mary Anne's timer went off—do you want me to rinse out her colour?' asked Terri in a loud voice, hovering nervously next to a daybed near the door.

Therese rolled her eyes, just privately to Cora, and said, '*Yes*, Terri,' as if Terri was the dimmest person she'd ever encountered, and Terri flushed with humiliation and went back to the Coiffure.

'I'm sorry,' said Therese, who was never truly sorry, 'but that girl is as thick as a brick.'

She spooned three sugars into her tea and helped herself to several biscuits, and Cora stared at her for a moment, marvelling to herself at how Therese and Ed Johnson used to be the most glamorous couple in town, the top of the pile, and what a ghastly mess it had all become. Cora turned back to the newspaper and said, 'Nasty prang on the coast road,' and Therese said, 'Tourists.' And then they chatted for a while, which really meant that Therese chatted—nicely now about Ed and meanly about Terri—and then Barbie Robinson came in, and after that Lil Chapman from next door.

Cora stood behind the counter, like she always did in this scenario, which was altogether regular. This was Curios every day, with Cora hosting an ongoing merry-go-round of friends, acquaintances and customers who kept her stimulated and entertained and connected. Often someone would bring treats from the bakery. The kettle would boil again and again. Sometimes they'd all watch daytime soap operas on the small white television that Cora had behind the counter. This was the reason Cora loved her store and never wanted to close it: it was like a social club and she was president. So how strange it was now to have the pleasure of this dwindle inside her and to feel suffocated by the relentless activity.

'The policeman came around—who's the fat one? Bonnie Franklin's son?' Lil Chapman was speaking now.

'That's Gus Franklin, but I think he's just got a big bone structure,' said Mary Anne, who had arrived with a large blow wave.

Therese was standing in front of her, fussing at it with her hands. 'Bloody Terri. I'm sorry, Mary Anne, I should've come back in and done this myself.'

'I like Terri,' said Mary Anne.

Mary Anne had a tendency to be generous, which was perhaps why Therese referred to Mary Anne, behind her back, as 'a bore'.

Lil Chapman went on about how she'd suddenly remembered—'like a bolt from the blue'—the out-of-town lady who had crouched down and spoken to the man who'd died on the footpath.

Cora looked up, unsettled by this new information. 'What woman?' she said sharply, and Lil described her as best she could.

Cora's mind ticked over, recollecting the out-of-town lady who'd been interested in the watch cabinet that day the man had died. A sophisticated blonde woman, hair so perfect she looked like an advertisement for shampoo. She'd asked to see several of the watches with thin gold bands, and then

Cora was sure she had seen her in the crowd after, when the ambulance men were there and the police were asking questions. Were her hands a bit shaky when she inspected the watches? They were. Her hands shook—tremors like tiny earthquakes—and Cora remembered the surge of pity she'd felt, for such a refined woman to have the shakes like that. What an embarrassment it was when the decline was so visible. Yes, a clear picture of the woman was fixed now in Cora's mind as Lil was talking.

'I said to Bonnie Franklin's son that if I had to say, I would say she looked just like Nikki from—' and Cora Franks cut Lil off with a squeal.

'From *The Young and the Restless*!' said Cora, and she and Lil fell about laughing like a pair of schoolgirls.

Oh, yes. That was funny. Cora laughed and laughed and thought: even though Lil Chapman couldn't spell or use correct punctuation, she did have a good eye for detail—probably on account of her quilting—and even though she always stank of menthol cigarettes, she wasn't an awful person. That was a relief. Cora was so grateful for Lil Chapman in that moment. And perhaps the closer everyone got to knowing who that dead man was, and how he died, and why it had to happen right there outside the window, then perhaps Cora Franks would begin to feel like her old self again.

23

It was late in the afternoon when Constable James Hall returned from Clarke with his pie crumbs of information about the brief amount of time the unknown man had spent there between getting off a train and getting on a bus.

Simmons was in the kitchenette making a Nescafé and he stood there, solid and sweaty next to Jimmy's rangy body, while Jimmy explained himself.

Hall had met two constables from Clarke at the train station. One was outright condescending and the other was just mildly so. The two constables stayed for about three minutes before they said sarcastically, 'Best of luck, mate,' to Jimmy Hall, and left him to carry on with the investigation on his own.

'Fuckers,' said Simmons. 'It was supposed to be O'Leary meeting you. Did they pass on my message about the pie cart?'

They had, that was good, but that was about the only thing they had contributed, apart from a racial slur about the operator of the pie cart—they had called him a 'wog'.

Hall had looked at the bench the unknown man had sat on while he waited for the bus, and then he looked at the pie cart. It was such a short distance between the two, and there were not many other options if you were hungry. In that part of Clarke it was either a pie or a snack from the newsstand, and given the contents of the unknown man's stomach, Hall approached the pie cart—Mick's Famous Pies—and spoke to a cheery man called Mick.

'Are your pies really famous?' asked Hall.

'Could be,' said Mick, with a toothy grin. A gold tooth, in fact; it sat right up in front of his mouth and glinted in the sun. 'You want to try a pie and see?'

'Do you remember a man in a brown suit who may have bought a pie from you on Wednesday? It was an old-fashioned suit.'

'Oh yeah, that guy,' said Mick easily. 'Yes, yes, I remember.' And he relayed to Hall his recollections.

The man in the suit had come from the station—or that general direction—on Wednesday morning. Mick was in his cart, serving a lady who bought fifteen pasties, which turned out to be both a good and a bad thing. Good because it was always pleasing to sell so many pasties, but bad because it really upset the man in the suit that the fifteenth pasty was in fact Mick's last one.

'You never know with pasties. Some days I end up with so many pasties at the end of the day, you understand? And I don't love pasties. Or I'll say that pasties aren't my *favourite* of my products.'

The man in the suit had waited calmly as the woman made her purchases. Then, she went off with her paper bags full of pasties, and he approached the cart.

'One pasty,' he said.

But Mick had no more pasties.

So Mick explained this cheerily to the unknown man, and he put forward an alternative proposition: that perhaps the man could tolerate a pie.

'Ah,' said the man in the suit, shaking his head. He appeared distressed. 'No.' He seemed very opposed to the notion of a pie, and very concerned about the lack of pasties. He really had his heart set on a pasty. He stepped back from the cart and looked up and down the street, peering at the few other shops. Mick felt he was scanning them for potential pasties.

'That's when I go, "Mate! It's just structure. That's the only difference, my friend! *Structure!* A pasty is folded over and a pie has a lid on top. But, my friend, the middle is very often the same, you understand? What would be the matter if it folds over or if it has a lid?"'

The man in the suit had considered this deeply.

'Then he goes, "Okay." He said something like this. And I said, "Yes, mate. That is all it is—it's the structure."'

Simmons looked at Hall as he told his story, an amused expression on his face. Franklin had wandered over too; he was sitting on a stool eating a biscuit.

'So what happened?' asked Simmons, leaning forward.

'He agreed to a pie,' said Hall. 'Then he sat down at the bus stop and ate it. And that's it.'

Simmons hooted and Hall, who wasn't sure what was funny, smiled cautiously. Then Simmons sighed and soured and said, 'Seriously, though, that's everything?' and he rubbed his temples.

Unfortunately, it was.

Hall had questioned the man who ran the newsstand, who had no memory of the man in the suit. He questioned two people who worked at Clarke train station and were present on Wednesday morning, but they had no memory of the man either. Then he canvassed the rest of the area, shop to shop, but either the unknown man hadn't visited any of them or everyone just failed to recall it. Indeed, the only person in the vicinity of Clarke station who had anything to report was Mick—whose name was actually 'Danilo Batez, to be truthful', as he admitted when signing his official statement.

'Yugoslavian,' said Hall, and Simmons nodded.

They sat in silence for a few moments, thinking.

'Any accent?' asked Simmons.

'I'm guessing Yugoslavian,' said Franklin.

Simmons looked over at Franklin. 'I mean our guy, mate.' And then to Hall: 'Did you ask Mick if our guy had an accent?'

'Yeah, I asked what kind of voice he had. City accent or country accent, that kind of thing. Mick didn't reckon he said enough for him to be able to tell. He said he had a normal-sounding voice, whatever that means.'

'Hmm,' went Simmons. He was uncomfortable, it was hot. They needed a fan in the kitchenette. 'And nothing about this Mick guy felt off?'

Hall shook his head. 'No. He definitely didn't serve the guy an arsenic pie.'

'No,' said Simmons.

'I mean, boss, if I'd felt there was anything . . . but there was nothing. He's been running the pie cart for years. He obviously didn't know the guy. And I made a couple of calls—you know me. He's got a young family and no criminal history.'

Simmons put his hand up and swiped away some imaginary thing in the air. 'Yeah, yeah, good,' he said, and then he made the rhythmic sucking sound for a while—*tock tock tock*—before adding that it was something, at least. That they now had someone who had actually spoken to their guy.

Franklin finished his biscuit and adjusted himself. He held his media release in his lap. It said APPEAL FOR INFORMATION ABOUT UNKNOWN MAN along the top, and had Franklin's typed text below it.

'Someone got this poison into him somehow—or he got it into himself,' said Simmons. 'Jimmy, what do you reckon?'

Jimmy Hall sighed and shrugged his shoulders.

'I thought "wog" meant Italian or Greek,' said Franklin.

'Also Lebanese, I think,' said Hall.

'It's a bit of a catch-all,' said Simmons. 'What do you think about our fucking guy, Jimmy?'

'I think our guy really wanted a pasty,' said Jimmy Hall.

24

The afternoon was still bright as Benny drove along Valley Road on her way to Odette's house. She went through the town and soon approached the big sandstone bridge, with the river running deep and brown beneath it. Benny drove across, glancing at the sign on the wooden rail that prohibited a person from fishing from the bridge, or jumping off it, or stopping on it. She looked down quickly and saw ducks below, sitting on the rippled water.

Benny Miller found everything very beautiful along the route up the mountain—the tall gum trees with long strips of bark peeling off them, occasional banksias with their thick yellow flower heads. As the road grew steeper and the trees grew thicker, she watched the odometer to make sure she didn't miss the turn.

At the LIMES ETC sign she left the sealed road, and excitement swelled inside her at the thought of seeing Odette again.

She wondered if tonight they might speak properly of Vivian, and of Odette herself, and the vibrant ecology of her life.

Why had Odette kept a box of her mother's books in the shed? This was something Benny wanted very much to ask. Had she been holding on to them out of sentimentality, or as a favour? Had they been an unwanted gift? Yet of course Benny could not ask these questions without revealing the undignified fact that she'd been snooping, so she would certainly not ask.

She thought more about the books themselves—the novels and travel guides. Frank Miller had told her that Vivian had gone off to Europe, and Benny had found a French phrasebook and foreign language dictionaries. She had flipped through them, just quickly, and found notes inside the front covers: French or German words or phrases were written there in her mother's handwriting, alongside the English translation. *Bus stop*, *bookshop*, *hotel*, *train station*, *glass of wine*—common traveller's words. Benny thought of Vivian Moon in Europe, smoking in a Parisian cafe or reading some intellectual tome on a park bench in London, and she was filled with a puzzling kind of envy, the source of which confused her.

Coming along the dirt road, Benny slowed over the cattle grid at the start of Odette's driveway. The cows were eating from a small pile of vegetable scraps, right up next to the fence, and the white birds were standing beside them. When Benny turned the engine off and got out of the car, she was struck by the quietude. Long light stretched across the paddock and, even though the cows were several metres away, Benny could hear so loudly the sound of their big hooves squishing around in the mud and carrots.

From the bush to her right, some birds.

Below her, the crisp sound of her own boots on the tough grass as she walked towards the house.

And then, 'Hello! Welcome!' as Odette, wearing an apron, opened the front door. Bessel trotted forward. And Odette's strong, warm arms went around Benny so that Benny closed her eyes and nestled there for a brief moment, against the woman's shoulder, before Odette released her and said, 'Come in, I'm cooking,' and Bessel walked around in excited circles.

Odette's feet were bare and she wore loose pants, and swished back through the house in them to the open kitchen. Benny followed, stopping to put her bag down near a coat stand.

'Do you mind anchovies?' asked Odette.

'I like them,' said Benny, who wasn't certain that she had tried anchovies.

'Oh good, I know some people find them a challenge.' And Odette stirred some onions frying in a pan, and began to chop herbs on a wooden board.

Benny knelt down and patted Bessel, and then she stood and looked for a moment at some of the photographs that hung on the wall next to the bookshelves. Odette was chopping and chatting—telling her what they would eat—and Benny

nodded and peered at a picture of a hillside of houses in
some foreign country. Lots of white rectangular houses with
identical roofs, sloping down to a bay full of boats. .

'Would you like a glass of wine, Benny?' asked Odette,
going to the fridge.

Music was drifting from the record player—jazz music
with a clarinet—and Benny said, yes, she would like a glass
of wine. So Odette fetched two glasses and poured white
wine into them, and Benny looked at another photograph,
a black-and-white one of Odette when she was much younger,
standing with a shirtless man in a fisherman's cap. They were
both leaning up against a white wall, smiling, and Odette had
her hand up over her face to shield it from the sun.

Benny went over and sat on the stool on the other side
of the kitchen island. She set down the paper bag of biscuits,
embarrassed now by her offering, but Odette thanked her
graciously and began to speak about her day—she'd had lunch
with a friend from a nearby town—and then Benny told
Odette that she'd met Cora from next door, that Cora had
brought over food in plastic containers, and Odette laughed
at that.

'That's good of her,' said Odette. 'She likes to be part
of the action, old Cora.' And then she started talking about
Cedar Valley Curios & Old Wares, telling Benny that it was
a Cedar Valley institution. It'd been there for over twenty-
five years and showed no sign of closing. Odette was never

sure how Cora made any money, but she guessed Fred was supportive. He'd been an engineer before he retired.

'You know, if you ever need anything, you can ask Fred. He's a good man—and he's got this great head of hair, a bit like Bob Hawke's hair. Just give him a yell over the fence. He's a bit more your speed, I imagine. Not so pushy.' And she smiled knowingly at Benny.

Benny nodded and sipped her wine and wondered for a moment if Odette Fisher was so perceptive that she could read Benny's mind. From the first moment they met, the way Odette had gazed at her, Benny had felt transparent. It was as if this strong and graceful woman could look right inside her and see her—she could see the very truth of her—without any effort at all.

The two of them talked more as Odette prepared their dinner—easy conversation about everyday things, like the best spots for swimming at the river, and how it was a bother not to have a proper agricultural supply store in Cedar Valley, because Odette needed some supplies. They made a plan to go to Clarke together in the next few days—Benny wanted to see it. And Odette was so pleased to hear that Benny had been in to the Royal already and Tom Boyd had given her a trial.

'I guess Tom looks like an old man to you but *God*, be still my beating heart! I think he's terribly handsome. Annie Boyd is a lucky woman—and don't think I haven't told her that.' Odette laughed as she poured some olive oil into a jar.

'Yes, he's very nice,' said Benny, feeling herself blush, and she told Odette about her day at the pub, how she had got to know the workings of the place pretty well and had poured lots of beers for the locals. Everyone had asked her who she was and where she was from, and she had been quite conversational, speaking at length with an elderly gentleman about the Cedar Valley cattle market and the difference between steer weaners, heifer weaners, yearling weaners and plain old cows. Benny had learned a lot and she liked the people she'd met; she liked talking with them, and they had been welcoming and kind. In fact, the only person she didn't warm to was the man called Ed who ran the kitchen.

'Ed Johnson's got tickets on himself,' said Odette. 'He's probably got eyes for you, you know. I don't think he's noticed that he's not twenty-one anymore. Apparently some women find him charming but I really don't see it.'

Benny told Odette how she'd been allowed a free lunch from the bistro and had ordered hot chips and a side salad and eaten it happily at the end of the bar. Tom had given her a Royal Tavern T-shirt at the end of her shift and she was going to wear it there on Sunday. He'd been friendly, if a little reserved, and what Benny didn't tell Odette was that while he surely did look like an old man, Benny found herself drawn to the cropped thickness of his grey hair and the rough shape of his skull, and she'd spent a portion of the afternoon thinking about Jules Cowrie, and how—even though he was twenty-one, the same age as she was—he seemed to her, now, just a boy.

Odette went to the oven, pulled out a tray of blackened capsicums and set them on the bench to cool, then she whizzed something in a food processer that came out like a thick green paste and smelled of garlic.

'It used to belong to a real shit, the Royal,' said Odette. 'This old racist called Tick Finch, he'd refuse to serve Koori men from the mines back in the day, even if they had one of those ridiculous certificates. Then Tick died, and his son Finchy—I don't even know what his actual name was—took it over. He was slightly better, even though he still wanted women to only drink in the parlour. That was when your mum was here, and we'd go in and rattle the chains and sit in the main bar. Finchy had no idea how to handle a woman like Vivian.'

And just like that Vivian Moon came alive in the room, and it was like someone opening a door in winter: a cold prickling on Benny's skin.

'What do you mean?' she asked.

'Well, Vivian was so defiant,' said Odette. 'And very spirited about it. She just thought a lot of those cultural norms were so backwards, and of course they were.'

'No,' said Benny. 'I mean about her being here?'

Odette wiped her hands on her apron and looked at Benny in a quizzical way.

'Oh, Benny, we really need to sit down and compare notes,' she said. 'I keep assuming you know things about Vivian that maybe you don't know. Your mother lived here, honey. In Cedar Valley. She lived with me at the cottage. She had that same bedroom you're sleeping in now.'

25

'How's she coping?' asked Lil Chapman, once Therese had gone back to the Old Paris Coiffure.

'Oh, she's okay,' said Cora, sitting on her stool behind the counter. 'She asked Ed about it directly and he denied it. So what can she do?'

Lil gave a withering look. 'For God's sake, of course he's going to deny it!' she said.

And Cora said, 'Yes, well,' and ordinarily Cora would have found some terrible delight in telling Lil Chapman about Ed Johnson having it off with Chicken Linda—under the pretence of 'feeling bad for Therese', but really just enjoying the scandalous thrill of it—but on that day Cora made the very uncharacteristic, and some may say wise, decision to keep all that to herself.

'That woman—the blonde woman who you saw talking to the dead man—she was in here for quite a while, you know,' said Cora. 'She had shaky hands, I think. Now I wish

I'd talked to her more. It was just a quick hello and I showed her the watches. Therese had already left. But you remember her, don't you, Mary Anne?'

Mary Anne had pulled up a stool on the other side of the counter and was wearing the expression so common to her: a kind of flinch, like someone was about to hit her in the face.

'Well, yes, I *think* so,' she said. 'But you know what I'm like with my memory.'

'Oh, I'm the same,' said Lil. 'I just sat up in bed the other night—bolt upright—and I thought, bloody hell! That woman talked to him! I don't know why I didn't remember it earlier, when the police were asking us.'

Lil had one hand pressed up against her cheek, which gave her a worried look, and her face was grey and lined from many years of smoking, except for her nose, which was red from many years of drinking.

Then she smiled and took her hand down and a glimmer came across her milky eyes.

'I know it sounds silly, but I said to Barry last night in bed, I said, "What if she killed him!" And Barry just laughed at me.' Lil laughed at herself now, too. 'But then he got out his KGB books. You know Barry loves his spy stories. And they're always poisoning each other with nerve agents and whatnot else—like in that James Bond movie where a lady has the poison in her shoe. Barry was telling me about this case in London, a real-life one, where a KGB man poked a Bulgarian spy with a poisoned umbrella. He died, Cora! From an umbrella!'

Lil started to laugh huskily, and Cora hooted and said, 'Lillian Chapman! Our man was not murdered by the KGB!'

'A silent assassin,' said Lil, grinning. 'Barry also suggested something else: a cyanide pill—like the Nazis. But I think that's for when you commit suicide.' Lil giggled again and it turned into a small coughing fit. Then when she was done, she wiped a tear away and helped herself to a biscuit.

'Maybe she was just asking him if he was okay?' said Mary Anne sensibly, not laughing. 'I mean, it's terrible that he sat there all day and no one asked him, don't you think?'

The mood lowered at that, and Cora leaned back against her lumber support and frowned, wondering if Mary Anne was accusing her, or Lil, or even Therese, of neglecting a stranger in need.

'But I walked straight past him myself,' said Mary Anne sadly. 'I just thought, I wonder what that man's doing? But I didn't think to ask. And you couldn't have seen him very well from here, Cora—not with that couch in the way.'

'No,' said Cora. 'Well, I saw him sit down, but, you know, there was Therese and then you and I were talking, Mary Anne. And then I was up the back for a lot of the afternoon. I couldn't have seen him from up the back.'

Feeling vindicated, she mentally replayed her resuscitation fantasy to make herself feel better still, while Lil and Mary

Anne chatted away about memory and how strange it was, and how poor old Elsie Simmons was really losing it. At such a young age! She was only seventy-six. But the last few times at book club she just hadn't been on the ball—she kept getting confused about *The Bridges of Madison County*—and she was going downhill fast in terms of her short-term recollections.

'She told me Barbie Robinson had been over on Sunday afternoon,' said Mary Anne. 'But Barbie and I went to the pictures on Sunday afternoon. So I said, "Elsie, are you sure it was Sunday?" And she just didn't seem to know.'

'Golly,' said Lil Chapman. 'Poor Els.'

'It seems so unfair, don't you think?' said Mary Anne. 'She's always prided herself on her memory. Never forgets a face and all that. Plus, she loves to read, and now her eyes are packing it in so she can't read. I just hope she doesn't get wandery. That's what happened to Nevin Oates—he got wandery, remember? They found him on the golf course and he had no idea how he got there. He was *so* sunburnt.'

Cora sat on her stool, remembering the movie *From Russia with Love*. She had the book version on the shelf in the back of the shop. Fred loved James Bond films and she'd watched that one, with that manly-looking woman who had poison in the tip of her shoe.

Lil and Mary Anne chatted away for a while longer, and then Mary Anne left and three women came in—tourists—and one of them bought a tartan scarf and an oil painting.

Lil went back next door to the Quilting Bee and Cora was alone for two minutes before Fran—who Cora liked very much—popped in and the two of them spoke about what dates they'd close this year, for Christmas and New Year, and how they needed to come to some kind of consensus at the next Shop Night. Cora sensed, though, that the real reason for Fran's visit was the dead man. Fran had been held up in the traffic jam on the way back from Clarke that afternoon and had missed the whole episode. She asked Cora several questions about it and seemed genuinely moved. ('Such an unceremonious end to a life, isn't it? Just on some footpath where no one knows you.') Then Fran handed Cora a brown paper bag with a spinach and cheese pasty in it, knowing how much Cora loved those pasties, and Cora smiled and said, 'Oh Fran, you spoil me,'

'Therese okay?' Fran asked as she was leaving.

'Therese?' said Cora, a little surprised. 'Yes, I think so.'

'Oh good. Just wondering,' said Fran, and Cora watched as Fran left though the front door and walked off across the road—she really was so fond of her.

Cora went to the back of the shop and flipped through *From Russia with Love*—perhaps she should read it, for fun—and she laughed a little to herself about Lil Chapman, even though Cora herself had wondered if someone had murdered the man in the brown suit and left him to die on the footpath.

But, no. That was ridiculous.

As Tony Simmons had said: it wasn't a crime scene, it was just a scene.

Cora put the book back on the shelf and went along to the counter. She thought of Elsie Simmons and it pained her. It was ever so difficult, watching a friend decline. Cora took the pasty out of its paper bag and set it on a porcelain side plate with roses on it and she took a few neat bites.

Cora Franks savoured the pasty—it was absolutely delicious—and she resolved to visit her friend Elsie Simmons in the morning to see how she was faring.

26

Benny got home from dinner at Odette's house with her mind full of thoughts. She pulled her car into the bricked driveway and sat for a moment, overwhelmed. Light was spilling out the windows next door—from Cora and Fred's house—and Benny saw their door was open. She could hear the faint sound of a television and some kitchen noises; someone was washing up. Benny felt glad they were there, Cora and Fred. Though she didn't care much for Cora Franks, she was comforted nonetheless by her proximity.

Benny got out of the car and went inside the green cottage, switching the lamps on in the living room and the kitchen. The house was still, and she turned on the radio and changed into her bed shirt, half listening to R.E.M. Then she lay on the couch, where her quilt and pillow were from the night before, and she thought long, confused thoughts about all the things Odette had told her over dinner, and what it meant about her mother, Vivian Moon.

Her mother had lived here—in Cedar Valley.

Here in this house.

And Benny didn't know why this was so surprising to her, but it was, it had blown her right over.

Odette had said, 'Look, Benny, why don't we sit down and eat, and just start from the beginning.'

So they had sat down at the table to eat, and Odette explained how she had come to be friends with Vivian Moon, and Benny listened with every inch of herself, while acting in a way she thought was very casual, trying to hide the intensity of her interest.

Odette Fisher had met Vivian Moon not in Sydney, as Benny had always assumed, but in Greece, in 1965.

Odette had a thirst for travel back then, and she had been abroad for seven months by the time she arrived in Athens. Indonesia, India, London, the major cities of Europe—Odette was enamoured with exoticism and newness. She just wanted to see everything she could see.

From Athens she took a ferry to Hydra with her boyfriend at the time, a young man who fancied himself a philosopher. They arrived at a wharf in a horseshoe bay and Odette fell in love with the houses that went up the slope of the hill. There was clear blue water in the bay and the village was home to several western artists. It was meant to be a weekend visit, but Odette stayed for two years.

'And then, one day, there was your mother,' she said to Benny. 'I'd been living there maybe six months. And Vivian arrived with a man. We met them at a restaurant one night and Vivian and I got talking—I was so glad to meet another Australian. I guess we just didn't stop talking.'

Odette looked at Benny with such composure then, like she always did, but Benny thought she could sense something like sadness underneath.

Vivian and Odette became instant friends. They would walk up the steep hill to Odette's white house with a bag of fresh sardines. They would cook and drink and swim in the bay.

'She was exquisite,' said Odette. 'Charming, smart, intense. I just loved her right away. And at that stage, I was a bit lonely, I suppose. I was very fond of the island, but I was beginning to tire of the philosopher. That's him in the picture over there on the wall. Vivian took that picture.'

Odette pointed, and Benny looked up at the picture she had seen earlier. Young Odette and a shirtless man, leaning up against a white wall. He was a good-looking man, in a cap and wooden beads. It was only then that Benny noticed the shadow that slanted out across the bottom of the image: the shadow of the photographer, her mother.

Vivian was younger than Odette, but that never mattered. It was almost as if it were the other way around, because Odette looked up to her so, and marvelled at her intellect. Vivian would recommend books and Odette would read them.

They would talk about their families, their boyfriends, their aspirations and ideas. Vivian's boyfriend at the time was a Jewish poet who Odette found deliberately obtuse, but she liked him all the same. They would all hang around together, often, and had lively dinners that went long into the night.

Odette was so saddened when Vivian left a few months later to follow the poet back to London, but she'd said she'd stay in touch, and Odette was so pleased when she did. Her letters arrived frequently from all over Europe. And when Odette returned to Australia, and then moved to Cedar Valley, the letters continued on.

The women would enter into long discussions over several missives, often philosophical in nature, and always stimulating. Vivian Moon had such a rousing, restless nature. She loved to be perplexed. She loved to have some conundrum in need of solving.

'What happened to the poet?' asked Benny.

'Vivian's poet? Oh, who knows. I can't even remember his name. But she never had any trouble finding men to fall in love with her . . .'

Perhaps it was the slight crease of surprise on Benny's face that made Odette stop speaking then and become suddenly reticent. She rubbed at the back of her neck as if there was an ache there, and she looked across at Benny thoughtfully.

'I don't know, Benny. This is difficult because I don't know how much I should tell you about her. I lay awake last night wondering which bits to leave out! You see—I'm just not sure what she would want you to know.'

Odette picked up her water glass and took a sip. They were sitting opposite each other—plates in front of them, a delicious meal—and yet Benny had hardly eaten, such was her concentration on Odette's recollections of Vivian Moon.

'I guess I feel torn,' said Odette. 'Because here you are— you're an adult and you're asking. Benny, I can see how much you want to know about her. And you have every right to know. But she was my dearest friend. I mean, for a long time I considered her my dearest friend. And now, I don't know. I don't know if "dearest" is the right word. It's probably more accurate to say that my friendship with Vivian was the most *intense* friendship I've ever had. Although sometimes, I'm not quite sure what to think about a lot of it.'

Benny didn't know what to say, so she said nothing. She took a bite of bread and chewed slowly. 'You don't want to betray your friendship,' she said finally.

'No, I don't,' said Odette, leaning back in her chair. 'But it's more than that. It's that, if she were alive, and you came here asking about her past . . . Well, I don't think I'd tell you. I'd say it wasn't my business to say. You know? So I lie awake and wonder: why does that change just because she's died? I don't know—does it change?'

Odette sighed and took a sip of her wine, and Benny said that, of course, she understood. Nothing needed to change, and Odette needn't continue if she didn't feel comfortable about it. And, inwardly, she felt the gorgeous flash of Vivian—just a shadow in an old photograph—and she was enveloped in her own desperation for her. For her mother. How tactile it was, the way Benny longed to be near her; just to be present while Vivian went about her daily activities. Benny would have given anything for something so simple: to have sat on a bed and watched her mother getting ready for the day.

But this rush of longing didn't last and, in an instant, Benny felt something else sharply. Perhaps it was anger—or shame—and Benny felt it bitterly, towards herself. Her eyes went to the table then, thinking of how she was acting, so prying and undignified, rifling through boxes for any little scrap of Vivian and putting Odette in such an awkward position. Why couldn't she erect a boundary around Vivian Moon, a stony wall, and just go on with her life?

The record had stopped and Odette rose from her chair quite abruptly, and Bessel followed her over to the record player. Soon some piano music sounded, and Odette went to a side table, took something from one of the two large drawers, and came back to the table.

'Here,' she said, and she handed Benny a small wad of photographs with a little nod.

Benny was not expecting that.

She took them and held them in her hand, and for a moment she couldn't bring herself to look at them.

Benny owned several photos of Vivian, she'd had them for years, and she could look at them with a necessary kind of detachment. Photos of Vivian with Odette; an image of her at the foot of a bush trail; Vivian standing by a counter in a shop; and the one in the silver frame that Benny kept on her bedside table. But photos Benny hadn't seen before? Well, she had no idea what Vivian would look like in them. What would she be wearing? What would be the content of her expression? How much would the pictures disturb her?

So Benny held the photographs for a few moments, and then she looked—of course she looked—and with a mix of relief and disappointment, she saw that the photo on the top of the pile was not of Vivian at all.

It was of Benny.

She flipped through the pictures. There must have been ten or fifteen of them, and they were all of Benny. Benny as a newborn. Benny sitting up, in a singlet and a nappy. And they went on from there chronologically. Benny's kindergarten picture; one of her painting in the garden at Rozelle; Benny in a tent that Frank had put up in her bedroom; Benny in her high school uniform.

Odette was watching her from the other side of the table, her expression was something Benny had not seen before. It was distress.

'She sent me those,' said Odette. 'Vivian left Cedar Valley to go back to Frank, and then she fell pregnant with you. She would send me pictures as you grew, with letters that got shorter and shorter. I'd write back, of course. Her return address was always a post office box in Sydney. I tried to arrange a visit—to see Vivian and to meet you—but, I don't know, there was always some excuse. And eventually the letters stopped. The last one I got was eight years ago. I never quite understood it. I guess I always wondered if I'd done something to upset her, but in the end I decided that life just goes on, you know. I thought she was probably too busy being a mother.'

Benny sat, gripping the photos in her hand. They were all familiar to her. Frank Miller had taken most of them. Her grandmother, Irene, had taken a few. All of them—or copies of them—were in albums or drawers at Frank's house in Rozelle. He had the kindergarten one in a frame in the living room.

•

Later, lying on the couch in the cottage, Benny turned the evening over in her mind, and she didn't know what to make of any of it.

Long after dark she got up, switched off the kitchen radio, dragged the quilt and pillow back to the bedroom, and lay on what she now knew to be Vivian Moon's old bed.

She looked over, just quickly, at Vivian—at her mother—smiling in the photo on the bedside table. Then she picked up the frame and turned it face down, and it made a sharp sound against the wood.

It took Benny a long while to fall sleep.

She stared at the ceiling, but there was no noise from the python, and so she listened to Odette's voice in her head instead. She replayed in her mind what Odette had said to her while Benny was sitting, aghast, holding the photographs.

'Benny, I can see how much you need to understand it all.'

Did Odette say this with pity? She had looked at Odette across the table, searching the woman's face for any indication, but she couldn't tell. Then she had looked down at a photo of herself as a child: such a leavable child.

Benny Miller did not want pity. She did not want to be any kind of imposition. She just wanted to recall exactly what Odette Fisher had said at the dinner table, while Benny sat straight in her chair, absorbing the words like sun into her skin.

'I don't blame you, Benny. If I were you, I'd be doing exactly the same thing. I'd be driving off to look for someone who knew everything I needed to know. I'd be asking every question I could think of. Don't go thinking it's wrong to have those feelings. It's so natural, Benny. Do you understand? *You're* so natural.'

27

With a nod of approval from Detective Sergeant Anthony Simmons, a detailed description of the unknown man in the brown suit was sent to all local media in the Gather Region, for immediate release, late on Friday afternoon.

APPEAL FOR INFORMATION, it said, describing the gentleman as being Caucasian, approximately fifty-five years of age, one hundred and eighty centimetres tall, with brown hair and blue eyes. The man had no distinguishing marks—no scars, birthmarks or tattoos. He had arrived at Clarke station on the Sydney train, and travelled by bus to Cedar Valley on the morning of Wednesday, December 1st 1993. In lieu of a sketch, this was as thorough a representation as the police could manage.

'If any member of the public has information concerning the identity or movements of this man,' said the man on ABC local radio, 'please contact local police.'

Tony Simmons had the radio on in the kitchen on Saturday morning, and he read the article in the paper while sitting at the table with his instant coffee. Jenny Simmons brushed their youngest daughter's hair in front of the television, and their older daughter sat nearby and watched the cartoons. Then Jenny went to put the washing on and the girls fought over the hairbrush, the two of them pulling it back and forth and then Hayley, the oldest, ran off with it down the hall, leaving little Dawn to whimper on the living room carpet.

Simmons hated it when the girls fought. He did not like the sound of cartoons. And Jenny Simmons seemed to have the shits with him lately too, and Tony didn't know how to remedy that. He had snuggled up to her in bed that morning, into her back, and put his hand under her nightie in a way that announced his arousal. Then he pushed himself, hard, against her very lower back and breathed heavily, moving his hand down, but Jenny Simmons had sat up and sighed loudly.

'Tony,' she said, facing the wall, 'are you serious?'

She had walked into the ensuite and shut the door loudly and he'd heard the shower run, and maybe he heard her crying in there, he wasn't sure. Or he was sure, but he didn't like the idea of it, so he decided he wasn't sure. And he wasn't sure why she had rejected him like that, the same as last time, but Tony Simmons didn't want to know the reason for that either, and he certainly didn't want to ask.

The whole thing made him angry and uncomfortable and he rolled over in bed, considered relieving himself with his right hand, but even the thought of doing that always made him so full of hot shame. Instead he closed his eyes and made a low grumbling sound like distant thunder until the rage and discomfort slowly passed.

An hour later, sitting at the kitchen table, he stared at the newspaper article and was satisfied with the description Gussy had written.

Dawn said, 'Dad, Dad, Dad,' from the living room, the sound of her voice below the radio, and Tony wondered if anyone would come forward with information. Why wasn't anyone missing a man in a vintage suit? Had he no family? No loved ones? Perhaps he didn't. There was certainly something about him that seemed itinerant, but maybe it was just his lack of belongings.

And something that kept returning to Tony's mind was the man's shoes. They were so newly polished. He couldn't have walked a kilometre in them—the soles were near immaculate.

Tony needed to start piecing all of this together in some logical fashion. He needed to speak to Ping Williams first thing on Monday and discuss the further analysis of the organs. The stomach, liver, kidneys; the blood and the urine samples. The more he thought about it, the more he knew Gussy was right: the man didn't want anyone to know who he was—but why would that be?

Dawn went, 'Dad . . . Daaaaaad,' somewhere in the outer edge of his consciousness.

They would all go to see his mother in a few hours, the whole family. He was so worried about his mother, Elsie Simmons. She was beginning to forget things that had happened just a day earlier, or she'd tell him the same story two or three times. The week before, he'd been helping her change the batteries in her radio, Elsie sitting there in her armchair holding two spent AAs while Tony fixed the new ones in the plastic slots, and, mid-conversation, she'd looked down at her hand and said, 'What are these for?' Tony had never seen anything like it. Wily old Elsie, so confused.

'Tony!' said Jenny's voice now, with anger in it.

He wheeled around and saw little Dawn on the floor of the living room, trapped under an armchair. She'd managed to tip it somehow and got herself wedged there and was crying.

'Daaaddy,' she wailed, big tears rolling down her cheeks.

'For God's sake, Tony, she was calling for you,' said Jenny. She lifted the armchair off Dawn and wrapped her arms around the girl, and Dawn cried, 'Daad . . . Daaad.'

Tony Simmons said, 'You're okay,' to Dawn. And then to Jenny, more coldly, 'She's fine,' and he got up and tripped on the cat dish as he went to put his coffee cup in the sink.

28

Even though it was only a short distance by foot, Cora Franks drove her car out of her garage, up to Valley Road, along past the park, and turned right at Bell Street, where Elsie Simmons lived in a yellow weatherboard house with a frangipani tree out the front and a plastic Christmas wreath hanging on the screen door.

Cora was tired. As of this morning, she had an ache in her right hip. And it was peculiar that such minor complaints, which previously she would have brushed off with an aspirin and a lie-down, had taken on a heavy kind of significance since the unknown man had died against her window. She drove to Elsie's, because the thought of walking in the December sun, even with her parasol, was beyond her, and her weariness and pain weighed on her as potent symbols of her own mortality.

'Els, it's Cora,' she said loudly, a brown bag of banana bread in her hand.

Stooped Elsie came along the dim hall in her housedress and slippers.

'Oh, love,' she said. 'Good.' And she opened the door so the two women could embrace there on the landing.

'Good,' said Elsie again. 'Come in, Cor.'

The hallway of Elsie's house was narrow and carpeted, and framed photos of a young Tony—a twiggy kid—hung along the wall, as well as a set of flying porcelain ducks and some of Elsie's needlework. Cora followed Elsie down the hall and Elsie popped the kettle on, and Cora set the banana bread on a board so she could cut off two thick slices for them to eat.

Soon enough, the two women were sitting in the living room, where Elsie had a small fan.

'It's a bit dark in here, Els. You want me to open a curtain?'

'Oh no, Cor, don't,' said Elsie. 'My eyes have gone off. I like it better like this. When did I see you last? I remember seeing you, but I don't remember when it was.'

Cora forced out a smile. 'I'm afraid to say it was last week. Or was it the week before? Oh, bugger, what if my mind's going too?'

Then the two women laughed and sipped their tea and were happy that it didn't matter when Cora was last there, for she was there now and they were so fond of each other.

'I could tell you every detail of the day Tony was born. All of his school years. A book I read ten years ago. A book I read *one* year ago. All of it! But all of a sudden it's the day-to-day stuff that just disappears. You know how I never forget a face? I've always said that, Cor, because it's true. Now I'm worried I'll start to forget faces.'

'Oh, Els, I know. But I bet you'll remember my face,' said Cora, and she put her cup down and gave a big theatrical grin, her hands on either side of her cheeks.

Elsie laughed loudly. 'Cora!' she said.

Big Tony Simmons, in his police uniform, stared out proudly from a framed photo on the side table. There was a doily under the frame and a lamp next to it with a frilled shade. Another photo showed Tony with Jenny and their two daughters, and there was one of Elsie with the girls when Dawn was just a baby. But there was not a photo on display, anywhere in the house, of Elsie's husband, the late Neville Simmons.

'He's been very good, Tony has,' said Elsie. 'I do worry about him moving here because of me; he did love living in Clarke. But he's been very good. He brings me dinners.'

Cora said, 'Well, he's not just here for you. Jenny loves it here; she tells me so when she comes in, and that's quite often. She bought some big terracotta pots last week. Lovely woman. I like her.'

'So do I,' said Elsie. 'I just hope Tony doesn't bugger it up.' And she shrugged and laughed faintly, which was a thing Elsie did when she felt bad about something.

Cora knew what Elsie meant, since they'd discussed all that before. All that and much more, over the many years they had known each other. In fact, being there in the sitting room with Elsie was the calmest Cora had felt since all the kerfuffle with the man dying on the footpath. All those feelings of wanting to be alone had grated on her, and had made her not want to come and sit with Elsie. But now that she was here, it reinforced for Cora what an altogether decent person Elsie Simmons was, especially given the things she had endured.

'I have a new neighbour,' said Cora.

'Who's that?'

'Remember Vivian Moon?' said Cora, raising her eyebrows.

'Oh, of course I do. I haven't heard that name in a long time,' said Elsie Simmons.

'Neither had I,' said Cora, and she paused. 'She died, Els.'

'*No*,' said Elsie. 'How? She would've been young.'

'I don't know how,' said Cora. 'Can you believe I didn't ask?'

Elsie Simmons chuckled so that tea almost spilled out her cup. 'I do find that hard to believe,' she said.

'I'm trying to be more sensitive,' said Cora, grinning, and then she set her teacup down and picked up a plate with banana bread on it. 'Well, Viv had a daughter. Her name's Benny. Odette has her staying at the cottage. You should see how much she looks like her mother!'

'She had a child?' said Elsie. 'Gosh. I can't picture Viv nursing a baby. Benny—what's that short for?'

'I didn't ask that either,' said Cora, and Elsie laughed again.

Then they discussed Benny Moon—or whatever her last name was—and how thin and shy and young she was, and how pleased she'd been when Cora brought her some home-cooked food. Imagine her on her own like that in the cottage? Cora would make her something else, too. The girl had to eat. And you really couldn't hold someone's mother against them, especially when that mother had died.

Elsie thought that was very good of Cora, given the circumstances, and the right thing to do. And besides, as Cora said, what a time for her to arrive! She no sooner sets foot in Cedar Valley than a man drops dead on Valley Road.

'Oh, yes,' said Elsie. 'What's that all about? I heard it on the radio, I think. Or maybe Tony mentioned it the other day. He just keeled over, did he?'

'No, he sat,' said Cora. 'Right outside Curios. I was inside with Therese and—oh, you've missed a bit of book club drama—but Therese was there and Mary Anne. I saw this man sit down against the front window, and I thought, what's he doing? But then I was serving and talking, you know, and the next thing I know I went to close and he's still sitting there. And he's stone dead!'

'Oh, for heaven's sake,' said Elsie. 'What did you do?'

'Well, Lil and I called triple-o. And then everyone came over to have a look, as you can imagine. It was quite dramatic.'

'Goodness me,' said Elise, quite entertained. Then: 'Oh, this is delicious, Cor,' as she had a bit of banana bread, spread thick with butter.

'It did look odd,' said Cora. 'He was in this lovely vintage suit. A proper wartime suit. With a jumper, too—in December. I don't know what that was about. And he was just slumped there, quite a good-looking man. He looked a bit like an old movie star. And now they still don't know who he is, or what killed him. Can you believe that? It's our own little valley mystery.' Cora was enjoying being able to relay the whole saga to an interested audience.

Elsie was gazing at her, rapt, and then her eyes moved to the fan. She stared at it, her mind off someplace else all of a sudden.

Cora looked at her friend and thought: Oh God, here she goes. Poor old Elsie is losing her mind, and this is what it looks like. Look at her, staring at the fan; she's entered a fugue state, right here in the living room.

But Elsie hadn't lost her mind at all.

'This is very familiar,' said Elsie, looking back now at Cora Franks. A little crumb sat at the side of Elsie's mouth in the way that crumbs tend to stick to older people.

'What is?' Cora asked. 'The banana bread?'

'No, Cor, not the banana bread,' said Elsie. 'I'm from Adelaide—I grew up in Glenelg. You know that.'

'I do.'

'Well, something just like this happened, not long after the war. We talked about it forever! A man in a brown suit was found dead on the beach at Somerton. He was a normal-looking man—not unhealthy. He sat down and people walked past him, not sure what he was up to. And then he just died. And to this day—*to this day*—as true as I'm sitting here, Cor, they don't know who he was, or what killed him.'

Cora Franks stared at Elsie, wondering if this was all a strange figment, some symptom of her deterioration, but Elsie went on.

'The Somerton Man,' said Elsie. 'That's what they called him. It's famous in Adelaide. And you know there's a lot of darkness in Adelaide, a lot of mystery. Somerton Beach is the next one along from Glenelg, which of course was where the Beaumont children went missing. That was in the sixties, after I'd left.'

'Oh God, I remember the Beaumont children,' said Cora. 'Were there three of them?'

'That's right,' said Elsie. 'Three siblings, and they never found them. Never found out what happened. Oh, it was awful. Just awful. But the Somerton Man . . . I mean, I know the poor man died, but it was almost a bit *fun*, as far as mysteries go. Is that a terrible thing to say? It's just that you wouldn't believe the strange clues and things they found, trying to work out who he was. Codes and hidden messages, stuff like that. Some people think he was a spy. That's what I think. It was just at the start of the Cold War. Apparently, there were Russian spies everywhere, with communism and everything. Remember all that, Cor? Remember communism?'

Well, that last bit had Cora on the edge of her armchair. To think that Lil Chapman had just been making jokes about the KGB! All of it sounded like utter madness, yet she could see that Elsie Simmons had her wits about her.

'The Somerton Man,' said Cora. 'I've never heard of him.'

'Well, now you have,' said Elsie Simmons matter-of-factly. 'You telling me about this fellow on Valley Road brought it all back. I haven't thought about the Somerton Man since Mum was alive. Isn't it funny that this man outside Curios sounds so similar?'

29

Benny Miller considered walking the distance to the river, but the sun was hot and the air was clammy, so she decided to drive instead. She put her swimmers on and a dress over them, and took a bath towel from the linen cupboard. Then, with the map Odette had given her, she set off with the windows rolled down, turning left before the big sandstone bridge, and driving to the swimming spot that Odette had marked with an X.

Benny parked her car where the narrow dirt road ended. It was a picnic area with a few tables under a grove of trees. Another car was parked there and Benny could see two men upstream fishing. She went the other way, to where the water was deep, and she lay the bath towel on the thin sandy grass near the edge.

At this spot the river was a wide, slow-moving thing. From the bridge it had looked brown, but up close it was clear, with smooth flat rocks along the bottom. Benny pulled off her sandshoes and stepped in so the water covered her feet. She bent down to pick up a particularly nice stone—oval, with some rough indents in the edges—and cupped it firmly in her hand.

Then she stepped out again, her feet dripping, and rested the stone on her towel—it would go in her collection—and she sat down and lay back on her elbows, watching the river, wondering if Vivian Moon had ever swum at this exact spot. And then her mind went to another river that was apparently good to swim in: the Murrumbidgee. Odette had spoken about it the night before, and how it provided a beautiful swimming hole for the people of Hay, New South Wales. That, Benny had learned, was where Odette Fisher was originally from.

'Where's Hay?' Benny had asked.

'Exactly,' said Odette. 'My brother sent me a bumper sticker for my birthday that says, *Where the hell is Hay?*'

So Odette had explained to Benny a little about Hay: where it was; its general character. Hay was in the Riverina, halfway between Sydney and Adelaide, an agricultural town on the alluvial Hay Plains, which were mostly treeless and extremely flat. 'The second flattest place on earth,' Odette had said.

'What's the flattest?' asked Benny.

'Oh, I don't know. The Sahara? The salt flats of Bolivia? I think it's just something people from Hay say.'

Odette took a bite from one of the chocolate biscuits Benny had bought from the bakery. After she had chewed and swallowed, she said, 'I was happy to go to boarding school. Can you imagine that? I was desperate to go! And I took my elocution lessons at Ascham *very* seriously. I thought I was so posh.' Odette laughed and shook her head.

After boarding school, and university, and her travels, Odette had bought the green cottage in Cedar Valley in 1967. Houses were cheap then, and she had a little money from her parents. She had spent school holidays in the area; she loved it. The mountain was so dramatic and the coast was so close. She had an old friend who lived nearby, in a small town to the north, and this friend introduced Odette to the man who would eventually become her husband.

Lloyd.

'What happened to Lloyd?' Benny had asked.

'*I* happened to Lloyd. But we'll get to Lloyd some other time,' said Odette, and Benny could not tell what kind of emotion went with that statement, or if there was any emotion at all.

Vivian Moon had come here to Cedar Valley to visit as soon as she returned from Europe—while Odette and Lloyd were romancing. She came back again and helped Odette repaint the inside of the cottage, the two of them dressed in men's shirts and headscarves, listening to Jacques Brel. Odette had had a job in town at Hargraves Books.

'I loved working there, and that's what got me into editing. One of our customers, Arden Cleary, was a writer. I was an early reader for him, and then I became his editor. I've done eight books with him now, and I somehow managed to pick up more work as I went along.' Odette ran a hand along her thick braid, the colour of a storm.

Vivian was drawn to Cedar Valley, just as Odette had been. When Odette and Lloyd decided to buy the land on the mountain, Vivian decided to set herself up in the cottage in town.

'That was 1971, and I was pregnant.' Odette's smile went away. 'But that didn't work out. And I will always be indebted to your mother—she was so supportive. She let me cry on her shoulder. I think I cried for months.'

Vivian stayed in the green house for over a year, with Odette and Lloyd mostly, although they spent more and more time up at the bush house, sleeping in a makeshift shed while Lloyd laid the slab, and built the frame, and wandered around collecting firewood in his striped pyjamas.

Vivian had met Frank already by this stage, but Odette wouldn't speak much about that. Frank was up in Sydney, chewing his fingernails and restoring his furniture, and Vivian found a job in Cedar Valley, and she lived in the green cottage and walked and read books.

'My dad always said she was in Europe then,' said Benny.

'Oh, did he? Well, no. And now I've gone and landed him in it, haven't I? This was the kind of thing I was afraid of, Benny—saying the wrong thing and confusing matters. But that is how it was. She'd been in Europe a long time, but after that she was here in Cedar Valley, until she went back to Frank. And the next thing I heard, she was pregnant with you.'

Benny lay on the towel on the thin grass now, thinking it all over. Maybe her dad just hadn't known where Vivian was and thought Europe was likely. Or maybe he had lied. If he had lied, why he would do that? She stared at the branches and listened to the sound of the river, which was a constant watery sound, and she felt troubled by all of it. If Frank Miller had lied about Europe, then what else had he lied about when it came to Vivian?

'Where did she work while she was here?' Benny had asked Odette, who by that stage was lying on her back on one of her long couches with Bessel in a ball at her feet.

'Vivian? Oh, she worked at the pharmacy. The one in town. My friend Maureen works there now. It's still run by the same chemist—Dieter. He's very unusual. He wears white clogs all year round because he wants everyone to know he's German. Wasn't Vivian's father a chemist, back in Adelaide?'

'He was,' said Benny, and she considered her grandparents for a moment, Clive and Nola Moon, and how they would send her money. She'd always sensed they pitied her, but not enough to visit.

Benny Miller, down by the river, stood up and pulled her sundress over her head, and then walked over and put her toes in the shallow water. It was cold and it took her a long time to wade in up to her waist. The rocks were so hard and slippery under her feet and reeds brushed her ankles. The fishermen were too far away to bother her; just small shapes on a faraway bank.

Eventually Benny pushed herself forward with her legs and dived under the water. She resurfaced, gasping at the temperature, and swam across fast towards the other side, and then back to the deep middle, stopping there and moving herself around with her arms. She looked across towards the grand old bridge, and the sun was sparkling on the water. It felt good to be swimming and she stayed in until her skin was wrinkled and her body was cold to its core.

When she was ready to leave, Benny gathered up her towel and her new stone and walked barefoot back to her car.

Another vehicle was parked there now, near her own. A white ute, dented and dirty, with extra lights fixed to the bonnet—lights that could illuminate a field.

A man sat in the cabin, and another man was sitting on a picnic table, his feet on the bench, drinking from a bottle in a paper bag. Benny knew straight away from the look of them that they were dangerous men and that they frightened her.

She kept her eyes on her feet and held her towel up under her armpits as she walked to her car, wondering how long they had been there, and if they had been watching her swimming.

'Where you from?' said the man in the car. He was fair with tufts of rough hair on his chin.

Benny didn't answer him. She opened her car door and threw her things on the passenger seat and got in.

The fishermen were out of view now; tree trunks were in the way, and the ute was as well, with this man in it.

'Where you from?' the man said again, more insistently this time.

Benny fumbled her keys into the ignition and started her car, just as the man opened his door, kicking it hard with his foot.

He got out—swaying a bit in the breeze—and Benny reversed, full of fear. She looked across as he took a step towards her car, and she struggled with the gearstick, shaking as she pushed it hard into first.

'In Australia we say fucken *g'day*,' he said at Benny through her rolled-down window, and she took off in her car with a small jolt that made the dust come up as she drove out of the parking area.

Benny Miller, her heart racing, drove fast along the dirt road by the river and back towards the main part of town.

30

L unchtime sun came in through the big windows at the Royal Tavern as Tom Boyd set down a counter lunch on the wooden bar and nodded at Tony Simmons.

Simmons sat on a stool in his weekend clothes—a T-shirt and a pair of shorts—and said, 'Thank you kindly,' and had a good sip of his beer. He picked up his fork and steak knife and began to eat while the locals chatted away around him and Smoky Dawson played on the stereo.

'You escape, did you?' said Ed Johnson, sitting one stool up.

'Something like that,' said Simmons, who'd had a shit of a morning. 'Jenny's taken the girls to see my mum.'

It was true. Jenny had taken the girls to see their nanna. And Jenny had preceded that by not speaking to her husband for several hours. She'd made Anzac biscuits, hatefully. Simmons had gone outside and mowed the lawn. Jenny walked out and said, 'Are you going to say something?' and he said, 'About what?' But of course Jenny didn't explain about what.

She'd just said, 'Don't bother coming,' and then she'd left to take the girls over to his mother's house without him, which would ensure that Elsie knew there were troubles afoot, and Tony did not like it when Elsie worried.

Tony had stared at the grass while the girls yelled their goodbyes from the house. There was so much onion weed in the lawn, he thought. And white clover, too, over near the fence, where the bees hovered.

'How is old Elsie?' asked Ed.

'Not the best,' said Simmons. He dipped a chip in a ramekin of mushroom sauce, and Ed nodded and said that he missed his dear old mum, especially on special occasions, that was when you really copped it. She was a good woman and hadn't deserved the early grave that cancer had gifted her. Simmons listened and commiserated in single syllables while Tom Boyd set dirty schooner glasses in the washer behind the bar, a tea towel over his shoulder.

'Cora was going over to see Elsie this morning,' said the voice of Freddy Franks, who sat a couple of stools up from Ed. Simmons had known old Freddy Franks since he was a boy being dragged along by Elsie to book club at Cora's house, and Fred would let young Tony hang around with him in his shed.

'That's good of her,' said Simmons, who didn't much care to think of Cora Franks in his spare time if at all necessary. That Elsie Simmons was so fond of Cora astonished him. What did his mother see in the woman? She was nosy and opinionated and didn't pay any mind to personal boundaries. But the complexity of relations between women was a universe that Simmons didn't like to dwell on. It was foreign and confusing and it caused him significant discomfort.

So here he was with Tom Boyd, who he found a little too reserved; Ed Johnson, whose bawdy humour vaguely entertained him; and Freddy Franks, who suffered the same affliction as Elsie Simmons: a fondness for Cora Franks. It was a chore in many ways, getting to know the dynamics of new people in a new town.

'Any luck with the dead guy?' asked Fred Franks. 'Or are you sick of people asking?'

'The latter,' said Simmons.

'Lucky you just missed Les,' said Tom Boyd. 'He's got a few good theories.'

'I timed it just right then,' said Simmons.

Ed Johnson laughed at that, and Simmons was reminded of how Ed Johnson's laugh always sounded a little cagey, like the laugh of a guilty man.

'You hear Tom's got a girl working behind the bar?' said Ed, smiling. '*Very* nice.'

'Is that right?' said Simmons.

Tom Boyd kept on with the glasses, resting clean ones top down on the tray near the beer taps.

'I heard she's Vivian Moon's kid,' Ed said. 'Remember Vivian, Fred?'

Freddy looked up from his fishing magazine and gave a big slow nod, his arms folded over his polo shirt. Ed Johnson whistled in the way a man does when he finds a woman pleasing to his libidinal urges, and Fred went, 'Hmmm,' very non-committal.

'Who's Vivian Moon?' asked Tom Boyd.

'She used to live next door to me and Cora, in Odette Fisher's place,' said Fred. 'Years ago—before your time, Thomas. Now her daughter Benny's living there. Cora met her. She said she's a nice kid. Looks like her mother, apparently.'

'Oh, she does,' said Ed Johnson. 'Very similar in the face. When Maureen said she was Vivian's daughter, I thought, of course she is. I knew that face pretty well. I wonder what Vivian's up to these days?'

'She's dead, Ed,' said Fred Franks, looking sideways at Ed along the bar. 'You didn't hear that bit? She's just died recently.'

Simmons glanced up from his steak, chewing a big mouthful. The name sounded familiar to him: Vivian Moon. Why was that? He swallowed and felt himself looking stern in concentration. Perhaps she'd been in trouble with the law, was that it? Or, no, it was more like she'd been one of his high school teachers, that's how the sense of the name 'Vivian Moon' felt to him: distant yet unpleasant. He hated it when something unearthed a faraway memory and he couldn't find the proper road to reach it. He ate a chip and then picked up another.

Tom Boyd had stopped what he was doing and leaned forward on the bar with both his arms, taking in this news about Benny's mother with a look of some concern.

'Dead? No kidding? That's a shame,' said Ed Johnson, very nonchalant. 'She was a stunner back in the day, don't you reckon, Freddy?'

Freddy said plainly, 'She was.'

Simmons kept wondering about the name—Vivian Moon—a chip aloft in his hand.

'Sensational tits,' said Ed Johnson.

31

Benny pulled into the drive at the green house, still a little shaky, to find the lawn outside the cottage freshly mowed and Cora Franks sweeping the little pathway between their houses.

'Fred ran the mower over the grass earlier and I just thought I'd tidy it up a bit,' said Cora, who had donned a navy King Gee work shirt and long fawn culottes for her yard duties.

'Oh,' said Benny, getting out of the car. She looked at Cora and appreciated the older woman's outfit for a brief moment before returning to annoyance.

'I can do that,' said Benny.

'Oh yes, but I just thought I would,' said Cora. 'There,' she added, as she emptied a large metal dustpan full of leaves into a waiting bin.

Benny stood and watched, still wearing her swimmers, the bath towel draped around her.

'You've been swimming,' said Cora.

'At the river,' said Benny.

'I used to love swimming. But you get older and it's hard to get into the river, and then the pool's so awful on the hair. Just hold on a tick before you go in,' said Cora, and she strode back into her house while Benny waited near her car. Dirt, brown and chalky, was caked under the wheel wells and the front and sides were filthy with it. Benny had forgotten to put water in the windscreen wipers, too, and the windshield was thick with dust. She liked the look of her car like this, covered in country. She thought about the men in the ute at the river, and she looked at her car now with some small sense of pride. It looked—as much as a Volvo station wagon could—rather rugged.

A screen door slammed and Cora was coming out again, carrying a cake tin.

'Here you are,' she said. 'It's banana bread. I was making one anyway so I doubled the recipe.'

Benny took the tin and said, 'Thank you.' She had eaten half the carrot cake already and, while she hoped this wouldn't keep happening forever—Cora making her food—she was hungry and glad to have banana bread.

'If you need anything else . . .' said Cora, looking now at Benny's Volvo as if it were an abomination.

Benny stood steadfast and hoped the woman wouldn't offer to clean her car.

'Thank you,' she said again, 'I'm fine.' And she moved towards the green cottage.

'Well,' said Cora, clearly wishing for more words to come out of Benny, yet realising that this was not going to be the case, 'your mother would have wanted someone to look out for you.' This was delivered in a tone that Benny couldn't decipher.

Everything that Odette had told Benny the previous night was still sinking in. So only now did it occur to Benny that—of course—Cora Franks would have known Vivian Moon. She would have been her neighbour.

Cora gave Benny a proprietorial look, letting the statement sink in, and then she squinted up at the sky. 'No rain till next Friday, apparently. I better do the pots.' Then she smiled and went back up the steps to her verandah and disappeared inside.

Benny, clutching the cake tin, went into the green house, thinking about what Cora had said. How well had she known Vivian Moon? She set the tin on the kitchen bench and opened the lid. It looked good and Benny was hungry and she got a knife from the drawer and cut a big wedge from one end.

And it was then, when the knife moved the baking paper that was wrapped around the edges, that she saw there was something slipped in there, against the side of the tin.

She pulled it out and looked at it: an old photograph of a group of women sitting together around a dining table, with cups of tea and books. Benny recognised a young Cora

Franks, back and centre; she was the only one not seated. She had her hands on the back of a chair and a pair of reading glasses perched on her nose. To her left Benny saw a young Odette Fisher, smiling obediently. And next to Odette was her mother, Vivian Moon, looking soft and beautiful in a white knitted jumper.

Benny felt her mind go numb at seeing her mother—in a different setting, an uncomfortable pose, a strange jumper. Her hair was neat and pushed back in a way Benny hadn't seen before.

She turned the photograph over. *Book Club, 1971* was written on the back in faded blue pen.

Then—in a different pen, stronger ink—it said: *Benny, I thought you might like to have this. I was sorry to hear about your mother. From Cora Franks.*

32

By Sunday afternoon, two days after their media release, Constable Jimmy Hall and Constable Gus Franklin had taken a total of three in-person visits and eleven phone calls with information relating to the unknown man. Hall had paced back and forth to the kitchenette, making several cups of tea and attending to the seldom-ringing phone. Franklin had sat at his desk, flipping through photos of the dead man, and patiently listening to people excitedly telling him things he already knew.

Three local Cedar Valley residents, for example, had called in to report the man's strange stretching movements as he sat outside Curios ('prancing about with his hands'; 'like he was doing ballet'; 'raised his arm up all the way and then let it drop down limply'). A few people back in Clarke had noticed him sitting at the bus stop, waiting for the bus. ('An eccentric,' was how one man described him. 'Why do all these eccentrics catch public transport?') And a woman from Clarke who had caught the bus in question and alighted at Barrang, where she was a member of the bridge club, came all the way to Cedar Valley that Sunday to tell James Hall that the unknown man's suit was right out of the 1940s—the real deal—and whoever this man was, he was clearly 'a connoisseur of vintage fashion'.

'It was very similar to this one, see?' said the woman, whose name was Margot Young but who appeared very old. She held up an image of a man in a suit from an advertisement in an ancient magazine.

'Yes, it was,' said Hall politely. 'Are you some kind of clothing expert, Mrs Young?'

'I am somewhat of a connoisseur myself,' she said, in a faintly British accent that one did not often hear in a person who resided in the regional town of Clarke.

'Thanks very much for coming in,' said Hall, who didn't have the heart to explain to Margot Young—who'd demanded her husband drive her all the way to Cedar Valley in her Sunday Best—that the police were in fact in possession of the man's clothing, and did not need to be shown a faded picture of what that clothing resembled.

Gussy Franklin had taken a call from a Miss Leonie Wallace—an employee of the Harvey World Travel in Clarke—who'd been sent to Mick's Famous Pies for a pasty run, to cater for an office party that Wednesday morning. She'd stood there at the pie cart with the unknown man behind her—he was waiting to be served—as Mick counted out her fifteen pasties.

The woman had turned to the man in the suit and said, 'They're not all for me,' because, as she explained to Franklin over the telephone, she was a little embarrassed, as a woman on the larger side, to be ordering fifteen pasties in one go.

Instead of sharing a smile with her, as she expected, or offering a jovial remark to allay her discomfort, the man just nodded and kept his eyes to the ground.

'I almost went, "Oh, come on, mate, have a laugh," but he seemed . . . I don't know. He seemed pretty off in his own world. Like, not *rude*, but just awkward. I felt a bit sorry for him.'

'Why was that?' Franklin asked.

'Because he seemed lonely,' said Leonie from Harvey World Travel. 'And probably quite hot.'

Franklin hung up and relayed all this to Jimmy Hall.

'Not much of a talker, was he?' said Franklin.

'Apparently not,' said Hall, stretching his fence-pole arms up above his head and producing a neat cracking sound from his shoulders.

'Well, I got one thing,' said Franklin, looking down at the photographs, which he had spread out like a fan. He blinked for a moment at the figure of the man slumped against the window.

Constable James Hall tipped his neck to one side and then the other. 'What is it?' he said.

'Nige Haling popped in just earlier, when you were in the kitchenette. He was talking to Stevie about those rifles he's had stolen,' said Franklin. 'Apparently, Nige's wife saw a couple of dodgy-looking guys in a ute coming back down their road that day, so he's come in and reported that to Steve. Then he sees me here with the photos and he pipes up that he was in town returning his videos on Wednesday and saw our guy outside Curios. He walked right past him but didn't get a good look . . .' Franklin paused theatrically, making sure he had Jimmy's attention. 'Because there's a blonde woman crouched in front of our guy, and she was talking to him. Nige says they were definitely talking.'

'Oh, that's pretty good, isn't it?' said Jimmy Hall.

'It is, mate,' said Gussy Franklin, nodding. 'Nige says she's this rich-looking lady, all dolled up, talking to this fancy-dressed bloke on the footpath, and Nige has had a laugh to himself about the kind of people you see when you come into town.'

'Well how about that,' said Hall, and Franklin beamed, very pleased with himself.

He looked down at the photos again, and then pushed them all back together into a neat pile. 'Where are the ones of the people in the crowd?' he asked. 'I thought you took more of the crowd.'

'I did,' said Hall. 'They're at the start of the next roll. It's in a different pack.'

He got up and went into Simmons's office and didn't come back for a minute or so. 'That first roll ran out, so I had to put another one in,' he said loudly.

He came out again, empty-handed, and went to the desk used mostly by Senior Constable Steve Howard, which looked as if a burglary had occurred on it. Hall sifted around in the mess. 'Here,' he said, producing a pack of photographs.

It was a roll of thirty-six, just developed, and about twenty of those photos were of the inside of Nigel Haling's shed.

'We missed these ones, did we? Lemme see,' said Franklin, and he held one up to his face to examine it.

There were the people gathered around on Valley Road, all of them there to witness the spectacle of a dead body. There was Cora Franks and Lil Chapman and Therese Johnson; Keith Hand and a group of locals from the Royal; there was silly old Les; and many more tourists than Franklin had remembered being there at the time.

Hall had captured a lovely little moment of flirtation between the ambos: the male officer whispering in the ear of his female colleague and her laughing and looking delighted by it. Franklin smiled at that. Then he ran his finger along, over the faces—people standing, people sitting on the bench up opposite the Coiffure. Franklin set down the first photo and picked up the second. There was Maureen Robinson from the chemist, talking with some tourists, one of them holding a pie bag. And look, there was Gussy himself—gosh, he could do with losing a few kilos—and then Gussy's finger stopped at the person he was looking for.

'There,' he said, his mind still half wondering if he really looked that big in real life.

He turned the photo around, pointing to the face of a sophisticated blonde woman in a cream blouse. She was standing alone, staring intently in the direction of the dead man, with one hand covering her mouth and large dark sunglasses covering her eyes.

'There she is,' he said. 'Our mysterious blonde who looks like what's-her-name from the soap opera. She stuck around.'

Constable James Hall looked at the photograph and grinned widely.

Franklin grinned back. He said, 'I reckon if we can't get any more on our guy, let's get a bit more on our lady.'

33

Benny Miller spent the rest of the Saturday at the pale wooden house filled with an unshakable sorrow.

In the afternoon, she sat on the couch in the living room, reading her book. She lay for a while on the floorboards of the kitchen, her legs up against a cupboard door, looking out the window over the sink. The trees rustling, sunlight flickering through, and the tin of Cora Frank's banana bread on the floor next to her, half eaten. An ache of grief would arise in her, close to every hour, and Benny would press her eyes together and will it to pass.

As the sun lowered, she walked down the path to the shed, allowing herself only a brief glance at the cardboard box up on the shelf, full of Vivian's books. She had resolved not to look at them again—for a few days at least—and instead she left a peach, cut in quarters, next to the old washbasin where the possum slept. She took a handful of gardening magazines from the dusty pile and carried them back to the house.

On the small radio in the kitchen, Benny experimented with frequencies. She came across a local station with a Christian theme that played old pop songs and, every now and again, the announcer read out a verse from the Bible. Benny found it quaint when a wobbly elderly voice said: *'Then Peter came to Jesus and asked, "Lord, how many times shall I forgive my brother when he sins against me? Up to seven times?"'* and she left the station on while she sat at the kitchen table with the gardening magazines and drank half a longneck of beer.

By twilight, she had somehow rationalised further intrusions, and she went through all the drawers in the kitchen, and the cabinet in the living room, and the hallway table, looking in vain for some old relic of her mother. She found coloured pencils, a jar of small change, batteries, a Dave Brubeck record—*Jazz Impressions of Eurasia*—and an ancient joint in a tin on top of the fridge.

She stared a while at the photo Cora Franks had given her, and eventually she put it inside her cardboard box with the rest of her collection. She would ask Odette about it, she thought, and then she sat on the bed next to the box, flipping through letters that Jules had sent her from Canberra. She felt a rare yearning for him then, and wished he was there with her, even just for an evening.

In the nighttime, Benny turned on the lamps and had a long bath in the pink-tiled bathroom and smoked the joint she had found in the tin. She rested her head back and closed her eyes as her throat burnt happily. It was close to midnight when she ate the rest of Cora's carrot cake, standing in the kitchen, her mouth as dry as dust, feeling unusually positive about a Phil Collins song that was playing softly on the radio.

At first light she was woken by a deep sliding noise from the ceiling and she lay in bed for the next hour, half sleeping, half awake, listening to the slow, restless snake and thinking about her mother, and whether she had slept under this very quilt, on this very mattress. What were the contents of her dreams in this room? What kind of person was Vivian Moon, in the dark mossy parts of her that she kept so well hidden?

The telephone rang just after seven.

Benny sat up, startled and weary, unsure if she should answer it or not. She got out of bed and went up the hall.

'Hello?' she said, expecting Odette.

'G'day, Ben,' said a familiar voice.

'Oh. Hi, Dad,' said Benny, and sadness washed around inside her, like waves over rocks.

Frank Miller paused on the other end of the line, then said, 'How you going?' His accent, as she heard it now, was a city accent. It wasn't stretched and broad like the men she poured beers for at the Royal Tavern.

'Good,' said Benny. 'I was just waking up.'

And there they were together, on the phone: Frank and Benny Miller, father and daughter, who, having cohabited in their distant way for eighteen years, had never been good at communicating with each other, even when Frank had had a beer and was in a good mood. That morning, as Benny could easily tell, Frank was not in a particularly good mood.

'So, how's the house?' he asked.

'It's good, Dad,' said Benny, and it pained her how awkward this was, speaking to her father on the phone. It was always this way with Frank. As if any words he might have to offer were trapped inside him and couldn't find a way out.

Standing there in the hallway in the slanted light of morning, an old memory surfaced in Benny—of when she was little, running under the sprinkler in the back garden at Rozelle, while Irene Miller watched on from a chair.

'When my mum comes home to live with us we're going to get a swimming pool,' Benny had said to her grandmother; where such a fantasy had come from, Benny did not know.

Irene had made an odd sort of scoffing sound. 'Benita, your mum's not coming home. And there's really no room here for a swimming pool.'

Benny held the telephone receiver and looked down at her bare feet on the rug, a Persian runner that went the length of the hall.

'The house is very nice,' she said. 'I like it here. Odette's been good to me.'

Frank went *uh-huh*, *uh-huh* and she could picture him, chewing his fingernails.

'How are you, Dad?'

'Oh, you know,' he said, 'pretty well. Just thought I'd ring you. See how you were going.'

Benny wanted quite badly then to simply hang up and walk outdoors, just for the clear air. And at the same time, in light of what Odette had told her, she wanted to ask Frank a hundred questions.

Did you know Mum lived here? In this house? Did you know she worked at the pharmacy in Cedar Valley? Why did you say she was in Europe then? What is it about me that made her leave?

But instead they went back and forth with unbearable courtesies and the banality of it caused Benny to shut her eyes tightly in discomfort, imagining her drab father who had once been handsome and perhaps even interesting, and who now was forlorn and couldn't manage an even slightly animated conversation with his own daughter. When had he lost his charm? For Benny thought she remembered, from her childhood, some fire between him and her mother. Some flame of vitality in *him*. His sinewy arms would lift Benny above his head and onto his shoulders; and Frank Miller was so clever he could take a car engine apart and put it back together again. There was even a time when Frank had friends. Sometimes there'd be a group of them, men and women, they would come over and cook sausages on the barbecue and Frank would play Neil Young records and turn the speakers around to face the yard.

'Better go then,' he said, and he cleared his throat. Benny could hear the noises of the old Rozelle house in the background.

The hum of traffic and the television, which Frank would leave on throughout the day as a kind of lifeless companion. She did not miss these noises, nor the house in Rozelle, and it saddened her that she did not in any way miss her father.

Perhaps I will miss him later. This was what Benny said to herself, while knowing inwardly that she wouldn't.

'Okay,' she said into the phone. 'Thanks for calling.'

She meant that in a way. She was pleased that he'd thought of her, but he was probably just worried, and she didn't want his worry. In fact, she worried for *him*, was the truth of it. It had always been that way, from when she was ten or eleven and began to take on the cooking of their dinner. She would iron her school uniform and then the shirts he wore to the auction house. She had worried about him and she had pitied him for being so hopeless, and it seemed ridiculous to her now that she hadn't understood earlier why Frank was so sad.

Frank Miller was still in love with Vivian Moon.

Benny saw this now. That he was mourning her—her death—in a vivid way, but that he'd been mourning her for Benny's whole life.

They said their goodbyes and Benny hung up the phone. And she walked out into the wild garden, where it was so cicada-loud, and the sad waves moved around inside her for this father of hers, who was so lost and lonely and sad.

34

Constable James Hall and Constable Gus Franklin walked into the chemist on Monday morning shortly after 9 am and found Maureen Robinson behind the counter, affixing price tags to bottles of vitamins.

'Oh, good, it's you two,' she said, looking at them over her reading glasses. Her shirt was pale blue and offered the name of the chemist on the breast pocket—*Cedar Valley Pharmacy*—and a logo of a mortar and pestle with a heart on it. She also wore a name tag and a wry kind of smile.

Hall and Franklin had already stopped in at the newsagent, the bakery, the craft and crystal store and the cafe that morning, appealing for any information about the blonde woman who had spoken to the dead man. No one in any of these establishments recalled a blonde woman, but at least Franklin had an excuse to buy a neenish tart.

Cora Franks had been helpful—she'd come into the station first thing, and was more than happy to do so. Lil Chapman told Cora she should go up and talk to them. And, well, Cora Franks could talk the leg off a chair, and she didn't need much encouragement to get more involved. She went straight up there after breakfast and her only disappointment was that Tony Simmons wasn't in yet and she had to speak to Franklin and Hall.

Cora told them what she recollected: the woman was very interested in the watches, the ones with thin gold bands in particular. She tried on three and bought none. She was elegant, clearly not local, and did indeed bear a resemblance to Nikki from *The Young and the Restless*. Finally—and Cora didn't know the medical reason for this kind of thing—the woman had a bad case of the shakes.

'Like this,' said Cora, who demonstrated by holding out her hand and shaking it.

Franklin nodded.

'And now, I need to talk to Tony. When will he be in?'

'Detective Sergeant Simmons is due in this morning,' said Franklin. 'Anything we can help with?'

Cora considered this carefully, tilting her head at Gussy Franklin. 'No, I think I'd better talk to Tony,' she said. 'Tell him it's about a chat I had with Elsie. His mother. Elsie Simmons.'

Franklin nodded again and Cora left, and then the men began their canvass, and Gussy Franklin finished his tart on the bench outside the chemist before they went in.

'Is Dieter around?' asked Hall, referring to the pharmacist, Dieter Bernbaum, who was known to wear white clogs and be weird.

'He's stepped out,' said Maureen, fondling a bottle of B12. 'I'm glad you're here. I was going to come up to the station on my break.'

'Good-o,' said Franklin. 'Did you hear we're asking after a woman who may have had a chat with the man who died?'

'Oh, are you?' said Maureen, barely listening. 'How's your mum, Gussy? Before I forget, will you tell her we've got her orthotics in—or should I ring her?'

'You go ahead and ring her, Maureen,' said Franklin. 'Did a woman come in here last Wednesday, to your recollection, a blonde woman? Cora and the ladies from Curios reckon she looked like a soap star. Ring any bells?'

Maureen tapped the vitamin bottle against the counter, thinking about it. She leaned forward and looked up to the ceiling.

'Oh, yes, her,' she said. 'I remember.'

Franklin and Hall exchanged a look.

'Just a minute,' she said, and the two men stepped back to allow an elderly woman with a metal walking stick to approach the counter and purchase a box of cotton buds and some Mercurochrome.

'Hello, love,' said the old woman in a phlegmy kind of voice.

'It's healing okay?' Maureen yelled at the woman.

'She'll be right,' rasped the woman, and Maureen took her money and gave her change and came out from behind the counter to escort the woman to the footpath. They hugged, and the woman raised her stick in the air as a goodbye before struggling off.

Maureen returned to the counter. 'The rich woman, yes. She looked rich. Nice clothes, nice jewellery, very sophisticated. She looked like she'd just stepped out of the salon. And it *was* that day, wasn't it? I think I saw her over the road after they'd found him.'

'You did,' said Hall. 'Here.' And he held up the photograph of the crowd, pointing to the woman in the cream blouse and the large sunglasses.

'That's her. She came in asking for sleeping pills, but she didn't have a prescription so I could only give her the over-the-counter kind. I think she asked for a sedative, actually, which is a bit sad, isn't it? To use the word "sedative".'

'Hmm,' said Gussy Franklin, wondering what was so sad about the word 'sedative'.

'Anything else you can remember about her?' asked Hall.

'Well, she was one of those well-to-do women that kind of look down their nose at you,' said Maureen. 'You know, a bit superior. She was looking around the shop like it was a pile of crap. But at the same time, she was just a bit too desperate for the pills. You see that sometimes in my line of work. Like someone has demons. And, you know, it's the demons they want to put to sleep.'

Maureen laughed darkly and Hall looked back at her, nervously blinking.

'Oh, and she had a tremor,' added Maureen, and she held out one hand and trembled it. 'Like this,' she said.

Franklin wrote that down. And Maureen Robinson began to talk about the dead man and how strange it was to see a dead body like that, just sitting on the footpath.

'It's really shaken up some of the customers,' she said. 'Especially the older ones. Everyone's been talking about him. I think because death is usually kind of *hidden*, you know? Happening someplace else. But when it's just sitting there on the footpath in a nice suit—it makes people take stock of their lives. Betsy Dell was in this morning and she thinks we should have some sort of commemoration for him, which is a funny kind of idea, but I think it would be good to give everyone a chance to come together and talk about it. It's just not an everyday thing for people to see.'

Maureen put her elbows on the counter and leaned in a little, so Franklin and Hall leaned in also.

She lowered her voice. 'And that's what I was going to come up to see you about. You know Elsie Simmons? Tony's mum? Well I was over there last night for tea and we were talking about it, and Elsie said it was just like a thing that happened in Adelaide after the war. You should have heard this story! It was *so* similar, I couldn't believe it. And of course she hasn't told Tony any of this. I told her to call him last night but she didn't want to bother him at home, for some reason. So I told her I'd go up to the station today and have a word in his ear.'

'Oh yeah,' said Franklin. 'Elsie's solved the case, has she?'

Hall repressed a smile.

'Have some respect, Gussy,' said Maureen sternly. 'I've known Elsie Simmons for twenty-five years and let me tell you, she may forget a few things here and there, but she knows her stuff. The Somerton Man—that's what they call him in South Australia. I think you should look it up. Elsie says it's *still* a mystery, never solved. A man died just like our man did, in a nice brown suit on the first of December. I thought about it all evening. And I don't think Elsie Simmons is one to make up stories, do you?'

35

Tony Simmons sat in his hot office with the fan going around and Senior Constable Bob Kurnell, a good bloke, standing in the doorway banging on about a couple of stolen rifles and how he'd had a run-in with the boys from Clarke over some yobbos in a ute who may or may not have stolen them.

'That mate of yours, O'Leary, he's come down here about it just now, because the bottle-o under the Clarke Plaza got held up by these two guys with rifles—which are probably Nigel Haling's rifles. And I just said to him, "Mate, if you're gonna give us help on our end, fine. But if you're not, then youse can just get in your car and piss off back to Clarke." And they pissed off back to Clarke!'

Ha ha ha. Simmons had such a scraping laugh. 'Of course he did, the lazy prick,' he said, and Kurnell shook his head and went back out to his desk laughing, and Simmons heard Gussy

Franklin's voice, talking softly with Hall, and the high-pitched alien calls of the fax machine.

Simmons was waiting for Ping Williams to return his call. He'd left her a message an hour ago, enquiring after the second analysis of the dead man's organs. He'd hung up and busied himself with paperwork, ignoring a note on his desk, in Franklin's writing, telling him that Cora Franks wanted to talk to him, regarding his mother. The last thing Simmons wanted to do was talk to Cora Franks about anything, especially his mother. So he worked and he waited and at some point, staring at the fan, it occurred to Simmons that he had a lonely man's yearning for Ping Williams.

The first time he met her was many moons ago, at Clarke Base Hospital, after a dreadful car crash from which he had dragged a child. Ping Williams was the size of a child herself, in a white coat and thick glasses. 'Will she make it?' Simmons had asked her. Simmons remembered that day well—how his shirt was dark with blood. Ping Williams had looked at the blood, had looked at him, and said softly, 'We do all we can, don't we, Sergeant? Perhaps a singing bird will come.'

The young girl had died and Simmons was nauseous for three days. The bird had not come.

Now, years had passed, and the voice on her answering machine had moved him in an uncomfortable way. Then the phone finally rang and Simmons picked it up like lightning, and he felt a stirring in his loins for Ping's calm whisper when she said, 'I still feel the only possible cause to be an undiscovered barbiturate or glycoside, but as you can probably tell by my use of the word "undiscovered", I'm sorry to say we still haven't found any.'

'Right,' said Simmons.

'I should tell you that Dr Stanton disagrees with my analysis. He feels the findings *exclude* the possibility of a poison—or certainly a common poison. But Dr Stanton does agree that a physical specimen such as this man would not just sit down and die. There must have been a cause, you see? And after further examination of the stomach, I am certain we are looking for something injected, but we can't find any mark of a hypodermic needle. It is truly perplexing, Detective.'

Simmons felt a little jolt when she called him 'Detective' and he had spoken to Ping for a while longer, realising he was asking more questions than usual—he liked having her there on the phone. They went around in circles, positing various theories and then hitting brick walls. No matter how they came at it, the fact was that Ping Williams's conclusions were frustratingly inconclusive.

'I can't really say, Detective. I feel certain that this man was poisoned, but the evidence does not warrant that finding. And even if I was correct, I can't say whether the poison was self-administered or administered by some other person in the form of a murder.'

Simmons thanked her and hung up the phone and he watched the fan for a few moments, smiling absently at the way Ping said the word 'murder'.

Hall was on the phone. Simmons could hear his muffled voice out there in the common area. The boys had been preoccupied all morning. Simmons stood, stretched and went out to the kitchenette, where he made himself a coffee and ate a biscuit, crunching it with his mouth open while standing there, thinking. Hall was over at Franklin's desk now, showing him a fax.

'Morning, boys,' said Simmons loudly across the room. 'Sit rep.' And he strode back into his office for a situation report, invigorated by his conversation with Ping Williams.

Franklin came in first, and then Hall, who was carrying a notepad and the lengthy-looking fax. They assumed their positions and, as was customary, waited for Simmons to speak.

'Ping Williams still reckons it's poison, even though she can't find any trace of it.' Simmons was in a good mood now; he smiled while he said this. 'She doesn't know if it's murder or suicide; she basically doesn't know bloody anything. But she's a feisty little woman, isn't she? Very sure of herself.'

'So what happens?' said Hall.

'Well, it'll have to go to an inquest, I imagine,' said Simmons. 'Which is not what I would have expected last week, but there you go.'

Franklin cleared his throat and told Simmons about the sightings of the blonde woman, the sedatives, the shakes. 'It seems that she definitely talked to our unknown man, so now we definitely want to talk to her.'

'Shit, yes,' said Simmons. 'Very good.'

Simmons was the one to check in about the sketcher. Hall was organising someone to come down from Sydney to do it, based on the photos he took in the morgue.

'Amazing we haven't had one person come forward to report him missing,' said Simmons. 'Who the hell was he not to have anyone asking after him? That's why we need to get a good drawing done. Someone will see it and they'll recognise him. What about the prints?'

'Nothing,' said Hall. 'Parramatta sent them Australia-wide and got nothing.'

'Hmm. Anything on the chemist angle?'

'Nah, but it's pretty hard to run with. Suffice to say no one's reported a missing chemist,' said Hall.

'It's starting to feel like we've got nothing, boys,' said Simmons.

'Yeah, but your mum might have something,' said Gus Franklin with a broad smile.

'What's that?' said Simmons, who would be certain to level any person who said a lewd word about his mother, Elsie Simmons.

Gus Franklin realised the mistake in his tone and his face went pink as Simmons glared at him—a sharp and flinty stare—and Gussy shuffled in his chair.

Hall, the earnest saviour, swooped in. 'Boss, Maureen Robinson told us that your mum said our dead 'un reminded her of a case back in Adelaide. I understand she's from Adelaide originally. And look, we thought it was probably nothing, but you know me—I made a call.'

Tony Simmons was squinting across the table now in disbelief. He didn't want to lose his temper with Franklin or Hall, they'd been good boys. But why were they sitting here talking about his mother? Hall was not prone to practical joking, yet that's what this nonsensical information sounded like—some strange kind of joke.

'It turns out that there's this old unsolved case in Adelaide,' said Hall, speaking quickly. 'This guy in a brown suit sat down at the beach in Somerton and died. This was in 1948. But it happened on the first of December, just like our guy. Isn't that weird? And they still don't know who he was or how he died. I have a mate who's stationed at Norwood, in Adelaide, so I called him, and he knew all about it. He thought our guy sounded pretty curious. He's sent over a few pages, and he's gonna call me back.' Hall held up the fax paper.

'What the fuck are you talking about?' said Simmons.

'Listen to this. The guy in 1948—the Somerton Man, that's what they call him—well, they think he died of poison, but they couldn't find any poison. He had no ID and, get this . . .' Hall paused.

'Get fucken what, Jimmy?' said Simmons.

'All the labels on his clothing had been removed,' said Hall.

'Ha!' went Simmons loudly. He was sitting forward in his chair now, his hands on the pinewood desk. 'What else?' he said, smiling now, back in the game.

'And the only things he had on him,' said Hall, reading now from his pile of folded fax paper, 'were cigarettes, a box of matches, half a pack of Juicy Fruit gum, a bus ticket, a train ticket, and two combs.'

36

Benny's Royal Tavern shirt did indeed swim on her. It was a men's small, but the sleeves still went down to her elbows, and the shirt itself fell midway to her knees. She found a pair of scissors in the utensil drawer at the cottage and cut it shorter, then she tucked it into her denim shorts and rolled up the sleeves. After that it was okay, and she liked that she got to wear one while she worked behind the bar and made conversation with the locals.

The Sunday shift had gone well. The rest of Cedar Valley was closed on a Sunday—roller shutters down, deadbolts fastened, unlit interiors along Valley Road. Even Fran's World Famous Pies shut at 1 pm and then Fran herself, pie-round and bonny, wandered up the road to the Royal for an afternoon beverage. She was like a minor celebrity in Cedar Valley, Benny discovered, and when Fran was at the bar the main thing you could hear was Fran. She was well versed in community matters, and was diplomatically opinionated.

At one point that Sunday afternoon, Ed Johnson had said, 'Frances, with all your ideas on what this town needs, maybe you should run for mayor.'

And Fran said, 'I'll be thanking you for your vote, Edward. I'll be thanking our whole street for their votes,' and the two of them clinked their glasses and chortled. Evidently, Fran and Ed were neighbours.

'Seriously, though, this guy we've got now—what's his name? Watson? Awful! We haven't had a good mayor since Neville Simmons, in my opinion,' said Ed Johnson.

'Hear, hear,' said Don in the terry-towelling hat.

'Dear old Neville Simmons,' said Fran. 'I was, what, thirty-five when he died? I couldn't care less about politics then, but I was as sad as if he were an uncle. The way he made fun of himself in those big speeches at the Clarke Show? I *loved* that.'

That led into a discussion about the good old days in general, and how things were changing with the technology and the tourism, then talk turned to federal politics and the issue of native title, and finally wound its way back around to local politics and the brilliance of the former mayor, the late Neville Simmons. Benny fixed drinks and found this all to be genuinely interesting, and then she chatted a while with two sisters, Maureen and Barbie Robinson, who lived together in a house near the school. Maureen was clearly the older and more dominant sibling, while Barbie sat there obediently and smiled in agreement at everything Maureen said.

'And now we have Neville's son tending to our law enforcement,' Fran was saying.

Ed Johnson nodded.

Then Tom Boyd said, 'Tony Simmons has his work cut out for him this week.'

And this seemed to be Fran's cue to speak at length about the dead man, and how odd it felt to her that she'd missed the whole thing. There'd been a terrible crash on the coast road and traffic had been backed up for hours.

'You were a couple of cars ahead of me Edward. I saw you when we finally started moving,' said Fran.

Ed Johnson appeared surprised. 'Big hold up, that was,' he said.

'I just keep thinking how sad it is that not one person knows him,' said Fran. 'Nobody! I just think that's awful for him—and that's on top of dying.' And she went on to say that Betsy Dell, who owned the grocery store, had raised the idea of holding some kind of funeral service in his honour, and Fran thought Betsy was right on the money. Ed laughed at that but Fran persisted. A wake could be held there at the Royal, she suggested, and Tom said that would be just fine, and then Tom took his break in the little back room that he referred to as his office.

•

On the Monday, Benny sprayed Norsca on her shirt and wore it again. She worked the lunch shift, smelling like a forest. Her confidence grew by the hour and she spent a good while talking with the red-faced woman called Linda, who had a rostered day off from the chicken factory but lied to her husband about it in order to drive to the Royal Tavern to drink all day.

'He'd just want me doing housework, and I'm done with all that, I'm done,' Linda slurred, and Benny saw that underneath the beer puff, Linda Carlstrom (who had held out her hand for Benny to shake and introduced herself by her full name) had once been a pretty woman. And Benny listened to Linda talk about her son and her deadbeat husband, who cared a whole lot more about car parts than he ever cared for Linda. Then Linda cupped Benny's hand in both of hers and said, 'You're a good egg,' in an emotional way, just as Odette Fisher appeared in the doorway, with Bessel beside her.

'Here's trouble,' said Tom Boyd as Odette approached the bar.

'Hi, Benny,' said Odette warmly. She sat on a bar stool and, although Benny would not have imagined Odette Fisher in a pub, she looked just as at home there as she did in her wooden farmhouse on the mountain. Bessel sat down on the floor beside her.

'Hello,' said Benny to Odette, and Odette put an arm across the bar and rubbed Benny's shoulder.

'You got a T-shirt,' she said. And then, 'I thought I'd pop in and see how you were going. Hi, Tom.'

Benny stood there grinning, for she was so pleased to see Odette.

'You having a drink?' said Tom.

'I should think so,' said Odette. She assessed the beer taps. 'I might get a beer. A small one.'

So Benny poured Odette a middy of beer, and before Odette could get her purse out of her big leather bag, Benny had pulled money from her own pocket and paid for the drink herself.

'Please,' she said, when Odette protested, so Odette nodded and said, 'Thank you.'

Odette sipped her beer. 'How's Annie?' she asked Tom Boyd.

'She's good. She took the girls up to Port Kembla yesterday to get pipis.'

'Oh, I love pipis. Tell her Carol's finally decided on a book for January. We're going with *The English Patient*.' Odette looked at Benny. 'Annie and I are in a book club together.'

'I thought you were in a book club with Cora,' said Benny.

Odette paused, surprised. 'I *was* in a book club with Cora. That was years ago. How did you know that?'

'Cora told me,' said Benny. 'Kind of.' Odette seemed a little bemused, and Linda Carlstrom burst into a coarse laugh at the other end of the bar, where she and Ed Johnson were smoking together.

'Well, now I'm in the splinter group,' said Odette. 'Me, Annie Boyd and about six others. A couple of us used to be in Cora's club, but there was a rebellion.' Odette laughed and sipped her beer again. 'I might get a packet of chips,' she said.

Tom Boyd opened a packet of chips and emptied them into a basket and set the basket in front of Odette.

'This lot think they read better books,' said Tom to Benny.

'We do,' said Odette, and she ate a chip.

'Have you spoken to Annie about our dead guy?' Tom asked Odette. 'She's got wind of some theory.'

Odette pushed the basket over and Benny leaned across and took some chips.

'I love it how everyone's calling him *our* dead guy,' said Odette. 'And no, I haven't. Why?'

Tom explained: Annie had spoken to Maureen Robinson. Maureen had been round to see Elsie Simmons, and now they were all on about some other man who'd died in the 1940s. He, too, had been sitting on the ground in a suit and tie. And there was something Tom didn't quite catch about codes or poetry.

Odette stared at Tom. Her mouth opened a little. She looked as if a penny was dropping inside her.

'Elsie's from Adelaide,' she said, thinking. Then she looked at Benny. 'That's the case I was talking about the other day.' She set her beer down and slapped the bar. 'That's right—he had a message in his pocket! They found it much later, and it was linked to this old book of poems. God, doesn't that sound mad? But it's all true.' She shook her head, grinning.

'How do you know about all that?' asked Benny.

'Well . . .' Usually so composed, Odette seemed suddenly unsure of what to say. 'Actually,' she said, 'it was Vivian who told me about it. I mean, she knew the story because she's from Adelaide, but she was really fascinated by it. I remember her telling me all the details.'

Benny stared back blankly. 'Oh,' she said.

'It all sounds very weird,' said Tom Boyd, arms folded, leaning back against the bench.

'It does, doesn't it?' said Odette. She gave Benny a look of concern, and then she smiled. 'But don't you think someone needs to check our dead man's pockets?'

37

'Not only did he have this note in his pocket,' said Tony Simmons, 'but it was in bloody *Persian* and it had some special connection to a poetry book they found in a car!'

It was as if Simmons was performing sketch comedy, the way he was speaking about the Somerton Man. A bead of sweat had formed near his ear and soon enough it dripped down to his jawline as he laughed at the pure ridiculousness of the revelations before him. 'This is fucking mad is what this is.'

'So your mum never told you about it?' asked Hall.

'I wasn't born yet, Jimmy,' said Simmons. 'So no, she didn't.'

'What's with Adelaide?' said Franklin after a pause, and the others didn't know what to say.

Hall and Franklin and Simmons had spent the past couple of hours making enquiries in relation to the Somerton Man. The fax machine had beeped and emitted its stuttering groan as ancient newspaper articles were sent through. The men had read things quietly to themselves; they had read things aloud to each other; they had applied highlighters and made notes. Simmons had become so excited by the sheer number of similarities between the two cases—the Somerton Man and the Cedar Valley Man—that he made a call to regional homicide to share the recent developments.

The detective who took his call was unconvinced. 'So you reckon because your unknown sounds like this—I'm sorry—this unsolved homicide? Was the one in Adelaide a homicide?'

'Oh, well, I'm not sure; no one's sure,' said Simmons, wondering then if he'd jumped the gun by calling homicide.

'So what was it?' asked the detective, who seemed to find the circumstances presented to him rather preposterous.

'Ah, well, it's still a bit of a mystery, as I understand it,' said Simmons. 'It's an unsolved *possible* homicide,' and a few moments later: 'I'll call you back.'

So he hung up the phone and gathered his thoughts, and by the end of that Monday they lay out what they knew so far about the enduring Australian mystery known as the Somerton Man.

•

Early on the morning of December 1st 1948, a man was found dead on Somerton Beach in the Adelaide suburb of Glenelg. He was in a seated position, on the sand, leaning against the sea wall, his feet towards the sea. He wore a brown suit, with a pullover under his jacket, a white shirt and a wide-striped tie. His shoes were near-new and polished, his hair neatly combed and his fingernails trimmed and clean. Upon inspection by local police, it was discovered that all the labels on his clothing had been removed.

Some witnesses reported that the man seemed calm and composed; others assumed he was drunk. A fellow called John Lyons was taking an evening walk with his wife and saw the man raise his arm as if stretching—extending it up and down again in an elegant fashion. No one spoke to this man, and he spoke to no one. And it wasn't until early the following morning—on December 1st—that people realised he was dead. John Lyons was walking past again, and he was the one who noticed something was amiss. Lyons, and two men with a horse, all up early for a beachside stroll.

The police had no idea who the dead man was, or what to make of him. A post-mortem examination was performed and the results were inconclusive. Pathologists at the time felt certain that a poison had been administered, but no poison could be found. The body of the man was pumped with formaldehyde in order to preserve it, while everyone wondered what to do.

It wasn't long before an unclaimed suitcase was discovered in the cloakroom of Adelaide railway station. It had been checked in on the day the unknown man had travelled to

Somerton Beach. Threads in the suitcase linked it to the unknown man, and authorities concluded it was his. But even though some items of clothing in the suitcase bore the names *T. Keane*, *Keane* or just *Kean*, police suspected the names were a deliberate plant, a misdirection, and, since they couldn't find anyone missing by the name of T. Keane anyway, it didn't lead to an identification.

Evidence was examined and re-examined and an inquest was held in June 1949, at which various pathologists testified. Rare, deadly poisons were discussed, and theories posited, but the inquest could not determine either the cause of death or the man's identity. Authorities described it as an 'unparalleled mystery'.

It was around the time of the inquest that, upon re-examination, detectives found a rolled-up scrap of paper hidden in the fob pocket of the dead man's trousers. The paper looked to be torn from a book, and it had the words 'Tamam Shud' printed on it. What did that mean? The police had no idea, so they appealed to the public for information: did anyone in Adelaide or beyond know what 'Tamam Shud' meant?

Well, a man called Frank Kennedy knew. He was a police reporter from the Adelaide *Advertiser* and he recognised the phrase as Persian. He contacted police immediately and told them to look into a book of poetry called *The Rubaiyat of Omar Khayyam*, written by a twelfth-century Persian astronomer.

'Tamam Shud' meant 'it's ended' or 'finished' and it appeared at the back of some editions of the book.

Police conducted a nationwide search to find a copy that had the phrase in it, and a photograph of the torn piece of paper was released to the media.

It was then that a local man came forward, a man who was never identified, but he was described as a professional of some kind. Some reports refer to him as a 'doctor' or a 'chemist', and on the day the man had died this doctor/chemist had parked his car on Jetty Road in Glenelg and left the windows rolled down. The doctor/chemist had been with his brother that day, and when he noticed a copy of *The Rubaiyat of Omar Khayyam* on the back seat of his car, he assumed it belonged to his brother. His brother assumed the same. Neither thought anything more about it until months later, when the book was suddenly a vital clue. The doctor/chemist handed it over to the police. Sure enough, at the back of book, a section had been neatly torn out. It was the same size as the scrap of paper found in the dead man's pocket bearing the words 'Tamam Shud'. Tests proved the paper to be one and the same.

But that wasn't everything.

Written there too, in capital letters, was what police believed to be some sort of cipher:

WRGOABABD

MLIAOI

WTBIMPANETP

MLIABOAIAQC

ITTMTSAMSTGAB

That's what was written, in black pen, with a few lines and cross marks here and there. And some letters were difficult to make out. Was the first letter a W? Or was it in fact an M? Was the cross mark a cross, or the letter X? No one could ever figure it out. Navy codebreakers worked for weeks in vain. An Adelaide newspaper offered a reward to anyone who could figure it out. Letters were received from across Australia, offering solutions and theories. Thirty years later, when defence department cryptographers took another look, they speculated that the letters might be little more than the meaningless product of a 'disturbed mind'.

Police made similarly little progress with the other thing found written in the back of the book: the unlisted telephone number for a woman who police referred to by the nickname 'Jestyn'. Jestyn, a nurse, lived in Glenelg, about four hundred metres from where the unknown man was found. When police interviewed her, she claimed not to know the man. She said she had no idea why her number was written in the back of the book. But as coincidence would have it, she did admit that, while working at North Shore Hospital in Sydney in 1945, she just happened to give an army lieutenant named Alf Boxall a copy of *The Rubaiyat of Omar Khayyam*.

Alfred Boxall.

He'd had a couple of drinks with this nurse, Jestyn, at a hotel bar and she gave him a book of Persian poetry. She left Sydney shortly after and married, and when Alf tried to contact her again she declined his advances. Then, three and a half years later, in 1948, a man shows up dead on Somerton Beach—walking distance from Jestyn's house—linked to the same book of Persian poems. What were the odds? This was what the police wondered, and they quickly concluded that the dead man must be Alf Boxall.

But he wasn't.

Police found Alf Boxall, alive and well, living in Sydney. He still had his copy of *The Rubaiyat*, too. It was signed in the front, to him from Jestyn, and she'd copied out one of the poems in her own writing on the title page. When police checked the back of the book, the words 'Tamam Shud' were still intact. Alf Boxall had no idea anyone thought he was a dead man until the police came knocking on his door.

So that left the unknown man from Somerton Beach—with the mysterious piece of paper in his pocket, the lack of identification, the unknown cause of death, the suitcase at the railway station, and the book of poetry and codes.

A taxidermist made a plaster cast of his head and chest, in the hope that it would one day lead someone to an answer. The body was eventually buried, and when flowers began to appear on his gravesite years later, police at the cemetery questioned an elderly woman who seemed to be paying particular attention to the grave—but she too claimed not to know him.

So the years passed, and the spy-related theories continued to abound. Laypeople sat in their living rooms, hunched over notepads, perplexed by the code. Newspapers reported every new and significant development. Adelaide police received letters from enthusiasts across the country, postulating about espionage and the potential involvement of the KGB. And, funnily enough, Alf Boxall himself had worked as an intelligence officer during World War II. He was questioned about this in '78, and about the theory that the Somerton Man was some kind of spy, but Alf Boxall played it down.

'It's quite a melodramatic thesis, isn't it?' he said in 1978—and now, in the Cedar Valley police station in 1993, Detective Sergeant Anthony Simmons cracked up laughing.

'*Ha ha ha*. Isn't it, though?' said Simmons, as he read from a faxed transcript of the interview, provided by Hall's mate from Norwood.

'He's still alive, you know,' said Hall.

'Who, Alf?'

'Correct. My mate in Norwood has been into the case for years. Not officially, more as a personal hobby. I told him he should write a book about it. He's read all the articles, all the files. He's got a VHS copy of the interview from *Inside Story*. He grew up in Glenelg and his parents were well into it too. He says Boxall must be eighty-five by now, but he's still kicking.'

Simmons set down the fax paper and clasped his hands behind his head.

'What an absolute cracker,' said Gussy Franklin, peeling a banana. 'What do you make of it, boss?'

'Madness!' said Simmons, beaming. 'Fucking madness.'

'So what do we do?' asked Hall. 'I mean, our guy obviously had a thing for the Somerton Man, yeah? Would you say it's like a copycat case?'

Franklin took a too-big bite of banana and struggled to keep his lips closed while he chewed it. He made a little *mmm* sound at the word 'copycat', which was either surprise or choking.

'Well, we've got our connection,' said Simmons. 'Even just his outfit says it all now, doesn't it? The labels and the suit and so forth?'

'It's a shame there's no cloakroom at Clarke station for him to have left a suitcase full of clues for us,' said Hall.

Franklin swallowed and cleared his throat. 'Why would you copycat this, though?' he asked. 'And why would you copycat it here?'

Simmons's eyebrows went up. He nodded. 'This nurse back in Adelaide—Jestyn?—she's clearly bullshitting. She knew him! She obviously gave him the poetry book, as well as giving one to Alf Boxall. Either that or it's the biggest fucking coincidence in Australian history, and you know what I think about coincidences. Is she still kicking too?'

'Still kicking,' said Hall. 'And my mate says everyone who's worked on it reckons she's bullshitting. To this day, she bullshits.'

'So our old dead mate in Adelaide, he was in love with her. Are you thinking this? Or else she's a spy too. Or she's a spy *and* he's in love with her. And she's killed him somehow. You with me?'

Franklin was chewing again, a confused look in his eyes.

'Should I call my mate in Adelaide and tell him you've solved the unparalleled mystery?' said Hall.

'You might just have to do that, Jimmy,' said Simmons.

Franklin took yet more banana into his mouth, as if this was even possible.

'So you reckon the nurse killed him because she didn't fancy him,' said Constable James Hall. 'And she had access to the special poison because she's a spy.'

'Plausible!' said Simmons, enjoying himself. 'And now maybe *our* guy—our dead 'un—maybe *he* has a nurse. So to speak. A "Jestyn" of his very own in Cedar Valley.'

'Who's killed him?' asked Franklin. 'But wait: how does he get someone to kill him so it looks like the Somerton Man? Does he just ask nicely?'

'Fuck, I don't know!' said Simmons. 'How's your banana?'

Constable James Hall grinned, and a little twinkle came into Gussy Franklin's eyes.

'Does it have to be a nurse again?' he said.

Simmons slapped the desk, hooting with laughter. 'Yes, Gussy. It has to be a nurse who works for ASIO on the side,' he said. 'Or wait—the Russians! We're talking about the Russians, aren't we? *Ha ha ha.*' Simmons really was having a wonderful time. He pushed his chair back and put one leg up on the desk—*plonk.* 'Seriously, though, Jimmy,' he said. 'Your thoughts?'

Constable James Hall stopped smiling and applied a look of concentration. 'Well, yeah,' he said. 'Of all the towns in Australia I guess he must've had a reason to sit down in this one.'

Simmons stared at Hall, nodding, as a thought came to him.

'We should probably check—' Hall began.

'We should check his fob pocket,' said Simmons.

38

Cora Franks was sitting with Therese Johnson at the counter of Cedar Valley Curios & Old Wares when Benny Miller, wearing a Royal Tavern T-shirt, stopped outside the big old antique store and looked in the window.

'That's her,' said Therese, who was perched on a stool facing the street with a cup of tea in her hands.

'Who?' said Cora, looking up from the little television.

'The new girl Tom has working at the Royal,' said Therese, as Benny entered the shop and began inspecting a dresser covered with crockery and decorative plates.

'Well, hello there,' said Cora loudly.

'Hi,' said Benny, giving a small wave, then she wandered around the front of the shop—inspecting a ceramic phrenology head and picking up a vase—while Therese looked her up and down, and was clearly displeased with what she saw.

•

Benny Miller's desire to visit Curios had arisen earlier that afternoon. So far she had seen it only through the window— on the night the man had died, and when she had walked up Valley Road and seen the closed sign hanging inside the door.

Even from the street though, she'd got a good sense of its charm. It was unlike the musty, claustrophobic places that Frank Miller had dragged her to, wedged so tightly with furniture that some heavy item would always have to be moved in order for some other item to be looked at. Curios looked spacious and quite lovely—and the dead man had been sitting up against its wide window, which Benny had certainly found interesting.

But given what Odette had said earlier that afternoon, that interest had become an acute fascination. That a man in Adelaide had died in the same fashion? And that her mother, Vivian Moon, had been intrigued by the case? How was it possible that Benny Miller had arrived in Cedar Valley in search of information about her mother on the very same day that a man had died in the same strange manner as some person from the 1940s? An unsolved mystery that had perplexed Vivian Moon?

Tom Boyd had offered some economical comments: 'It's just a bit ridiculous.'

And Odette had said, 'I *love* ridiculous! You know, Benny, I think Vivian sent me a letter about it. I remember her talking about it when we first met. And then it came up again when she was travelling, and she sent me this long letter with all the details. I'm going to dig it out. And I might just have to call Elsie Simmons.'

Benny had tingled with excitement. 'Can you tell me everything?' she said, more eagerly than she had intended.

'I'll tell you everything, honey,' Odette said, and just the sentence itself had felt like a gift to Benny Miller, standing behind the bar in her new T-shirt, her cheeks sore from smiling.

Later, she finished her shift and walked down Valley Road to Curios to look again at that spot where the dead man had sat slumped against the glass, and to thank Cora Franks for the photograph of her mother. She wondered if Cora might have a lot more to say.

But then here was this other woman sitting at the counter too, her red-dyed hair perched atop her head like a hat.

Benny smiled as she walked past Cora and the woman.

'How are you, Benny?' asked Cora.

'Good, thank you,' said Benny. 'Thank you for the banana bread. It's delicious.'

'You're welcome,' said Cora, and she winked at Benny. A wink, of all gauche things, and neither Benny nor Cora herself was quite sure why. Benny went along to the back of the shop, attracted by the fluoro cardboard signs of the book section. She crouched down in front of the bookshelves and looked through *Fiction*, where, among many other titles, there

were three copies of *The Power of One*. Then she pretended
to look through *Misc.* which was mainly Readers Digests and
books about craft.

But really she was wondering if the other woman might
leave soon, so she could mention the photograph to Cora, and
see what Cora might say. Cora seemed like a person who liked
to divulge. Had she known Vivian well? Were they friends?
And, on a different matter altogether, what about the man
who had sat down and died on the footpath? Benny wanted
to ask all these things, but she felt that she couldn't with the
other woman sitting there too.

Benny flipped through a book about wildflowers. She
could hear the sound of a soap opera coming from the television up behind the counter. Cora and the women were
drinking tea and watching it.

Eventually Benny put the book back and wandered back
past the counter, giving Cora a quick nod.

'See you again,' said Cora, and the other woman wasn't
even civil enough to smile.

•

'Tsk, tsk, tsk,' went Therese, as Benny Miller left the store.

'Oh, stop it,' said Cora Franks.

'She's Vivian Moon's daughter,' said Therese, as if being
Vivian Moon's daughter was the same as being a deviant
criminal.

'I *know*,' said Cora to Therese, who really was in a particularly bad mood, even for Therese.

'Why are you baking Vivian Moon's daughter banana bread?'

'Because she's staying next door in Odette Fisher's cottage,' said Cora. 'And I'm very neighbourly.'

Therese laughed at that, and Cora allowed herself to laugh too.

'Oh, I don't know—she looks like a lost puppy,' said Cora. 'You heard that Vivian died?'

'Yes I did, and I won't be crying for her,' said Therese. 'The way she went about when she lived here, waving her tits around? *Please*. And how about the way she treated you? Come on, Cora.'

'Yes, I remember,' said Cora, biting into a biscuit.

'Just because Freddy's so upstanding and you don't have to worry about those kinds of women,' Therese said.

'I thought Ed took you to the Riverside and showed you a good time?' Cora said. 'You said it had all been in your head.' Cora rippled with discomfort, and an abrupt image appeared in her mind: Ed Johnson thrusting away at Chicken Linda, her face like a beetroot.

'Yes, well,' said Therese. 'It better be all in my head.'

Then Therese looked so sad for a moment that Cora almost reached out to touch her. Cora wanted, just in that moment, to touch her cheek, to brush it with her thumb like she used to do with her own son when he was crying. But Therese was so prone to turning awful that the feeling of tenderness deserted Cora as quickly as it had arrived.

'If it's all in my head then at least I won't have to kill him,' said Therese, with a kind of furious humour. 'Or *her*.'

Cora sighed. 'Oh dear.'

'Did you know that in France, if you kill your husband because he's cheating on you, or if you kill the woman he's cheating with, you don't go to jail? It's called a *crime passionnel*,' said Therese, in a terrible French accent.

'Is that true?' asked Cora doubtfully.

'It's true,' said Therese. 'Because the French are sophisticated. And sometimes I think Ed should take me to Paris, not to the Riverside.'

Cora sipped her tea and stared at Therese, who really was an awful person. Earlier, when Cora had excitedly told Therese what Elsie had said—about the man who died in Adelaide—Therese hadn't cared an inch about it. How could she not care? Everyone else had cared. Therese had just stood in front of the mirror near the counter and fussed with her hair and she hadn't asked after Elsie either. And now she'd been outright rude to young Benny.

Cora's mind went to Benny now, that lost puppy. It was interesting that she had come in. Benny must know that Cora owned the store. Perhaps she wanted to talk? Maybe that photograph had upset her; Cora still wasn't sure if she should have slipped it into the tin like that. But in the end, she just couldn't help it. She could sense that Benny needed something, and perhaps Cora could assist her. And with Nathan having moved away, she so missed her son, he didn't often come to visit, and there was no one to cook for in that particular way a mother cooks for her child.

And then, of course, there was Therese, sour as a grape and ranting away.

'All that needs to happen is for someone to find out. The husband finds out, or the wife finds out. And that's it! Honestly, people get murdered *all the time* for going to bed with the wrong person. Not just in France. Everywhere. And you know what I think?' said Therese.

Cora didn't say anything.

'I think it serves them bloody right!' said Therese, and she smiled a truly frightening, truly maniacal kind of smile.

39

Detective Sergeant Anthony Simmons stood over his large wooden desk, hands on his hips, bent over and staring.

On the desk, upended from an archive box and now in a heaped pile of brown paper bags, of various sizes, was the clothing of the unknown man—items that bore a fresh kind of significance in light of the forty-five-year-old unparalleled mystery known as the Somerton Man.

Simmons's back hurt. He stood straight for a moment and twisted himself to the left and then to the right, and a noise emanated from his throat while he did that—'*nggghhh*,' he grunted—just like old Neville Simmons used to do when he had trouble with his muscles. Simmons winced at the pain, and he winced at the noise he had made; he was so disgusted with himself when he acted in any way like his father.

'Shirt in this bag, and that's the tie,' said Hall, who had upended the box and was sorting through the items. He looked inside the paper bag with the tie in it. 'This looks identical to the Somerton Man's tie in the photos. How did he get one the same?'

Franklin, sitting forward in a chair, shrugged.

'Jumper,' Hall continued. 'This is the jacket and . . . here we go: trousers.'

Constable Hall opened the bag and very carefully removed the brown trousers, slow and delicate, as if they were an injured marsupial. Then he held them up by the waistband, a prize exhibit, for Simmons and Franklin to see.

'You say you did check the pockets already?' Simmons asked.

'Oh yeah, we did, boss. We found the tickets and combs and stuff in those main pockets. Maybe we didn't check the fob pocket properly, though. What is a fob pocket?' asked Franklin.

Hall laid the trousers on the desk and looked at them, puzzled. 'It's usually here,' he said, pointing. 'You know that little extra pocket on a pair of jeans?'

'Oh, *that* pocket; I never understood that pocket,' said Franklin.

Hall stared at the trousers. 'These pants don't have one,' he said, looking disappointed.

'Let me see,' said Simmons, jostling Hall out of the way. He picked up the trousers and examined them, squinting at the main pockets and looking above them and around them, at the place he too expected a fob pocket to be. He put his hands inside the main pockets and felt around—they were empty. Turning the trousers around, he checked the pocket at the back. Then he looked at the front again, and unzipped the fly, and looked on either side of that. 'Hmm,' said Simmons as he turned his attention to the inside of the trousers, running his finger around the waistband.

'There,' he said. On the inside of the waistband, just to the right of the fly, was a tiny hidden pocket.

'Huh,' said Gussy.

Simmons put a finger inside the pocket. 'Well it's easy to miss, I'll give you that,' he said, looking down intently as he felt around.

Hall stood still, waiting.

Then, using his thumb and his forefinger, Simmons carefully extracted a tiny piece of paper rolled up tight like a cylinder. It had been wedged right down at the bottom of the hidden pocket.

'Well, fuck me,' said Simmons, smiling, as he held it up. It looked like a cigarette.

Franklin and Hall watched as he unrolled the paper with his meaty hands.

'What does it say?' asked Hall breathlessly. 'Does it say "Tamam Shud"?'

Simmons stared at the paper. A bemused look passed across his face. Then he turned the paper around so Franklin and Hall could see.

It did not say 'Tamam Shud', and it was not torn from some book of ancient Persian poems.

Written in capital letters, printed small and neat—was a single word: *GIFT*.

40

After her short visit to Curios, Benny went up Valley Road to the grocery store, where she bought garlic, spaghetti, a can of tomatoes and a jar of olives. The woman at the register with the enormous bosom introduced herself this time—she was Betsy—and she made some small talk with Benny about the weather.

'It was very dry last year, you know, and that was awful. Farmers lost livestock it was so dry. But this year's been better. You notice it's greener.'

'It is,' said Benny, holding a can of tomatoes. 'It is quite green.'

'You're Benny, aren't you?' asked Betsy.

'Yes, I am.'

'I thought so. You can't hide anything in Cedar Valley, love. Just cooking for yourself, are you? I try to do that too on most nights. It's a good way of being nice to yourself, isn't it, to cook yourself a meal.'

Benny had never thought about it like that, but she agreed that it was. Then—seeing Benny's T-shirt—Betsy made a positive comment about the Royal Tavern and said she expected to see Benny up there sometime, and that Betsy would be the one having a schnitzel.

'That'll be me,' said Betsy. 'Have you had the schnitzel?'

This conversation, which Benny was quite enjoying, ended when a man in blue coveralls, arms covered in engine grease, came in to buy a can of soup, and Betsy greeted him warmly.

'See you, Betsy,' said Benny.

'Hooroo, love,' said Betsy, and then: 'Now, Morry, might I sell you a bar of soap as well?' And Benny walked out to the sound of the man, Morry, laughing.

Benny turned left at the corner outside the grocery store and walked past the weedy vacant lot towards her street. She was hungry. It was a hot afternoon, with no breeze, and she walked the distance to Wiyanga Cresent quickly to get out of the sun. Bees hovered over the flowers of the bottlebrush tree on the corner, and parked cars gleamed brightly. Benny crossed the street to the green cottage and let herself in.

A thought was trying to find her, she could feel it, and she went straight to the bedroom where she kept her box of photos. She emptied the contents onto the bed—photographs and letters and envelopes of pressed flowers—and she sat beside the pile, sifting through it until she had collected all the pictures with her mother in them.

There was her favourite photo of Vivian Moon at the table with Odette, empty glasses around them. The background was difficult to make out, as it was mostly out of focus, but Benny saw it now as she hadn't seen it before. The windows behind them were the windows of the Royal Tavern. Benny stared at the picture and she smiled. What a satisfying feeling this was: to recognise something new in the picture she had stared at so often. She turned the picture over to see the *1971* written on the back. The year before Benny was born. The year that Vivian Moon lived in Cedar Valley.

Benny looked again at the photo Cora Franks had slipped into the tin with the banana bread. All those ladies at book club. Benny saw now, in the photo, the woman who had been at Curios earlier, sitting up at the counter with Cora. There she was in the book club photo, twenty years younger, an attractive woman with the same coiffured hair. Benny turned that photo over too, and read the date again: *1971*.

Then she set all the other photos in a line.

There were Vivian and Odette at the fence in the field. And Vivian and Frank in the back garden at Rozelle, Frank holding tiny Benny in his arms. Another showed Benny on her eighth birthday, when Vivian had made a rare appearance. Benny was sitting next to a cake—a cheap-looking, store-bought cake—and Vivian had her hand on Benny's shoulder with the awkwardness of a stranger. Benny looked at herself in the picture, and at her imposter of a mother, and she pressed her eyes shut, filled with unease.

But the thought that had been trying to find her flickered again, and Benny opened her eyes and remembered a different photograph: the one of Vivian Moon standing at a shop counter.

It must still be in the box.

She fished around and found it and pulled it out, and then she sat on the bed and stared at the picture.

Vivian Moon looked the same as she did in the other photos from 1971. She was standing by what Benny now recognised as the counter at Cedar Valley Curios & Old Wares. Vivian was smiling, holding a cup of tea, and looking very much like she worked there.

41

'So he was on his way in to Curios to buy a present,' said Constable Gussy Franklin, leaning forward in his chair, as the ceiling fan went around and around.

'Sure,' said Detective Sergeant Simmons, still holding the little piece of paper that had *GIFT* written on it. 'Wouldn't that be funny—if Cora Franks was right about that. She's been saying it: that he must've been on his way in to buy something.'

'And Terri from the Coiffure?' said Franklin. 'She was sure he was on his way to Curios because he looked so *antique-y*. Obviously the ladies are way ahead of us.'

Franklin was smiling, and Simmons chuckled, but Constable James Hall looked serious.

'If he just needed to buy a gift, why would he keep a note about it rolled up in the secret pocket?' he asked.

'More to the point, Jimmy,' said Simmons, 'how does a man buy a gift when he doesn't have any *fucking money* on him?'

Hall winced.

'Oh, yeah,' said Gussy Franklin. 'Good one, boss.'

Simmons wiped sweat off his brow with the sleeve of his shirt and let out an irritated sigh.

'Because he's copycatting the Somerton Man, so he needs *something* in his secret pocket,' said Hall cautiously.

'Yeah, maybe he couldn't find a copy of the Persian poetry book,' said Gussy Franklin. 'Maybe he wasted enough time finding the right tie.'

'Ha!' went Simmons.

'But he's gone to all that trouble,' said Jimmy Hall. 'He's remembered every detail about the Somerton Man and he's got all the same things in his pockets. It's not like he's someone who needs to remind himself to buy a gift, or steal a gift, or whatever. It's got to be more like the Somerton Man's note. Like a message. You know—for us.'

Simmons was perched on the edge of the desk now. 'That's sweet, Jimmy,' he said. 'You think he wrote us a little note?'

'You know what I mean, boss,' said Constable Hall.

And it was true; Detective Sergeant Simmons did know what he meant. It was possible that a methodical kind of person *would* write themselves a reminder note, just as another way of being methodical. But it did seem odd that a man such as this, a meticulous kind of person, would even need a reminder. And if he wouldn't write *himself* a note, and the note was indeed some kind of message—a deliberate clue—then what did it mean? And who was it intended for?

'What does "Tamam Shud" mean, anyway?' asked Franklin. 'I mean, I know it means "finished", but does that mean the Somerton Man killed himself?'

'That's what people thought,' said Hall. 'My mate says it never became a proper homicide investigation because most people assumed he killed himself and that "Tamam Shud" was his suicide note. But that doesn't explain why he checked his suitcase in at the railway station, or why he tossed the book in someone else's car. If he didn't want anyone to find it, why wouldn't he put it in a bin? And if he did want someone to find it, why didn't he just keep it with him?'

Gussy Franklin nodded.

'I guess it's possible that someone else could've put the note in his pocket,' said Hall.

'Oh, mate, that'd be a bit tricky,' said Franklin.

'But what about before he got dressed?' said Hall.

Franklin puffed out a lungful of air, and Detective Sergeant Simmons got up from the edge of his desk and sat down in his chair. The window was open and hot air came in—it was a blistering day—and Simmons could feel the sweat trickling down his sides, and under his shoulderblades and, to his great discomfort, on the insides of his thighs.

Silence ensued for a few minutes, while he tilted his head back to look at the ceiling and think, and Franklin and Hall looked over their papers. Simmons lifted a thick arm and wiped his brow with the back of his hand.

'You see this?' said Franklin, tapping a page with his finger. 'Guess what they found in the stomach of the Somerton Man?'

'What?' asked Hall.

'A pasty,' said Franklin. 'He ate a pasty!'

'No wonder our guy really wanted a pasty,' said Hall.

Simmons looked up at the boys for a moment—a pasty?—then he shook his head and went back to contemplating the ceiling, his mind swimming with information, all of it peculiar and competing for his attention.

The blonde woman who looked like a soap star; Simmons thought about her. She had been into Curios. She had the shakes, whatever that meant. And she had been looking at something to buy—what was it? Cora Franks had been in that morning and she'd talked to Hall and Franklin.

Simmons sat upright again. 'What about the blonde? Did she buy anything at Curios?'

'Ah . . . no,' said Franklin. He picked up his statement book and found the appropriate page. 'Cora Franks said she was in there for about fifteen minutes, and she looked at watches. She tried on a few with gold bands, but she didn't make a purchase.'

'Hmm,' said Simmons. 'Gold watches. Our guy wasn't wearing a watch. No wedding ring and no watch.'

Simmons thought for a moment about watches. He thought about antiques in general—watches, clothing, and whatever else Cora Franks traded in—and he glanced back at a piece of the fax paper that had lit a spark of curiosity somewhere in the recesses of his consciousness. Simmons picked up the fax, scanned it again, and then he got up slowly to prod at a large paper bag which contained smaller plastic bags within it, each holding an item found in their dead man's pockets.

'Right now I'm wondering more about the combs,' said Detective Sergeant Anthony Simmons, picking up the relevant bag and looking into it.

'What about them?' said Hall.

'Well . . .' Simmons held the fax in one hand and a clear plastic property bag in the other. 'Our guy had the exact same things in his pockets as the Somerton Man, right? He had the cigarettes, the half-packet of Juicy Fruit, the matches, the bus ticket, the train ticket and the combs.'

'Yeah,' said Hall.

'But the Somerton Man had two combs. That's what the inquest report says. He had two. And look . . .' Simmons held up the bag. 'Our guy had three combs. One, two, *three*. So what's with the extra comb?'

42

Benny Miller was in the kitchen making pasta sauce and listening to the radio when somebody knocked at the front door of the green cottage.

It startled Benny, who was deep in thought and not expecting a visitor. But perhaps in some way, after visiting Curios, she did expect to hear from Cora Franks. Funny old Cora, she was such a pushy person. The way she had made her advances already—barging in with food and secreting a photograph in the cake tin. Benny Miller found this behaviour so unusual, so *forward*, and yet Cora Franks produced in her a strange kind of compassion. Why was that? Benny had no idea, but she walked down the hall, almost smiling to herself, thinking about the awkward wink Cora had given her from behind the counter at Curios. She was sure it would be her now, and opening the door Benny decided she would invite her in.

'As I was knocking I realised I probably should have called first. But then, this is the reality, isn't it? People just pop in when you live in the country.'

It was Odette Fisher—and Bessel, who trotted in past Benny and went on down the hall towards the kitchen.

'Hi,' said Benny, blushing a little with surprise.

'Hello, Benny,' said Odette. 'I hope you don't mind. I needed to come get something.'

'Of course.'

And Odette too walked in past Benny as if she owned the place, which she did.

'Oh, that smells good. Are you cooking?'

'I'm making some pasta,' said Benny. 'I was so hungry I didn't want to wait till dinner.'

Benny followed along as Odette went into the kitchen and put a big cloth shopping bag on the counter and she watched as Odette took out a plastic bag with greens in it, and a carton of eggs.

'This is for you from the garden. Just some spinach and herbs. And these are from my girls.' Odette got a bowl and set the eggs in it, and put the empty carton back in her cloth bag. There were some rented videos in the bag, and Benny could see the cover of *Bagdad Cafe*.

'Thank you,' said Benny. She was pleased to have the eggs, since she had eaten the first lot already; and she was pleased to have the herbs, because she could put some with her pasta.

But mostly she was pleased to see Odette, and to have her here in the house. A sense of comfort and safety emanated from Odette Fisher, like warmth from a fire.

'The house feels good with you in it, Benny,' said Odette, glancing around the kitchen. And then: 'So. I went home to look for Vivian's letters. I thought about these two dead men, in their matching outfits, all the way home! It's just *so* unusual, isn't it? Part of me is laughing at myself, and the other part is just desperate to investigate.'

'Did you find the letters?' asked Benny, who had been thinking about the dead men also. She had been slicing garlic and thinking about them; and she had been opening a can of tomatoes and thinking about her mother. Then she had been stirring the sauce and staring out the window, wondering about the photographs.

'Well, no. That's why I'm here. I think they might be in the shed.' Odette walked out the double doors and down into the back garden, shooing Bessel from under the rosemary, where he appeared to be eating something from the dirt.

The sound of someone hosing came over from next door.

'Hi, Fred!' Odette said.

'Is that you, Odette?' said an invisible Fred from over the paling fence.

'I'm just here with Benny,' said Odette loudly. 'You well?'

'Very well,' said Fred, and Odette said she was glad to hear it. Then she turned to Benny. 'You can come and have a look if you like.'

Benny went back inside and turned the stove down and then followed Odette down the garden, Benny filled with a sudden anxiety that Odette would immediately realise she'd been snooping in there.

Odette opened the shed door and stepped inside.

'Possum poo,' she said, looking at the shelving and then into the washbasin. 'He must still be around. Is that a new towel in there?'

'Oh, yes,' said Benny. 'I thought it might be a bit softer. I've left him a few things—some fruit, and then some cashews this morning. He's eaten all of it.'

'Aren't you adorable,' said Odette as she went towards the high shelf at the back, where the cardboard boxes were. She chose the one on the right, heaving it down and setting it on the concrete floor. Dust rose up around her ankles.

It was the box of old bills and bank statements that Benny had looked in already. Odette sifted through the papers on top, then started lifting them out and piling them on the floor around the box. She pulled out the calendar from 1980.

'God, 1980! That was a while ago. My house up on the mountain wasn't finished properly till 1980. Before that it was just a shack and, when Lloyd left, I moved back here to town for a couple of years while I had the plumbing and electricity put in. And while I got over Lloyd.' Odette said this in her serene way. 'He never wanted any amenities. Sometimes I think he was a true transcendentalist, old Lloyd. "The tonic of wildness," as he liked to say. But after he left, I didn't want to live that rough on my own.'

Benny watched as Odette got deeper and deeper into the cardboard box, and the piles around it grew bigger.

'It looks like I just tipped the contents of the kitchen dresser in here. I think I must have. But I did keep letters in the dresser. Oh, here we go.' And from the bottom of the box Odette pulled a thick wad of envelopes and postcards, bound together with an elastic band.

Benny blinked at them and the wintry feeling began to rise inside her, a cold wind in her chest. To think that Vivian's letters had been sitting there in the shed this whole time. So near.

Odette crammed the piles of papers back into the box, and put the box back up on the shelf. Then the two women went back across the garden to the house.

Bessel settled inside the back doorway, surveying the garden, and Benny went to the kitchen and stirred the sauce. She filled a large pot with water, and lit another burner on the stove.

'Would you like some pasta?' she asked Odette.

'I'd love some pasta,' said Odette, and she slipped her shoes off and sat down at the kitchen table and put the pile of letters in front of her.

Benny, hopeless with curiosity, took oregano and parsley from the plastic bag and began to chop them on a wooden board.

'It's upsetting for you,' said Odette.

'I'm okay,' said Benny.

'I don't mean to be lighthearted about this,' said Odette.

Benny turned to Odette now, leaning against the bench. 'I'm okay,' she said more firmly.

'It's just, I know you want to know, Benny; I can see that, and I wrestle with it. I keep thinking: who am I to hide things from you, when you want to know? So this whole thing with the dead man—or the dead *men*—I mean, it's so bizarre. And it's a distraction. But I wonder if it's a good way in for you. It was something that Vivian was interested in, and now you're interested in it too. It's a nice connection, in a funny sort of way. Except for the fact that it's so . . . morbid.'

Benny smiled, and Odette did too.

Then Benny started to laugh and Odette, well, she didn't just laugh. Odette Fisher cracked up like Benny had never heard her before. What a glorious laugh she had! Odette laughed and laughed, her eyes crinkled up like paper, until tears ran down her cheeks. The two of them in the kitchen—Benny Miller and Odette Fisher—they shrieked with laughter like old friends.

'Psalm Twenty-Three, verse one: *The Lord is my shepherd, I lack nothing*,' said the ancient voice of the man on the radio, as the laughter of the women abated.

'What *are* you listening to?' asked Odette, wiping away a tear.

'Odette,' said Benny, suddenly serious, 'did my mum work at Curios?'

43

Elsie Simmons was sitting in her living room, listening to her radio, when Detective Sergeant Anthony Simmons arrived at her house.

'It's just me, Mum,' he said, opening the screen door. 'Don't get up.'

'Oh, good,' said Elsie, and got up.

She shuffled into the kitchen and put the kettle on, and Tony was struck by the sight of her meagreness. There was nothing of her. And she was so bent forward now, it was as if she'd permanently dropped something on the carpet and was about to pick it up. Tony could barely look at her. He went to the fridge and put a bottle of milk in.

'Thanks, love, I needed milk. Do you want tea?'

Tony nodded and the two of them were soon sitting in the living room next to the fan, and Tony wondered why his mother had the living room so dim these days, when it was so bright outside. She sat in this room with the curtains drawn and one lamp on, and it broke Tony's heart that a once-sunny woman would choose now to sit in the dark.

'How're you feeling, Mum?' he asked.

'I'm good, love. Just fine. How was your day at the station?'

Tony Simmons had left Franklin and Hall at the station with their fax paper and notepads and property bags.

They had gone around in several circles about the significance of a certain comb, they'd posited various theories, and Hall had suggested they consult an expert in antique hair care products.

When they'd run out of ideas, Hall and Franklin returned to their desks and Simmons brooded in his office for a while before rising and going to the door. 'I'm gonna head over and ask Mum a few questions,' he said.

'Sure thing, boss,' said Franklin. 'We just heard from the sketcher. He'll be here in the morning.'

'Very good,' said Simmons, and he'd left the station and driven the short distance to Elsie Simmons's house in the bright sunshine.

'Why's it so dark in here?' he asked his mother now. 'Should I open a curtain?'

'I like it this way,' said Elsie. 'It's easier on my eyes.'

'Mum, why didn't you ever mention the Somerton Man to me?'

Elsie laughed. She sat there with her hands resting gently in her lap, such a neatly comported woman she was, and she laughed softly at her son.

'The Somerton Man? Everyone wants to talk about the Somerton Man! And I don't know, Tony. I didn't not tell you on purpose, it just never came up. I've not said much to you about Adelaide. It's a place I'd rather forget in a lot of ways.'

'Because of grandfather?' asked Tony, who had the vaguest inkling that Elsie's father—his grandfather—had not been a good kind of father. And it had always struck Simmons, even if it was something he didn't care to dwell on for any stretch of time, how strange it was that his mother had endured such a father, and yet went on to choose a husband like Neville Simmons.

Elsie sipped her tea, and a look passed across her face—a blank and bottomless expression—and Tony knew not to ask any more questions about his grandfather, who he had never so much as met.

'I was just reading some articles at work. There was one about the Beaumont children. I remember when that happened.'

'Oh yes,' said Elsie. 'And it happened on the same beach, just about; it's really just one long stretch of beach. That was a long time after I left, though. Mum was so upset, and we talked about it a bit on the phone, but it was just too awful.

I don't think anyone *enjoyed* talking about the Beaumont children.'

'I read in the article that before she disappeared, Jane Beaumont was last seen buying pasties,' said Tony. 'And did you know the Somerton Man had a pasty in his stomach? That's a pretty weird coincidence. And you know what I think about coincidences.' Detective Sergeant Anthony Simmons, in issues pertaining to law enforcement—or anything else for that matter—believed there was no such thing as a coincidence.

'Oh, well, you're not from Adelaide,' said Elsie. 'I'd say if you opened the stomach of most South Australians in those days you'd have found a pasty.'

'Is that right?' said Tony.

'Oh, yes. Cornish immigrants! They brought their pasties,' said Elsie. 'We had the Cornish, we had the Germans. Did you know they had a German newspaper in Adelaide at one time? There were that many Germans.'

Tony was reminded sharply then of how savvy his mother was. How knowledgeable. After Neville Simmons died she would host dinner parties with her book club friends and there was no one better at Trivial Pursuit than Elsie. Elsie Simmons, who never forgot a face. And now, to have that memory and knowledge fading. Tony looked across at Elsie, in her housedress and slippers, with respect and regret.

'Do you remember a woman called Vivian Moon?' asked Tony.

Elsie looked taken aback. 'I do,' she said. 'Do you?'

'Should I?' said Tony Simmons, who'd had the name Vivian Moon floating around in his consciousness since hearing Ed and Fred talk about her at the Royal on Saturday. The name Vivian Moon, it meant something to him, but he sure as hell couldn't work out why.

'She was Cora's neighbour, a long time ago, when you were maybe twelve or thirteen. Do you remember? You and I came down from Clarke a few times to stay with Cora and Fred of a weekend. We'd have a meeting of book club and sometimes we'd socialise. Viv lived next door with Odette. You know Odette Fisher—she lives up in the bush now. Very fine woman, very smart. But Viv. Well, she was smart, too, but quite inscrutable. She was very . . . *free*. Maybe too free.'

Memories were coming back to Tony. He did stay at Cora Franks's house—he had forgotten they would sleep over—and Fred Franks was always so good to him. Freddy would let Tony sit in the shed while he worked on things, and did he take him fishing one time? Cora and Fred had a son, Nathan, a real wuss of a kid.

'Why would I remember Vivian?' he asked.

'She looked after you once,' said Elsie, 'while Cora and Fred and I went out to a dinner party. And to be honest with you, Tony, I regret leaving you with her.'

There was something sparking in Tony's mind now.

'She was a gorgeous woman to look at, but not very maternal, I suppose. And I don't think Odette knew what was going on, because she was up at her bush house a lot and Viv was in the little cottage by herself most of the time. But she had men come to see her. Just, you know, a lot of men. Married men maybe, I don't know. She was a different kind of person to me.'

And now Tony Simmons did remember.

That beautiful woman, the illicit essence of her beauty; and that strange, artistic house. Was that the house next door to Cora's? It was. Was that woman in his memory Vivian Moon? She must have been. It was all there, in his peripheries, and it stirred him up inside.

Simmons moved around in the armchair, disconcerted by his feelings.

'Oh, well; no law against it,' he said.

'I suppose not,' said Elsie. 'But I must say I'm glad you don't remember her. Are you okay, Tony? You look a bit funny.'

'I'm good,' said Tony Simmons, and he arranged himself in his chair, unsuccessfully, before putting his cup down and standing up and walking through to the lean-to, where a sliding door opened out to the garden.

'I might do the lawn while I'm here,' he said, separating the curtains so the light came in.

44

Freddy Franks was out back in the fernery when Cora got home, misting the maidenhairs with a spray bottle.

'You're doing it,' said Cora from the back pavers.

'Well you've been on at me,' said Fred, who wasn't normally a man to employ a spray bottle.

It was true that she'd been on at him. Cora felt that Freddy didn't pay enough delicate attention, in general, and it had become something of a disagreement.

'Did you do the ones in the pebble tray?' she asked.

'Just about to,' said Fred, and he walked towards her across the grass, and they smiled at each other on the back pavers, before both going into the house.

Cora got some chops out of the freezer and set them in a bowl of water in the sink. She took her shoes off in the bedroom and put them on the shoe rack. Then it took a while to remove her jewellery: she put her brooch and her earrings in a small wooden box of brooches and earrings; she hung her necklaces on the wall-mounted necklace hanger; and she took off her extra rings and her watch, putting the rings in a silver tin and placing her watch alongside her other watches, which sat in a row on a small velvet cushion.

Cora looked at herself in the mirror on the vanity then and brushed her hair with her soft-bristled brush.

'Therese says she wants to murder Ed,' she said to Fred from the bedroom.

She could hear Fred softly squirting the spray bottle at the houseplants.

'I would think there's plenty of women who want to murder Ed,' said Fred from the living room. 'Probably their husbands want to murder him too.'

Cora brushed her hair more than was necessary—she liked the feeling—and she stared at herself, and the deep wrinkles around her eyes. They were like ravines now, and she stood up abruptly, taking the shop copy of *From Russia with Love* from her work bag and plopping it on her bedside table.

'Did you find Vivian Moon attractive?' she said loudly.

Fred laughed and kept on with his spraying, and Cora went out to the living room and stood in the archway, leaning against the edge.

'Did you?' she said.

'I guess,' said Fred. 'She was a good-looking woman. That wasn't lost on me.'

'Did Ed sleep with her?' asked Cora.

'Oh, Cor, I wouldn't know. I'm sure he'd like some of us to think he did.'

'Did you sleep with her?' asked Cora.

Fred stood up straight, holding the bottle. He was so tall when he stood up straight like that. The spider plant, the one on the stand, looked tiny beside him.

'Are you serious?' he said. 'No. Of course I didn't. I could see she was good-looking because I have eyes, Cor, but she wasn't my cup of tea. And I have never done anything like that and you know it.'

Cora went over and sat on the couch. Then she shifted her legs up and lay down, flat on her back, and she looked up at the ceiling.

'I do know that,' she said quietly.

Fred came over and stood beside her, and Cora drew her legs up towards her chin, so he could sit down. And so he sat down, and then she extended her legs across his lap.

'Are you having a hard time with Therese?' asked Fred.

'Sometimes I don't know why I'm friends with her,' said Cora.

'Proximity?' said Fred.

'Yes, I guess that's it.'

Fred put a hand around one of her bare feet.

'What do you think people think of me?'

Fred made a little snorting sound. 'I don't really know,' he said.

Cora put her hands up on the mound of her belly and fiddled with her wedding ring—the one ring she never took off.

'I don't want us to die, Freddy,' said Cora. 'Especially not you. Especially not Nathan.'

Fred breathed in and out of his nose calmly and looked at her, his wife.

'Why doesn't Nathan visit more? Why doesn't he tell me anything, Fred? He never tells me anything.'

Fred was quiet on this for a moment, as if unsure of how to address it. 'Maybe it's just his nature,' he said.

'Sometimes I think people think I'm ridiculous. Do you think that's what they think? I catch myself sometimes, in the middle of talking to someone, and I think: what am I even going on about? Do you ever feel like that?' asked Cora.

'No,' said Fred.

'Well. I just think that people look at me sometimes and they think: uh-oh, here comes Cora. They think: here's that loudmouth. And they don't feel happy to see me. They probably wish it was someone else. Apart from Therese—she comes to see me. But Therese doesn't ever ask me a question! Did you know that, Fred? She comes in and she talks about herself the whole time and she never even asks me one thing about *me*. And then there's everyone else. I think they see me and, well, I do act ridiculously. Do you think I act ridiculously, Freddy? And that they think I'm just this loud and picky person? They think I'm ridiculous.'

Cora closed her eyes and Fred held Cora's foot on the couch, and he rubbed it while she lay there.

'I think Therese's hair is ridiculous,' she said. 'Nobody wears it like that anymore.'

'Does that make you feel better?' asked Fred.

'No,' said Cora plaintively, and she was silent for a while before she said, 'How do you think Vivian died?'

Fred sat there with his big hand around her toes.

'Well, I don't imagine she was murdered, if that's what you're thinking,' he said. 'Come on, Cor. Why don't we have some of those fried chip potatoes with the chops? Those crispy ones you like that I do on the barbie?'

45

Next door, Benny had made a delicious pasta and Odette really thought it was very good. Benny had sprinkled chopped olives and fresh herbs on top, and she set the table somewhat nervously. Odette Fisher seemed to eat so expertly that Benny found herself adjusting her table manners in order to mimic her. They had a salad made of leaves from Odette's garden, and at one point Odette hummed along to 'Unchained Melody' on the radio. Nothing pleased Benny more than having Odette there, and Odette thinking the pasta was very good.

Benny didn't have any wine—she regretted this, she must get some—but she offered Odette some beer and Odette accepted. Benny poured two glasses from a longneck she'd bought after her first shift at the Royal Tavern. Their conversation, after Benny asked Odette about Vivian Moon working at Curios, had gone like this:

'At Curios?' Odette said, surprised.

'Yes, did she work there?'

Odette sat at the table and put a hand to her mouth, thinking. She didn't say anything for several moments and Benny just stood there waiting. Then Odette took her hand away and looked up and said, 'I think she *did*. I'd forgotten that. Maybe Cora was being neighbourly and offered her work. I can't quite remember how it came about. But yes, you're right, she did work there.'

'Right,' said Benny, disappointed in some way by the information.

'Oh, Benny. I wasn't *not* telling you. I just forgot. I think maybe it didn't go well for some reason, because it certainly didn't last very long. Maybe only a few weeks or so. Did Cora tell you this? She would obviously know more than me.'

'I haven't spoken to Cora about it,' said Benny.

'I guess Cora and some of the other women in town— Cora's friends—they didn't really like Vivian all that much,' said Odette. 'I think she rubbed some people the wrong way.'

'But she was in the book club,' said Benny, holding her glass of beer. 'She was in Cora's book club with you.'

'That was because I invited her, but she didn't fit in very well. Some of those women are very conservative. They can be friendly, and I do like a lot of them. I like Elsie Simmons very much, and Mary Anne. But some of the others weren't very welcoming to Vivian. And then, later on, some of us defected. But it wasn't because we didn't like the people; we just got sick of reading schmaltzy books.' Odette smiled.

'Why didn't they like her?' asked Benny.

'Oh, I don't know. Vivian . . . The more I think about Vivian, the more I wonder about the way she presented things. Maybe she didn't always present things as they were. Do you know what I mean? Maybe she just never told me the negative things. But the more I think about her doing that, the more I think that's what everybody does. People present themselves in the way they want to be seen. And maybe Vivian was just better at it than most people.'

'Oh,' said Benny, and she sat there with this idea: that Vivian was someone who made herself out to be a certain way, when she wasn't that way at all.

Bessel got up, stretched, and then walked over stiffly and sat down again next to Benny's chair.

'I'd forgotten about her working at Curios. Probably because she never talked about it. And, you know, I was quite distracted at the time. I do remember her working at the chemist, though, she talked about that. She'd go on about Dieter Bernbaum and how weird he was; she'd catch him staring at her from behind his little pill shelf. I always found it odd that it didn't bother her—I would have told him to bugger off—but she was just fine about things like that. She worked there at the chemist until she went back to Frank.'

Benny poured some more of the beer into Odette's glass, and then she poured the remainder into her own.

'Didn't Cora ever talk to you about Mum? About why the ladies didn't like her?' Benny asked.

'Oh, God no. I mean Cora does likes to talk, but she'd never talk to me about Vivian. She would have known not to! I would've defended Vivian Moon till the cows came home.' Odette smiled and lifted her glass. 'We didn't do a cheers.'

The two women clinked their beers together.

'Cheers,' said Odette.

'To my strange mother,' said Benny.

'To Vivian,' said Odette, and then she reached across the table and rubbed Benny's shoulder. Her hand was strong and firm and she kept it there for a moment, and it wasn't so much the thought of Vivian—of commemorating Vivian—but the feeling of Odette's comforting hand that made the smallest of tears come into Benny's eyes and well there.

'Who can tell why people like other people?' said Odette. 'This is a small town, Benny. It was 1970.'

'1971,' said Benny.

'Then it was 1971—in a small town,' said Odette. 'The women around here, especially back then, they would have been threatened by a woman like Vivian. She was smart and she'd travelled and she'd talk about women's lib and the Sydney Push and all that stuff. I'm sure those ladies all thought their husbands would fall in love with her.'

'Do you think they did?' asked Benny, a grain of pride in her now with this fresh image of her mother. Her smart and worldly mother.

'Oh, I don't know. Probably,' said Odette.

'Is that what happened with Lloyd?' asked Benny. The question had come out before she had time to consider it. Perhaps the glass of beer had loosened her inhibitions. What an inconsiderate question it was; how hurtful and insulting.

'Oh,' said Odette, taken aback. 'No. Lloyd wasn't interested in Vivian like that.'

Benny felt herself sink inside with regret. She looked across at this woman who she respected so much. Did she look hurt or insulted? Benny couldn't tell. Odette merely sat serenely, wearing the look of self-possession that Benny was so fond of.

'I'm sorry,' said Benny. 'I just—I know you weren't close with her anymore.'

Odette sipped at her beer, swallowed and nodded. 'No,' she said. 'We weren't close anymore. But that had nothing to do with Lloyd, honey, and I don't mind you asking if it did.'

Benny shifted in her chair. The kitchen was aglow with afternoon light, streaming in the double doors that led to the garden.

'You know, Benny,' said Odette, 'meeting you and getting to know you a little—it's helped me. It makes me sad in a lot of ways, about how things could have been, and I've found myself going over that in my mind, in the way people do. But it's helped me to understand what happened—all this stuff that's bothered me for such a long time now. It's difficult to explain, and I'll explain it better when it feels more settled. But it is becoming a little clearer to me now, after all these years, what happened with Vivian.'

46

Tony Simmons lay in his bed that evening, while Jenny read stories to the girls in the next room, and he was flooded with uncomfortable feelings, and memories that he had always wished would go away.

Jenny's voice was muffled and he could hear his youngest, Dawn, asking, 'Why, Mumma? Why?' as she was so prone to ask of everything.

Tony lay there and had visions of himself as a boy. Young, small Tony Simmons. Jenny found the childhood pictures of him so funny—that he was such a twig of a kid, compared to the big man he became.

But Jenny didn't know a lot of things and she didn't know that Simmons spent his teenage years making sure he got bigger. He ate loads. He lifted heavy weights. He ran and boxed and played footy, aggressive in his every pursuit, and he ate more. He was a hulk by twenty and Elsie Simmons lamented it. 'I can hardly get my arms around you!' Elsie would say.

For before Simmons was big, he was a particularly small and defenceless child. His chest was sunken, his legs not much thicker than their bones. And his voice, birdlike and sweet, so high-pitched that he was often picked on.

But that wasn't the worst thing in the world, to be picked on by other kids. The worst thing in the world was to be picked on by his father, Neville Simmons, who would sneer at Tony's curly hair and thin body. 'You look like a girl. Are you a little girl?'

Tony tried to keep his distance when Nev was in a cutting mood—and of course that wasn't always. Neville Simmons was the elected mayor of the Gather Region. So Elsie Simmons would duck and smile in public and, in private, Tony would hear the icy sounds of Neville's scolding. How Nev kept his voice at such an even pitch while uttering his vile rebukes was somehow more terrifying to Tony than outright violence. The seething tension of it, so palpable—and then something of Elsie's would inevitably be broken. Neville would neatly smash an heirloom, or a new perfume he'd treated her to at the Clarke Plaza. Over the years, every piece of Elsie's mother's tea set, so prized by her, was shattered one by one. Neville Simmons was such a controlling and punitive man.

But Elsie was a tough old thing. She would sweep up pieces of porcelain without a word. And on bad nights she would tuck Tony up in bed as early as possible to keep him out of the way. Twice she made her son a morning promise that they'd leave, only to lose her resolve by the afternoon and be all smiles by the evening.

But Elsie didn't know what went on when she wasn't home. She didn't know and Tony never told her. What could he say? That he too endured Nev's precise and brutal humiliations? Like the time Tony, aged nine, missed the toilet and left some droplets on the seat. Nev took him into the yard and forced Tony to drink from the hose. He made Tony undress and wait by the back fence until he was ready to pee again, and then he made Tony urinate on his own bare feet as some kind of lesson.

It felt like all afternoon that they'd stood there in the cold yard—Nev in his suit and tie, thin Tony naked—waiting for the water to go through Tony's little body.

Simmons lay now on his bed, a grown man, remembering the warm indignity of his own urine as it splashed on his toes and seeped under his feet on the bricks.

Knock knock knock.

From the next room, knocking came through the wall, and then the quiet sound of waiting.

This was a game the girls liked to play. And even though Tony felt so nauseous that he might be sick, lying there in his memories, he lifted his arm up and knocked back.

Knock knock knock, he went, and hysterics came through the wall. The girls were squealing and Jenny was laughing too.

Tony smiled.

He closed his eyes and listened to the girls and Jenny laughing together, and it was nice. But then the thoughts of Vivian Moon came to him, too. They were clearer in his mind. The night she looked after him, and how it left him so full of humiliation. He could not quite picture her face, but he remembered her body all too well, and the sense of it was excruciating.

Vivian Moon. Or, as she was in his memory, Viv. And yes, she'd lived next door to Cora Franks in Cedar Valley. Elsie had left him there for the night when she and the Franks went out, and Viv had made up a bed for him in a spare room. There was a wardrobe in it, and a window that looked over the back garden. Recalling it now, he remembered the sound of wind chimes. Vivian Moon—Viv—had made the two of them something to eat, and afterwards he sat up in the spare bed reading comics while she tidied up in the kitchen. He was to stay the whole night. He had an overnight bag and a chest full of nerves.

Tony remembered with regret how he had stared at Viv while she cooked their dinner. He couldn't remember what she cooked, but he knew he had stared at her and then looked away when she addressed him directly. He shook his head now, disgusted at the memory of himself, and noticed that, in the room next door, Jenny and the girls had gone quiet.

Knock knock came through the wall.

Tony smiled. He waited, waited, and then knocked back.

Knock knock.

The girls and Jenny erupted, squealing and laughing.

Tony Simmons, full of his awful memories, sat up and put his legs over the side of the bed. He was so sweaty that he got his towel from the back of the door and he wiped himself down with it: his face and neck, his chest and stomach. Then he sat again, hunched over, and for the first time he let himself think about what had happened next. With Vivian Moon.

He recalled how a man had come over. There was a knock on the door when Tony was reading his comics, and then a man's voice talking and Vivian's voice whispering. It was the whispering of lovers, as he now understood.

The man left.

And Viv came back into the house and, knowing Tony was busy reading in the spare room, she went to the bathroom and had a shower. She left the door a little ajar, and light and steam was coming out of it when Tony got out of bed and crept into the hallway.

Oh, he was so desperate to see her. More than anything in the world he wanted to see her naked body. The way he'd watched, earlier in the kitchen, a white sweater tight against the perfect curves of her.

So, with a teenage boy's compulsion, he snuck along the hall and ever so slowly put his head around the edge of the bathroom door.

The noise of rushing water and the sounds of her washing—she may even have been singing—and little Tony looked in and saw her there, standing in the shower, which had no curtain, just a big bath with a nozzle over it, and Viv was standing in the bath, under the nozzle. He watched her and was covered in pleasure. He could remember the exact sensation of it, like being in a warm shower himself, and knowing so well that it was forbidden. The mere sight of her had made him gasp: the gentle roundness of her breasts and the way the water poured down upon her. And then the jolt of her looking up, and yelping in fright at the sight of him, and Tony running back to the spare bedroom and diving onto the bed, switching off the lamp with his heart thumping.

He listened in dread to the sound of the shower going off, and Vivian Moon getting out and walking barefoot down the hall.

Then she put her head in, silhouetted in the doorway with a towel around her, and she said with little effort: 'There's no shame in it, sweetie, forget about it. See you in the morning. If you're up early, your mum packed you some Weet-Bix.'

47

The next morning was a Tuesday and Constable Gus Franklin and Constable James Hall sat in the main common area of the Cedar Valley police station, watching over the sketcher while he worked away on a thick drawing pad.

Four photographs of the dead man lay across the table and the sketcher kept glancing at them as he drew. The face of the unknown man was taking shape there, in pencil, on his pad.

'You want a biscuit or something?' asked Franklin.

'Water's fine,' said the sketcher, a bearded man in a gingham shirt. He took a sip of his water and looked up at the policemen.

'If you wouldn't mind not looking over my shoulder? It's kind of off-putting.'

'Sorry,' said Franklin, and he rolled his eyes at Hall as they walked back over to Simmons's office.

'The drawing's looking pretty good,' said Hall from the doorway.

Simmons beckoned them in.

Hall sat down, upright, on the right, and Franklin sat down, slouching, on the left, and Franklin said: 'They released a photo of the Somerton Man. Why don't we just release a photo?'

'Because we're sensitive,' said Simmons. 'And I want him to look alive.'

Franklin said, 'Oh yeah. Dead people look different, hey,' and Hall nodded swiftly to agree.

'I just had a call from Maureen Robinson,' said Simmons, who had been in an efficient mood all morning.

'What did she say?' asked Hall.

'She said that Dieter Bernbaum saw our blonde woman last Wednesday.'

'Did he now?' said Franklin.

'Dieter was on his break when we went in to talk to Maureen,' said Hall. 'But didn't she say he'd been on his break when the blonde came in, too?'

'He *was* on his break,' said Simmons. 'He was getting a pie, and then he sat outside Fran's to eat it. Maureen mentioned the blonde woman to him at work this morning and he says, oh yeah, he noticed her coming out of the chemist, so he's asked Maureen to give us a call. Maureen says Dieter often notices attractive women at the chemist.'

'I bet he does,' said Franklin.

'But I bet attractive women don't notice Dieter,' said Hall, and the two of them had a laugh. But then Hall became serious. 'Dieter Bernbaum's really weird. I reckon there's something off about him.'

'I don't know the guy,' said Simmons. 'But off or not, he's got a memory. He sees the blonde walk out of the chemist, right, and then—you're gonna love this—Dieter says she made a call from the phone box outside Fran's World Famous Pies.'

Franklin clapped his hands together.

'Oh, very good,' said Hall, because Simmons always said that—'very good'—and Hall wanted to be a little more like Simmons.

'So after this, I want you to go and talk to Dieter—I'm sure you can handle it, Jimmy. Get the timing as accurate as you can, and then let's get onto Telecom and find out what number she called.'

Smiles all around as the three men sat there, feeling like they were inching forward in some small way.

Then Simmons sighed and said, 'I've been thinking more about these combs.'

It was true. Between phone calls, of which there had been several that morning, he had been sitting there in his chair, suppressing difficult memories, staring at the combs, thinking about them, wondering about the significance of a comb.

The Somerton Man had been carrying two combs. One was a narrow, aluminium, American-made comb; the other was plastic, most probably bakelite. The fact that the Somerton Man had two combs was clearly stated in the coronial inquest; Simmons had read over the faxed document. 'Two hair combs' it had said. It was public knowledge. And, accordingly, sitting in front of Simmons on his desk, in two separate sealed bags, was a narrow aluminium comb, and a brown plastic comb—what looked like bakelite—both found in the pocket of the unknown man who'd died on Valley Road.

How this guy had managed to get his hands on two antique combs to fit these exact descriptions, in 1993, Simmons had no idea. But it must be said: Simmons admired the attention to detail.

The more interesting thing though was the *third* comb, which Hall had retrieved from the man's other pocket. It sat on Simmons's desk in a separate bag and there was no mistaking that this comb was fancy. Sterling silver, it was stamped with small hallmarks declaring its authenticity, and Simmons had spent a good time squinting at them. The number 935 he could make out easily, but the symbols were more difficult. One of them looked like the outline of a bird flying left, its wings pointing north and south. Or perhaps it was a waning crescent moon?

And the symbol next to it?

That one was harder still. The hallmark stamps were so small and indistinct. Was it a house, a circus tent, a pentagon with something else inside? Simmons stared at it and could not tell. All he knew for certain was that the comb folded down neatly into its sterling silver handle and, while Simmons had never been a comb man, even if he had been, he'd have found this one far too pompous for his liking.

When he'd raised this whole extra comb issue yesterday, none of them had any idea what it meant. But they did know this: it had to mean *something*. It had to be significant, like the note in the hidden pocket. *GIFT.*

'What do you reckon, boss?' asked Constable James Hall.

'I think it's lucky we haven't had someone hand in a Persian poetry book with codes in it,' said Simmons.

Ha ha ha, Franklin laughed. 'True,' he said.

'Did you get onto your mate in Norwood again?' Simmons asked Hall.

'I did, after you left yesterday. I got nothing. He said the combs were never an issue. The Somerton Man just had two combs. That's it. He doesn't reckon anyone thought any more about it.'

'Did you think of a comb expert we can talk to?' asked Franklin, half smiling.

'Yeah, fuck, I don't know,' said Simmons. 'I made a call this morning to a mate in Sydney who should be able to help. He's got a contact who knows about hallmarks; he's calling me back. But it's hard to know how far to chase the goose, you know?'

Franklin nodded.

And then Simmons couldn't help himself—he leaned forward and picked up the bag with the fancy comb in it.

'Does that look like a flying bird and a house to you?' he asked, pointing at the hallmarks.

'Oh,' said Hall, 'I would have thought the one on the left is a moon maybe?'

'It looks like a banana and a skull,' said Franklin.

Simmons stared at Gussy Franklin and then put the bag with the comb back on the table and said, 'Brilliant.'

'We could ask Cora Franks,' said Hall. 'She knows about antiques.'

Simmons snorted out a laugh, rather defensively; he had no inclination to involve Cora Franks any more than was necessary.

Franklin turned to Hall. 'Maybe he was just really into hair products. He might have meant to sit down in front of the Coiffure and fucked it up. Got the wrong shop.' He grinned.

'Yeah, maybe we should ask Therese Johnson about combs,' said Hall. 'Hairdressers know about combs.'

Things were becoming troublesome when Detective Sergeant Anthony Simmons could not even tell if Jimmy Hall was joking—about asking Cora, or asking Therese—and he couldn't tell if he should be taking any of this seriously either. The boys were obviously having some fun. There was nothing like detective work when some unknown individual has taken the time to plant clues in his own pockets.

Therese Johnson floated around in Simmons's mind—so much rouge and hair—she always seemed so put upon.

Simmons barely knew the woman, but thinking of her brought to mind to something Elsie Simmons used to say: that some people connect to the world through their complaints about it.

Jenny had said something along those lines too: that when Therese would do her hair she'd just snip away and list her grievances; how she was so hot and cold on her husband, Ed; and how Jenny would rather just read a magazine.

'Maybe we should ask Therese Johnson about Ed, while we're at it. Like how is it that she hasn't turfed him?' said Franklin.

Jimmy Hall nodded. 'Fair,' he said.

'Why's that?' asked Simmons.

'Oh, Ed likes to get himself into strife,' said Franklin. 'He gets a bit on the side.'

'A bit?' said Jimmy Hall. 'I think Ed's been getting a lot on the side for a long time.'

'How do you know that?' asked Simmons.

'Everyone at the Royal knows,' said Franklin. 'Ed's not discreet. He loves the drama.'

Ed Johnson. Really? Simmons supposed Ed was funny, in a ribald kind of way, and he guessed he could probably turn on the charm. But the paunch, the pall of heavy drinking. Simmons thought, if Ed Johnson was some kind of ladies' man then he could not be sure of anything in this world.

'Are any of these women he has on the side married? Or is Ed the only one who's married?'

Franklin and Hall looked at each other and then back at Simmons.

'The one he's got right now's married,' said Hall. 'Linda. She works at the Ingham factory. She lives up in Goodwood.'

'Goodwood's a shithole,' said Simmons.

'Yeah, and she's a shocker. Her family are shockers. Ed usually goes for classier ladies. I think he's slipping,' said Franklin.

Simmons looked up at the ceiling, thinking, staring at the fan. 'I wonder what Linda's husband would do if he found out?' he said. 'I mean, just take her as an example. Small towns. People find things out. I wonder what any husband would do?'

Franklin did a slow nod.

And Hall said, 'Oh, well, yeah. There's probably a long list of husbands who'd do something pretty drastic if they found out what Ed Johnson's been up to for the past twenty years.'

48

Benny Miller sat in the early light of the garden on Tuesday with a cup of coffee and a bowl of Weet-Bix. She ate her breakfast slowly, facing the bush, listening to its morning noises. In her bare feet, she walked down to the shed and left a peeled banana on the shelf for the possum. She stared up at the cardboard box of books, considering them. Then she watered the wild garden and, at the base of the back fence, under the shade of the giant gum trees, she took a small rock from a crop of grey siltstone, carried it inside, and set it on the bedhead with the rest of her collection.

Benny dressed and put on her sneakers and it was already hot as she walked up to the town—for some exercise and something to do. She went the usual way to Valley Road and crossed the wide street towards the park, where galahs were eating at the grass. At the war memorial Benny stopped and looked at the plaque: OUR GLORIOUS DEAD with a list of names engraved. Then she walked in a new direction, away from the shops, past the library, her mind crowded with fragments of the previous night, and her long and winding conversation with Odette.

That Odette was beginning to 'understand' Vivian—well, that was a mystery to Benny still. Benny knew that Vivian had pulled away—this was what Odette had already said. Vivian had left Cedar Valley abruptly and returned to Frank in Sydney without much of an explanation. The two of them had settled into Frank's terrace in Rozelle, while Frank fixed furniture and Vivian worked at odd jobs way below her intellectual capacity.

Then the news came to Odette—via a letter—that Vivian was pregnant, and expecting a girl.

Well, it took the wind out of her, this news. For Vivian hadn't seemed especially devoted to Frank, nor especially keen to have a baby. Not like Odette, who had wanted a child so badly. This she told Benny while they picked at the leftover salad. She yearned for a child, and Lloyd did, too. The first miscarriage was a disappointment. The second, a great distress. But the third—the miscarriage she had in 1971—was a devastation. Odette Fisher was seventeen weeks pregnant when it happened. She was well and truly on her way, and the pain of it, the sorrow was an agony.

But, oh, how wonderfully caring Vivian had been.

'She soothed me more successfully than Lloyd did, really,' said Odette, putting her fork down and leaning back in her chair.

Then Benny had made tea and served the rest of Cora's banana bread on yellow plates. All the while the thick pile of letters and postcards sat in full view, just next to Odette's keys.

Somehow the conversation diverted back to the Somerton Man, and Vivian's interest in him, and that led to a discussion of Vivian's letters in general, and Benny sat unmoving in her chair, trying not to glance too obviously at the pile.

'I remember her talking about it. She was thrilled by it, really—just the mystery of it. She was fascinated by the Kennedy assassination, too; she loved conspiracy stories. And I guess the fact that the Somerton Man died right near their house when she was little—the story of it had been with her since she was a little girl.'

Benny nodded, wondering how she could find out everything there was to know about the Somerton Man: every single mysterious detail. If she were still in Sydney she could go to the State Library and look at the newspaper archives. There surely would have been articles. Perhaps someone had written a book about it, if the case was so famous in Adelaide. Benny could have searched through all of it and read everything available if she were in Sydney. But she wasn't.

Odette sat there, eating banana bread, relaying all the details fresh in her memory. She'd called Elsie Simmons as soon as she got home from the Royal. The Somerton Man, 1948. Found dead with nothing but a few simple items and a piece of paper that said 'Tamam Shud', torn from *The Rubaiyat of Omar Khayyam*.

'Elsie's convinced he was a Soviet spy, and she's really not one for histrionics,' said Odette—and she explained it all to Benny, about the copy of the *Rubaiyat* that was found discarded in a car near Somerton Beach and handed in to police, with the phone number and the unbreakable codes written in the back. Elsie Simmons couldn't remember the actual code, but she did recall that, back in Glenelg in the early months of 1949, she and her mother had tried to crack it. They'd sat in front of that odd string of letters on and off for weeks before giving it up.

'I wish Elsie had a copy of *The Rubaiyat* so we could have a look at it,' said Odette. 'Just for fun. I was sure Vivian gave me a copy when she was living here, but I couldn't find it on my shelf. It's a funny book. It's all about passion and living in the moment and enjoying wine. Quite hedonistic. I never really took to it, but I guess Vivian was so obsessed with it because it's all tied up with the mystery.'

Benny wrote the name of the book and its author down on the brown paper beer bag, and Odette laughed. Neither of them were quite sure how to spell it. And then Odette finally reached over and picked up the pile of letters and took off the rubber band that held them all together, and she spread them out on the table, sifting through them, turning some of the postcards over and looking at the pictures.

'Here,' she said, and, with some sense of gravity about the gesture, she handed Benny a postcard from Vivian.

It was sent from Paris, addressed to Odette Fisher in Hydra Town.

Benny knew her mother's writing so intimately, so hopelessly, and it pained her to see it there on the postcard, which said little more than 'hello', with a scant description of Vivian's activities. It recommended Odette read *Siddhartha* by Herman Hesse. *It has helped me with my 'sickness of the soul' and 'the quarrel of the universe'.* This was what Vivian had written, and Benny flinched at the thought of her mother being so afflicted, and expressing it in lofty quotations.

Odette glanced up at Benny, as if checking in on her, to see that she was coping, and then she handed another card, this one from London, and then another, from Brighton.

Benny looked at the pictures and then turned them over and read them anxiously. Why was it that she half expected to find a mention of herself? How utterly ridiculous, when she knew full well that she hadn't been born yet at the time of their writing. How urgent it felt, to read them, and how desolate too, to find they contained very little of interest.

Odette had opened some envelopes and was reading over a letter—Benny could see the double-sided pages teeming with words.

'This one is from Paris, but most of the letters are from Berlin.' Odette put one letter down and picked up another, and then another. 'This is the one I was thinking of—she's writing about the Somerton Man.' Odette kept reading, her eyes moving down the page quickly.

Benny looked down at the postcard from Brighton again. It was a colourised photo of a beach with a big, impressive pier. Vivian had written, *A little different from the Brighton Jetty in Adelaide!* in pen on the photo.

'Oh, how amazing,' Odette said. 'I'd forgotten this.' She turned the page over and read to the end of the letter, and then she set it down on the table.

'Vivian's talking about books she's been reading. We would often talk about that. She was saving some money to buy a German translation of *The Rubaiyat of Omar Khayyam* she found in a bookstore in Berlin—even though she couldn't read German. She never had *any* money, I don't know how she managed to travel for so long. Anyway, then she goes on to talk about the Somerton Man. God, I remember being so intrigued by this letter! She lists all the facts here. I didn't need to call Elsie after all. *Jestyn.* That's the name of the nurse. And listen, here at the end . . .'

Odette picked up the letter and began to read aloud: '"He'd never tell me yes or no. He'd just smile at me when I asked, and Mum wouldn't say anything about it. She thinks Dad is too caught up in it and she doesn't want to encourage him—and I think she honestly believes it would be dangerous to our family if people found out. The problem is it happened when I was six, and I remember it! I remember my parents talking about it, and there was something more than just being interested in the newspaper articles. So when I got older and read in the reports that the man who handed in the *Rubaiyat* to police was a chemist—and my father is a chemist—I asked him straight out. I said Dad, did you find that book in your car? And he just smiled at me and didn't say yes, and he didn't say no!'"

Odette looked over the top of the letter with her eyebrows raised.

Benny stared back, fascinated.

'*Well*,' Odette had said. 'How about that? Clive Moon. Your grandfather. Maybe he was a chemist with a secret?'

Benny Miller, walking now in Cedar Valley, thought about it all—the utter strangeness of it—and some of her sadness diminished. She walked, fast and springy, and the air was filled with bird sound as she let out a small wondrous laugh.

49

'H e's pretty off, yeah,' said Constable Gus Franklin to Constable James Hall after their brief visit with Dieter Bernbaum, the chemist at the Cedar Valley Pharmacy.

Dieter Bernbaum, egg-like in his balding, had sat on his chemist's stool—a modern-looking white leather contraption—and been oddly evasive for a man in possession of somewhat innocuous information: what time he had seen the blonde woman; any further details of the blonde woman. He hadn't looked at all closely when shown a photograph of the woman in the crowd, just to be sure they were talking about the same blonde. Instead, he kind of waved a hand, as if the photo were a bad smell, and went *mmmm* impatiently. In fact, Dieter Bernbaum went *mmmm* in response to almost every query, as opposed to the more direct 'yes' that Franklin and Hall would have preferred.

'Is that a yes?' Hall had to ask, so many times.

Mmmm, went Dieter Bernbaum, with his white clogs and his unconvincing smile.

'Why was he smiling like that?' Franklin asked Hall as they walked back up to the station, past the Old Paris Coiffure where Therese Johnson was standing in the window, looking out pensively.

'I think he was nervous,' said Hall. 'Seriously, that guy has creeped me out since I was a kid.'

Mmmm, went Franklin, which made Hall laugh.

Then back at the station, Franklin went to the kitchenette to make a coffee, and Hall went to his desk to call Telecom, hoping to discover what number was dialled from the phone box on Valley Road on December 1st 1993, at approximately 2.20 pm.

•

Simmons, in his sweaty office, was staring down at the completed sketch that lay on the desk before him. It was good—very good—and Simmons was pleased.

The unknown man, who looked a little grim in the photographs, especially the ones from the morgue, now appeared pleasantly alive, staring forward, his features captured in surprisingly lifelike detail.

'Nice work,' Simmons had said to the sketcher, and the sketcher—caressing his beard—asked if he might take a biscuit on his way out, and left via the kitchenette.

Now, sitting forward, his elbows on the desk, Simmons meditated on the dead man's face for a time—and he couldn't help but notice a particular quality about his countenance, his expression. What was it? It was something old-fashioned, something intrinsic. Was it *character*? Dignity? Simmons had seen a lot of dead faces in his time. He'd met a lot of men. But this man, this face—there was some attribute there that Simmons found commendable. Even in death—the way he sat up so neatly. What kind of man can accomplish such a neat and tidy death?

Simmons frowned and blinked, and then he yelled for Gussy Franklin to come in and take the picture away, write up the press release, and get it faxed out to the media, far and wide.

'Someone'll recognise him,' said Simmons to Franklin, and there was no doubt in his mind.

Then Simmons sat back in his chair, knowing full well that the best part of his morning—a phone call with Ping Williams—had already concluded, and that the rest of the day would be downhill from there.

He had called Ping as a courtesy—or so he liked to consider it—to tell her of the Somerton Man, to alert her to the striking similarities between the two cases, to advise her of the consequences of this development.

'What are those consequences?' whispered Ping.

'Well, we've notified homicide. Not that we necessarily think it's a homicide—but obviously we have to keep that door open. I've had to take it up the chain a bit—I've been on a few calls this morning. It just makes it a bit more interesting for everyone, doesn't it?' said Simmons.

'Why, yes.' Ping agreed that it did. 'Absolutely mystifying' was how she described it, and Simmons loved it most when she said: 'I would love to get hold of the original post-mortem reports on this Somerton Man. Would you be able to provide me with those, Detective?'

'Leave it with me,' he said, and he got off the phone rather hurriedly, with a discreet sense of embarrassment, a feeling which only settled when he went over—again—the list he'd compiled of similarities between the Somerton Man and the Cedar Valley Man. It was a list that spread over two columns, with a few haphazard arrows going here and there, connecting lines darting off in several directions, some words circled in red pen.

On another sheet, he had written a list of the things that were different. There were fewer things on this list—location, content of the note in the fob pocket, absence of an unclaimed suitcase with the name 'T. Keane' in it—and the most exciting thing, as far as Simmons was concerned, written in his own infantile handwriting: *Extra (third) comb.* Next to the list on his desk, he had placed a photocopy of the comb itself, which showed the hallmarks on the silver: the banana and the skull, as Franklin saw it; or the bird and the house, as Simmons saw it; and the number 935.

Simmons pored over the papers—thinking, thinking—until the phone rang—a call from his mate in Sydney with the contact who knew a thing or two about silver hallmarks.

'Mate,' said Simmons, 'give me news.'

Thankfully, Simmons's mate—Bob Watts—had news. Bob Watts had tracked down his contact: an older man who'd worked for several auction houses and was now an antique dealer. He had a fine eye for value, and a particular interest in jewellery and watches.

'What about combs?' asked Simmons.

'If it's gold or silver, he knows it,' said Bob, and he continued.

Most of the silverware this dealer handled was of British, Scottish or Irish origin, and every country had its own particular hallmarks, depending on the vintage and city. Most makers had their mark, too, and there were any number of assay offices or import marks, plus numbers or letters that indicated the fineness of the silver. It turned out the area of hallmarks was far more complicated than Simmons had imagined, but in the case of this particular silver comb, there was at least some simplicity.

The number—935—was the fineness mark. It was the number of parts of pure silver of one thousand possible parts. That meant this comb was 93.5 per cent silver, which was not a bad number at all, since anything above 925 is considered sterling.

'So it's valuable?' asked Simmons.

'Relatively,' said Bob. 'As far as combs go.'

'And what about the, uh, other marks?' asked Simmons, unsure of what they were.

Yes, well. Of course, it could be difficult to make out a hallmark when they were stamped so small, and every mark came out a little different, depending on various conditions, but the two little pictures on the handle of the comb were not a banana and a skull, and they were not a flying bird and a house either.

They were a crescent moon and a crown.

'A crown,' said Simmons, picking up the clear bag with the comb in it, and squinting at the little stamp. He had thought it was a house, or a pentagon with a smudge in it. But yes, as he looked again, he could see it was indeed a crown.

'That means it's German,' said Bob Watts. 'There's different stamps for different countries and cities. The British ones are all anchors and lions, the Britannia Standard, all that stuff. But my guy says the moon and the crown means it's German. He reckons early twentieth century, and it was probably part of a set, with brushes and a mirror and that kind of thing.'

Simmons could half hear the electronic musings of the fax machine dialling as Bob made a few more comments about the quality of German silver, the introduction of a national hallmarking system, and the fact that his mate, the antique dealer, would be interested to find the rest of the set.

Simmons, nodding and holding the bag with the comb, wound up the conversation and thanked Bob Watts.

Then he wrote *German* in blue pen on the photocopy of the crown, and made some more notes on his list.

He held up the bag again, lifting it between his thumb and forefinger, as if the comb would somehow become transparent to the light and reveal its secrets. It did not. But Simmons sure did spend a good while studying the squished stamps of a moon and a crown on this relatively valuable, sterling silver, German-made, early twentieth-century comb as it glinted in the hot light of day.

50

Benny Miller walked quickly back to Wiyanga Crescent, past the low-slung houses, the flowering trees, and up the steps to the door of the green cottage.

It had occurred to her midway through her walk what she wanted to do next, and she let herself into the house and went straight down the hallway, through the kitchen to the back doors. She unlatched them and stood for a moment, staring at the slanted shed. Then she went along the mossy brick path to where Vivian's old box of books sat on a high shelf.

In the shed, Benny lifted the box down carefully and set it on the dusty concrete, wiping away a newly spun spider web that went across the top. The books inside were as she had left them: stuffed back messily in uneven piles.

Now she unpacked them all one at a time, looking over each one carefully, as if they were artefacts from a museum. Novels by Evelyn Waugh, Iris Murdoch, Carson McCullers— the books took on the glow of some bygone treasure. Benny

looked again at the phrasebooks and foreign language dictionaries, a guide to Greece, collections of William Blake and
T.S. Eliot, a book of paintings by Marc Chagall. She opened
almost every cover to see the same name written there: Vivian
Moon. And every time she saw it, a tiny pulse went through
her, like another heart beating alongside her own.

It wasn't until Benny was near the bottom that she found
the book she was hoping for, and a shiver went across her
when she saw *The Rubaiyat of Omar Khayyam* nestled in there
among a selection of Australian bird books and bushwalking
guides to the Gather Region.

She lifted it out carefully, as one would handle a fossil.

It was a fancy-looking little book: a green cover with gold
letters and decorative inlay—*Translated by Edward Fitzgerald*,
it said in smaller text on the front. Benny opened it up to see
her mother's name written there, and then she flicked through
the pages. Almost every poem had some phrase underlined,
or notes scrawled in the margin.

Benny, who had been crouching, sat back cross-legged
and began examining the pages, slowly at first, and then
more quickly as she realised just how much her mother
had underlined, or circled, and how much her mother had
written.

On one page, a thick black box was drawn around the
lines: *A flask of wine, a book of verse—and thou beside me
singing in the wilderness—and wilderness is paradise enow.*

On another, Vivian had underlined in red: *Ah, my beloved, fill the cup that clears TO-DAY of past regrets and future fears.* And she had written alongside it in the margin: *The day on which you are without passionate love is the most wasted day of your life.*

All the lines Vivian had highlighted, the other lines she had written—all of them attributed to 'Omar K'—were about wine and death and love.

How sad, a heart that does not know how to love, that does not know what it is to be drunk with love. If you are not in love, how can you enjoy the blinding light of the sun, the soft light of the moon?

Benny sat reading, her heart throbbing for reasons she could not understand, sitting in the dank shed, feeling such unexpected disgust—or was it anger?—at the things her mother had been impressed by.

While you live Drink!—for once dead you shall never return. This was circled in pencil, and inside the back cover Vivian had copied out more quotes, and done some small drawings; Benny looked over them—they were just little shapes.

Then, in black wobbly pen, was written: *The fears and sorrows that infest the soul!* And underneath it, neatly in red, *Everything now is O.K.*, with a love heart.

Well. Benny had had enough of the fraught feelings this book was giving her.

Passionate love, overt despair, life and death.

Benny had had no inkling of these tumults in her mother. She had never been privy to her afflictions or desires. Did these lines belong to Omar Khayyam, or to Vivian Moon? Did Vivian possess them, or live in them? Did she live *for* them? How horrifying was the enthusiasm in the notes and markings—all over the book! Benny flushed with embarrassment and cursed her own shameful curiosity.

Then she threw the book across the shed. It thudded against a bag of mulch and landed splayed open on the concrete floor.

51

Constable James Hall knocked cautiously on Simmons's door at lunchtime.

'I got a call back from Telecom,' he said.

Simmons waved him in, and Hall sat down on the chair.

'So who'd she call?' asked Simmons.

'The time,' said Hall.

Simmons looked at him blankly. 'The time,' he said.

'Yeah,' said Hall, wide-eyed. 'You know, you call 1194 and it says, "At the third stroke," and then it tells you the time?'

'Yes, Jimmy, I know,' said Simmons, and the two men sat in silence for a moment, considering the peculiarity of the fact that, at 2.27 pm on December 1st, just before crossing the road and speaking to a man who would soon be dead, the blonde woman who resembled an American soap actress had stepped into a phone booth and called the time.

'But it looks like she took a call as well,' said Hall.

'How's that?'

'Someone called the payphone on Valley Road at two twenty-three, and the call lasted thirty-four seconds. It came from a silent number.'

Simmons nodded and said, 'Of course it did.'

'So do you reckon she waited in there for three and a half minutes after that, and then she called the time? Or maybe someone else took the incoming call and then she got in after,' said Hall.

'I don't fucking know,' said Simmons, and he sat back and considered their timeline.

As they had it, the blonde woman had been at Curios first. This was according to Cora Franks and Lil Chapman, who put the woman there a little earlier in the day, after Therese Johnson had left.

The blonde looked at the watches, tried on a few with thin gold bands, her hands shaking like leaves in a gale. In fact, so much was her shaking noted by shop staff on Valley Road that Constable James Hall had stopped in at Valley Road Family Medical to ask Janet Avery, the nurse, why a woman of a certain age would shake like that. Thanks to Janet, Hall had written a list of possibilities in his notepad: *Parkinson's (very serious); essential tremor; neurological disorders; inherited/genetic; alcohol withdrawal; prescription drug related etc.*

And, speaking of drugs, it was sometime after her visit to Curios that the blonde woman had turned up at the chemist and asked, sadly, for a sedative. Maureen Robinson sold her some mild over-the-counter sleeping tablets. And then Dieter Bernbaum, eating a pie, had seen the woman making a call from the phone box—to the time. All of this before she crossed the road again, spoke to the seated gentleman—had a proper conversation, as Nigel Haling described it—and later on she was photographed among the crowd, looking on at the deceased body—an innocent bystander—before disappearing without a trace from the town of Cedar Valley.

'Why wouldn't she just ask Maureen for the time? Or anyone on the street?' asked Simmons. 'If she's gonna go up and talk to our bloke in the suit—which is more than anyone else did the whole time he was sitting there—why doesn't she just ask someone for the time?'

'Maybe it had to be very precise,' said Constable James Hall. 'The talking clock is very precise.'

Simmons raised his eyebrows.

'Or maybe she knew our dead guy,' said Simmons. And he sat back, wondering what on earth was going on in the mind of the blonde woman, who was done up to the nines and wasted thirty cents on calling the time when any old person up on Valley Road would have had a watch on.

•

And while Simmons and Hall sat in the office back at the police station, Constable Gussy Franklin, in uniform, was sitting at the bar at the Royal Tavern having a counter meal and a Coke.

Tom Boyd, elbows on the bar mat, was discussing how Evander Holyfield compared, historically, with Ezzard Charles, and Franklin, who had been eating deliberately slowly, was pleased when Ed Johnson eventually took his regular lunchtime break and sat down on a stool with his apron on.

'G'day, Gussy,' said Ed.

'Ed,' said Gussy Franklin, cutting into his steak.

'Don't often see you in here on a work day.'

'Sometimes I get sick of a sandwich,' said Franklin.

Ed Johnson laughed—the man seemed to laugh at most things, a funny, wary laugh—and Franklin settled into a conversation with Ed, with Tom Boyd half involved, and Linda Carlstrom, wearing a Jack Daniels singlet and sitting a few stools up, pretending not to be listening.

'We're making some headway on our dead 'un,' said Franklin casually, after a lull.

'Oh yeah?' said Tom Boyd. 'I hear no one's claimed him. And what about this other bloke from back in Adelaide?'

'It's one of the weirder ones I've seen,' said Franklin. 'We've had no luck with the blonde, though. Jimmy came in here, didn't he, and showed you the photo?'

'He did,' said Tom. 'I never saw her.'

'Real attractive lady,' said Gussy Franklin to Ed. 'Nice clothes. Looked like she'd just had her hair done and that kind of thing.'

Ed Johnson nodded, his eyes fixed on the bar mat.

'You didn't see her, did you, Ed?' asked Gussy Franklin. 'You'd probably recall it, if you did. Real nice-looking lady. Apparently she had a chat with our dead 'un, which is pretty interesting. The whole thing is pretty interesting.'

Ed Johnson laughed, again, and it was funny how he would not look at Gussy Franklin directly. Instead his eyes darted left, towards Linda, who was now looking at Ed dead on, sitting back with her arms folded.

Ha ha ha, went Ed. 'Yeah, I don't know, Gussy. What would I know?'

52

Cora Franks had been waiting patiently on her front
verandah, potentially for a very long time—or this was
how it seemed to Benny Miller as she emerged from the
cottage that afternoon, dressed in her Royal Tavern T-shirt.

'Oh, you're off to work, are you?' said Cora loudly from
her wicker chair. Her handbag sat next to her on the boards,
ready to go.

'Yes,' said Benny.

'I'll walk with you,' said Cora Franks, and she rose swiftly
and started down the steps, her necklaces clinking together.
'I'm off, Fred!' she yelled through the screen door, and Benny
let out an 'oh' as Cora was suddenly next to her, squat and
smiling.

The two of them stood for a brief moment on the mowed
grass, and then Benny began to walk and Cora followed, and
soon they were walking together, awkwardly, towards town.

'I'm off to the Royal, too,' said Cora. 'It's Shop Night.' And she began to list the various groups and clubs she belonged to, noting that Cedar Valley was a small but very social town, very recreational, and that there was never any shortage of things to do. No matter what your interest—sewing, quilting, ceramics, fishing, books—you could definitely find a club for it. Cora was in three clubs, and Fred was in one. Fishing was Fred's thing, lake fishing mainly. And from that point it took mere minutes, thanks to Cora's deft conversational steering, to arrive at the topic of her book club—the *better* of the town's two book clubs—and the air hung with tension as both Benny and Cora wondered who would bring up the photograph first.

It was Cora.

'I wasn't sure if I should pop it in there. In the cake tin. But I thought you might like to have it,' she said.

'I'm glad to have it,' said Benny, who'd been feeling a strange kind of detachment since her morning discoveries in the shed. Feathery clouds lay across the sky and Benny, who had been wanting to speak with Cora about this exact subject, was now somehow lukewarm about the reality.

Cora Franks, in her peach blouse and grey skirt, made a few sallies towards the core of Benny's true sentiments. She approached from a couple of angles, testing the water with an air of false confidence. Some disingenuous remarks came out—of how saddened she was by the news of Vivian's death, and what a surprise it was for such a young woman 'to pass'.

'What a terrible shock that must have been for you,' she said, waiting for Benny to fill her in on the details. When Benny merely nodded, a feeling of distaste arose in Cora Franks at this young woman's rudeness, and a feeling of distaste arose in Benny at this older woman's lack of subtlety and tact.

'I know she worked at Curios,' said Benny, bluntly.

Cora Franks looked alarmed, and then somehow pleased.

'Yes, she did. I hired Vivian. She was a neighbour and she asked for work.'

Benny loped along with her eyes on the thick mowed grass underfoot. 'And what happened?' she asked in an unfeeling tone that surprised even herself.

'Well. It didn't last,' said Cora. 'A few weeks, maybe a month. But I had to let her go.'

They turned the corner and walked towards the weedy vacant lot behind the grocery store. The sun was still hot and Benny began to sweat with the heat and the conversation.

'Why?' asked Benny.

'Oh, well, Benny,' said Cora, and Benny could not determine her tone—it was either reticent or stealthily pleased. 'She gave me no choice really. I found out she was stealing.'

The last bit came out just as plain as day.

'Oh,' said Benny.

'I don't know the extent of it,' said Cora. 'But she was definitely stealing.'

'How do you know that?'

'Because things went missing! I know my stock, obviously, I know it very well, and of course I'd notice if something was missing. And I'd also noticed how she'd keep her handbag very private. She'd always have it a bit hidden away and zipped up. Well, I couldn't have it. I know she didn't have any money, but that's no excuse. I just said to her, I said, "I can't have it."' And Cora gave Benny a resolute look as they crossed the road to the pub.

Outside the Royal, Cora stopped on the footpath next to a yellow-framed window, hoping to continue the conversation in privacy before they went in. Benny stood there uneasily, confused by the information, her shoulders as even as a fence top.

When Benny didn't say anything, Cora said, defensively, 'You understand.'

And Benny—who did not understand why a person being a little private about their handbag amounted to stealing—nodded. She said, 'Well, I'm sorry about that.'

'Oh, Benny, you needn't be sorry,' said Cora with sudden kindness. And, in the clarity of having heard herself explain it out loud—all these years later—Cora suddenly wondered if the infamous instance of Vivian's thieving had ever really happened. For the first time in twenty years, Cora doubted it. And, of course, Vivian had protested at the time. She'd seemed to think she was so misjudged. And now here was her daughter, who Cora allowed herself to look at properly for the first time, without prejudice: her pure olive skin and the small glow of her that sat somewhere under the heavy sadness she wore like a coat.

A surge of maternal warmth overtook Cora Franks. She thought: this poor girl is even more beautiful than her mother was, and she doesn't have any sense of it.

Then Benny said, 'I'd better go in,' and she walked through the big yellow door of the Royal.

'Bye-bye then, Benny,' said Cora Franks, the words rushing out of her, and she stood on the footpath and caught her reflection in the pub window. There she was, next to an old sign for VB—her worried expression, too many necklaces, legs like little pylons. Good heavens, she looked completely ridiculous.

53

Tony Simmons arrived home from work and went directly to the fridge for a beer. He stood at the kitchen bench, his back aching, and swallowed close to half the bottle in his first sip, the coldness being such a blessing, and he looked out at the yard through the window. Jenny was out there, sitting on the grass in her house clothes—those unbecoming shapeless things she bought cheap at the Clarke Plaza—watching the girls in the shell pool as the day was getting on towards evening.

Jenny had left a box of Christmas decorations half unpacked on the dining table, and he could see she'd long forgotten about her tea. Her mug sat between two small bowls of spiral pasta, only somewhat eaten, and a messy pile of textas. Beyond that, on the side table, was a photo Jenny had proudly framed several years earlier: the two of them, all dressed up on the night he took her to Sydney to see Torvill and Dean.

Simmons finished his beer and opened another, and he poured Jenny a glass of white wine from the bottle in the fridge door and added two ice cubes to it, just the way she liked it, and when he brought it out to her—the girls squealing and splashing in the pool—the look on her face was as if he'd built her a castle made from diamonds, and he felt a crinkle of guilt at her gratitude.

They sat a while in the yard, the girls hollering, Simmons on a lawn chair, a cushion stuffed in behind him for his back—and he was about to ask after dinner when the phone rang. He went inside to answer it and heard Constable James Hall breathless on the other end with news from the station.

'You're still there?' said Simmons.

'I just thought I'd stay back a bit,' said Hall. 'You know me.'

'What have you got?' asked Simmons, a hand to his face, rubbing at his temple.

'A woman called from Sydney,' said Hall. 'She runs a little hotel near Central.'

'She saw the sketch?' said Simmons.

'She saw the sketch,' said Hall.

'Very good.'

Simmons looked out the back door at Jenny on the grass and, seeing her like that in the twilight, he felt that she was still a good-looking woman. She hid herself away since having the girls, always getting about in some tent-like thing so he couldn't see the edges of her. It was his fault; he knew that. He had criticised her carelessly and absented himself whenever possible. And when they fought, he heard the coldness in his voice as he reprimanded her over some minor detail. Tony Simmons, he disgusted himself no end—he was sticky with disgust—and it covered his vast body like sweat.

'The woman says our guy stayed there on November 30th—the night before he came down here on the train. He didn't say much, apparently, and he paid cash. But get this: he gave his name as T. Keane. You remember the name Keane?'

Simmons focused. Keane. Kean. T. Keane.

It was the name police had found on the clothing in the unclaimed suitcase at Adelaide railway station in 1948. The suitcase linked to the Somerton Man. It contained tools, stencilling equipment—Simmons had read all the reports. A tie, a laundry bag, maybe a singlet—all had some variation of the name 'Keane' written on them. At the time the police had thought it was a misdirection: a false name left deliberately to send them off on a wild-goose chase.

Simmons smiled to himself.

'I remember,' he said. 'He really went all out, didn't he?'

'And get this, boss,' said Hall.

'He had an accent?' Simmons said.

'How did you know that?' asked Hall, and Simmons could picture Hall on the other end of the phone, so keen, so lacking in cynicism. 'The hotel lady said he had some kind of European accent.'

54

Throughout Shop Night, Cora Franks could see Benny Miller though the glass doors of the bistro, serving drinks and chatting with the customers at the bar, like she'd lived in Cedar Valley her whole life.

Cora, at the head of the table, was surrounded by proprietors of the shops along Valley Road, who met in an unofficial capacity on the first Tuesday of the month for dinner and drinks, and to talk shop. That evening, Cora was much quieter than usual, rattled by her conversation with Benny, and fearing, as ever, that she had been misunderstood.

The conversation around her went through Christmas opening hours, the recent armed robberies of bottle shops in Clarke and now Barrang, the issue of drainage on the corner of Patsys Flat Road, and the upcoming Quilt Festival. Cora only half listened. She ate her fish and chewed slowly. And soon everyone was discussing the dead man, and Cora sipped her chardonnay and wondered: had Benny been there that night the man died? She had. Cora had an image of the crowd that was gathered there, everyone gaping and talking, and she suddenly remembered that yes, Benny Miller had been standing there among the local people, watching the whole thing impassively, thinking her very private thoughts.

It was Betsy Dell from the grocery store and Fran from Fran's World Famous Pies who brought up the idea of a funeral for the unknown gentleman. It'd been Betsy's idea originally, she'd taken it around to a few sympathetic townsfolk and now Fran had co-opted it and taken charge.

'And since no one's claimed him,' Fran was saying, 'he *is* ours. He's our responsibility.'

'I guess that's true,' said Maureen Robinson. 'He's a bit like the unknown soldier.'

'What a lovely comparison, Maureen,' said Betsy, who was having the schnitzel. 'And, as I said to Fran, finders keepers. He's ours and we need to honour him.'

Fran and Betsy explained their plan to the gathering, which included Carol and John Hargraves of Hargraves Books, Maureen Robinson from the chemist, Janet Avery and two general practitioners from Valley Road Family Medical, the owners of the video store, the bakery, the camping supplies store, the pizzeria and the cafe, and Yvonne Lourigan from Tender Thoughts. Therese Johnson, who was sitting next to Cora, had spent the whole night turning her head to check where Ed was.

Fran was the dominant speaker. The service was to be on Thursday at 5.30 pm at the Cedar Valley Public Hall. It would be an agnostic service, considering no one had any clue as to the denomination of the man in the suit. Betsy, an atheist since her husband had died, was very strong on this point. It didn't have to be churchy. Just a service. Betsy and Fran had organised everything, and all the rest of the town needed to do was show up.

It should be noted that a few of the shopkeepers present that night were not overly enthusiastic about the idea, and a few voices were raised in mild protest. Some people just didn't know how to come at it. But Fran, ever the diplomat, quelled the dissent, and had an answer to every potential objection.

'What about this business with the other man who died back in Adelaide?' asked Janet Avery.

'What about him?' said Fran. 'That's got nothing to do with us holding a funeral for *our* man. This is about our man, Janet.'

'What about the body? Don't the police need it for their investigation?' asked Keith Hand from Cedar Valley Brake & Clutch.

'We don't need the body,' said Fran swiftly. 'We'll just gather together and send him off. Everyone deserves some kind of funeral. Yvonne has been kind enough to donate flowers—thank you, Yvonne; they're going to be beautiful— and we'll make it all look nice. And then we'll have the wake here after. Cora, we were thinking that since you found him, maybe you could say a few words?'

Cora Franks, holding a glass of chardonnay, didn't hear her at first; she was irritated by the way Therese kept turning around every two minutes—who *cared* where Ed was?—and upset about Benny and the way she'd just walked off like that, with no goodbye. It was so dismissive, so ill-mannered. Cora was certain that Benny hadn't believed her, that Benny didn't believe her mother was a thief and she thought Cora had just fired her for no good reason.

'Cora?' said Fran, a little louder. 'We think you should make the oration.'

'Me?' said Cora, returning her attention to matters at hand. 'What would I say?' She was terrified at the prospect, and delighted to be asked.

'He had a lovely face,' said Lil Chapman. 'You could talk about how nice he looked.'

'Just anything you think,' said Betsy. 'But we have to do something. He died on Valley Road, and no one in Australia seems to miss him. Imagine if that were one of us? Just popping off like that and no one caring?'

'You're right,' said Cora, nodding thoughtfully, realising that she had the attention of the whole group. 'I'll put some words together. We have to do something.'

55

Odette had suggested to Benny that they drive to Clarke on Wednesday morning, since Benny wanted to buy seedlings at the garden centre—herbs and some different types of lettuce—and Odette needed to visit the agricultural supply to get some shell grit for her chickens and a new hoof knife for her cows.

Benny heard the car horn just after nine and she went out to find Odette there in her dusty old Land Cruiser (fawn-coloured with brown stripes along the side), and Bessel sitting in the passenger seat. He scooted into the back when Benny opened the door.

The three of them drove north out of town, along the coast road, with the windows down. Odette had a cassette of classical music playing and Benny watched the scenery pass and change; she found the mountain, to the west of the town, imposing and magnificent.

'It's very beautiful, isn't it?' said Odette. 'I remember thinking how striking it was when I first came here—the escarpment in particular. Driving in the Hay Plains used to bore me to death when I was a child. All there was to look at was sky.'

Benny looked up at the thick white clouds that hung above the mountain. 'Sky can be interesting,' she said.

'It can, but after half an hour it palls a little,' said Odette. Long grey hairs had blown loose from her braid and were whipping around in the wind. 'Did you hear they're having a funeral for the dead man tomorrow? Some of the women in town have organised it.'

Benny had heard about it; Fran from the pie shop had been up at the Royal talking to Tom about it on the weekend.

'Will we go?' asked Benny, and Odette said that of course they would, they would go together.

Everyone was going, as far as Odette could gather. Well, everyone who lived and worked in town and considered themselves a part of the community. Of course, some people in Cedar Valley were not so agreeable, and not everyone had a sense of occasion, but Odette was sure it would be a nice service—she loved the idea of it—as long as someone didn't come forward first and claim the dead man as their own.

The tape ended and Odette ejected it and turned it over and pressed play. And Benny listened to the music—just a cello by itself—and looked out the window as the trees rushed past.

They went through a little town called Galarra, which just had a petrol station and a general store and a bakery cafe, and after that was Barrang. They passed a beautiful old building—the Barrang School of Arts—and Odette told Benny that Tom's wife, Annie, would be exhibiting a selection of her ceramics there soon.

'You should come along with me to the opening. Annie's a fine artist.' And Odette continued to talk about Annie Boyd for what seemed like a while—she and Tom were a fantastic couple, and their girls were gorgeous, very creative, very bold—and Benny listened and nodded and felt a kernel of jealousy lodge inside her chest at the fact that Annie Boyd got to be married to such a decent and handsome man as Tom. And it was such a familiar feeling, this jealousy, that Benny realised, with some surprise, she had always been a jealous person. She had been jealous of the world her mother had inhabited. She was jealous of Europe; jealous of the past; jealous of the bed Vivian had slept in; and even of Odette, and the time she had spent in Vivian's company. It had always seemed such an injustice that Benny was denied entry to that sublime and sunlit world, and her mind swirled with it as Odette continued on talking about her renegade book club and how Annie always had such interesting opinions on books. Benny listened and made a noise of agreement every now and again, and she stared out the window as they went past a big lake, where a group of fishing boats sat together near two thin wharves. Then she closed her eyes for a time, her face in the wind, and when she opened them a sign announced their arrival at the outskirts of Clarke.

They visited the garden centre first and Odette advised Benny on her selection of seedlings. Benny bought potting mix and a pair of gardening gloves, and she politely declined Odette's offer to pay.

'You're a free human being with an independent will, Benny Miller,' said Odette, and Benny broke into a smile.

At Clarke Stockfeeds, Odette spent a while looking through the poultry supplies, wandering up and down in her navy overalls, and Benny went out to the large outdoor area, where there were piles of treated timber posts and steel tubing and metal gates. She looked around and eventually sat down on a pallet next to some hay bales and, when Odette finally emerged, she laughed at Benny and told her she looked just the part.

They stopped for fish and chips at a place near a metal bridge—a serve each of battered flathead—and Bessel sniffed along the riverbank and barked at the kayaks. Then they set off back to Cedar Valley, and they chatted about easy, everyday things for much of the way, and Benny felt so calm and full that she wondered if she might drift off to sleep.

'Do you have a boyfriend, Benny?' asked Odette, out of the blue.

'Oh, no. I did. But he moved to Canberra to go to ANU.'

'That's a shame. Do you miss him?'

'Kind of, not really. We write to each other sometimes,' said Benny, and she thought of Jules Cowrie, and how she had loved him in such a blinding flash and then spent close to two years trying to keep him at a safe distance. Benny hadn't known how to trust a person who showed such an open interest in her. And it was only just beginning to dawn on her, so recently, that Jules Cowrie was someone who deserved her trust.

'You know, Lloyd lives not too far out of Clarke,' said Odette. 'He has a shack up on the inland mountain. I guess that's one of the reasons I don't go to Clarke much. I always worry that I'll run into Lloyd, even though I never do.'

They left a stretch of straight fast road and came alongside the lake again. Cars were parked now on a patch of dead grass near the wharves.

'You asked me what happened with Lloyd, but there's nothing much to it really. I pushed him away—that's what happened.' Odette shot Benny a look that was full of regret, and Benny didn't say anything, hoping Odette would continue.

'He was a wonderful man. I'm sure he still is. But I blamed him for everything. When I couldn't get pregnant, I blamed him. When I had miscarriages, I blamed him. Isn't that crazy? I mean, I never blamed him out loud. But inwardly. And he could feel it. Over time, I think I bored away at his resolve.'

Benny sat still, her jaw clenched, not wanting to disturb the revelations.

'Vivian had all these adventures, you know. She had these experiences. And I would listen to her and, well, I guess I lived vicariously. She used to say Lloyd was "very dependable". God, I can still hear her saying it! But it wasn't a compliment. Even though she said it like a compliment, I knew it wasn't.'

Benny sat straight in the car seat and the wind blew her thoughts around—from Odette and Lloyd to the box of books in the shed and the notes Vivian had written all over them. *Ah, make the most of what we yet may spend, before we too into the dust descend.* Benny could not tell why these lines angered her so much.

Odette, lost in her own world of the past, stared through the windscreen with a dry kind of smile.

'I was so devastated by the final miscarriage. Losing our baby so late. I wanted to feel anything but *that*. Do you know what I mean?'

'Yes,' said Benny, as they went over a bridge above a wide lake.

'And Lloyd *was* dependable. Very smart, very philosoph-ical, very steady. I can't believe it now—how I'd lie there next to him just wanting *more*. And of course Lloyd didn't have the more I wanted. I'd have probably stood outside in an electrical storm at that point, just so I'd be struck. And so, I pushed him. And he pushed back. It's hard to think about even now. I said such awful things to him, Benny.'

Benny Miller wanted to say something very good at this point. She wanted to offer something helpful and even wise, because what Odette was saying to her was something she could understand.

'You were in distress,' said Benny, who felt much older in that moment, being admitted to the intimacies of Odette's history.

'Yes, I suppose I was,' said Odette, and she was quiet for a while before she added: 'That's a generous way of seeing it.'

The sign for Cedar Valley appeared and Odette turned off and drove along past a paddock of cows—an old bathtub sat near them at the fence, full of dirty water—and there must have been thirty of those white cow-birds standing with them, at least two birds to each cow. Soon the car arrived in the town, past the police station and the florist, and then right at the grocery store towards Wiyanga Crescent. Odette pulled to a stop behind Benny's station wagon. She turned the engine off and they sat there, with Bessel's head in between them, the dog panting in anticipation of getting out, his hind legs on the back seat.

'I was reading over Vivian's letters last night,' said Odette. 'That's why I'm thinking about it. She was describing this . . . this particular scenario. And I mean—the way Vivian felt about love? I think I thought that's how it should be for everyone, all the time.'

Bessel barked and Odette said, 'Okay, Bessel!' and her face lightened again as she opened the door and Bessel hopped out across her lap and went straight over to raise a leg at the gum tree.

Then Benny and Odette got out and went around to the back of the car and began to unpack the seedlings and soil. The bumper sticker on the back of Odette's car said: *Where the hell is Hay?*

'I guess if we see Lloyd at Stockfeeds next time, I'll point him out.'

Benny smiled. 'Okay.'

'Thanks for listening, honey,' said Odette, holding the chives, standing there by the dusty car in her overalls and her work boots. 'It's all a long time ago now. And what can you do? I didn't deserve Lloyd in the end. I'm spoilt just by the memory of him in his stupid pyjamas.'

56

Cora Franks sat behind the polished counter at Curios with a notepad in front of her and a pen in her hand, tapping the pen against the paper and wondering what on earth she could say.

She had spoken at four funerals. One for each of her parents, one for Betsy Dell's husband, and one for her father's sister—Lynette—who was such a horrible woman that it was very difficult to muster up anything nice to mention.

And now she was faced with this new challenge of what to say at the funeral of a man she had never met, and had no idea about whatsoever.

Cora tapped her pen and wrote down the only things she could be certain of: the quality and vintage of his suit, the date and approximate time of his death, the reassuring quality of his face. He looked like an old-fashioned movie star—that's what she had thought at the time. And she had felt he was very dependable.

Oh, how funny.

How she had formed such opinions, just by looking at his resting countenance. But oddly enough, Lil Chapman seemed to agree. They'd discussed it on the night he was found, over a glass of brandy, and Therese had rolled her eyes. Then Lil had reiterated it just that morning over tea. Just before she left to go back next door, Lil had said it like this: 'Don't you think he looked like a really decent person? Like, a bit noble or something?'

And Cora said, 'Yes,' and thanked Lil for her input.

Now, Cora wrote down *Decent* and *Noble* and then she sat back on her stool and sighed, and she was sitting there quietly thinking when Detective Sergeant Anthony Simmons and Constable James Hall walked through the door and approached the counter.

Cora Franks looked at them over the top of her reading glasses.

'Hello, Tony,' she said. 'James.'

'Hi, Cora,' said Constable James Hall, who seemed to Cora to always look like he'd just heard something rather surprising.

'Mrs Franks,' said Detective Sergeant Simmons.

And it just stuck Cora like a pin the way Tony called her that. *Mrs Franks.* There was something about the way he said it, so disdainfully, that made Cora wonder how any child of Elsie Simmons could have turned out so aggressive.

'I'm just putting some words together,' she said. 'For the funeral of the unknown man.'

'I heard about that,' said Tony. 'A funeral with no body. Don't you call that something else?'

'I think it's a called a commemorative service,' said Hall.

'You call it a funeral, Tony,' said Cora, and she took off her glasses and set them down on the counter.

Simmons grinned and he put one hand on the polished benchtop, another on his hip. He towered over Cora in a deliberately commanding position. 'Much to my disappointment, we're here to talk about antique silver,' he said, still smiling.

Cora nodded, desperately pleased that they were there on official business, and determined not to show it.

Simmons began to explain, quite vaguely, dispensing as little information as possible, how a particular piece had come into their possession—an antique—and they were wondering if Cora could take a look at it.

'You want my professional opinion,' said Cora.

'We thought it wouldn't hurt if you took a look at it,' said Simmons, as Hall casually examined the watch cabinet, taking particular interest in the watches with the thin gold bands.

'What is it?' asked Cora Franks.

'It's part of an ongoing investigation,' said Simmons, and Cora said, 'Well, if it would help in your investigation,' and then embarked on on a tangent about the funeral for the unknown man, and how Elsie Simmons had told Cora first

334

about the Somerton Man business, and that Cora was still astounded that it was so pertinent. Elsie was like an elephant with her memory. 'She may be getting a little forgetful here and there, but she can recall 1948 as clear as crystal; she's a wonderful resource.'

Simmons experienced the distinct discomfort he felt when someone spoke about his mother, even in friendly terms, and the instinct rose in him, as it always did, to come to Elsie's defence.

It had been his idea to come to Curios and speak to Cora Franks, even though it went against his personal preferences. He could have sent Franklin along with Hall, and avoided Cora altogether. But on his drive to the station that morning he knew he wouldn't do that. Despite his aversion to the woman, Simmons was a man who liked to see things for himself. He wanted to walk into Curios with the comb and watch her face as he showed it to her. Why? He wasn't entirely sure. There was just something about how it was all beginning to fit together in his mind.

Hall stood upright again as Simmons produced the clear bag with the comb in it from his pocket. 'This is it here,' said Simmons. 'It's a comb, obviously. Just wondering if you have any thoughts about it.' He said this casually and set it on the bench.

Cora Franks raised her eyebrows.

She put her reading glasses back on and picked up the plastic bag and held it so the silver comb was a foot from her face. Then she turned it over in her hand to inspect the marks on the handle, and looked up at Tony Simmons.

'Well I'll be damned,' she said.

'You recognise it,' said Simmons.

'It's just the weirdest thing,' said Cora Franks, plainly aghast. 'I was just thinking about it. Just yesterday.'

'You were thinking about the comb?' asked Hall. He looked at Simmons and then back at Cora Franks, whose eyes were wide and bright.

'Well if you want to *know* about it, it's German. I can tell you that for certain. German-made, sterling silver, either late nineteenth century or very early twentieth century. It belonged to a set. I have the brush and the mirror at home. I use the brush every night. It has lovely soft bristles.'

Cora looked quite pleased with herself now, being the custodian of such information, and Simmons stared steadily, careful not to react, even as he felt within him an engine firing up. It was deep down in his belly: a little motor of excitement.

'Huh,' said Hall, confused. 'Why were you thinking about the comb yesterday?'

'Well, because I had the whole set in my cabinet. It's the kind of thing you sell as a set. If you lose a piece—well, you can't sell them separately. And I was talking with my new neighbour, Benny; she's the new girl working at the Royal. You see, Benny's mother used to work for me. And I was telling Benny how I had to let her mother go.'

Hall retrieved his notepad from his pocket, and a pen from his other pocket and he wrote down the name *Benny* while Simmons just stood there, his arm on the bench, his body tingling.

'When did the woman work for you?' asked Hall.

'It was 1971,' said Cora.

'1971?' asked Hall, looking more surprised than usual.

Staring straight on at Cora, Simmons calmly breathed in and out of his nose. 'You're talking about Vivian Moon,' he said.

And Cora Franks narrowed her eyes, peering over her reading glasses, and she said: 'Yes, I am, Tony. I was talking about her yesterday and here I am talking about her again. What I'm telling you is this: Vivian Moon worked for me and I fired her for stealing this comb in 1971 and I've never doubted that decision for a second.'

57

Benny and Odette spent several hours in the overgrown garden behind the cottage, clearing away the weeds, digging out the long runners from the Boston ferns, pulling the overgrown vines off the fence and making a big long bed for vegetables. Odette dragged out several pots from the shed and they planted chives and parsley in them, and Benny set the pots on the deck near the back door, positioned for the morning sun. Then she opened a packet of garbage bags and they put leaves and weeds and small branches in five of them, until they were full.

At some point Odette had yelled for Fred over the fence, and he came over to help remove a clump of bamboo that had shot up alongside the shed but, even with the three of them, they made little headway. Fred Franks, with his Bob Hawke hair, was a man with a particularly pleasant demeanour and Benny liked him immediately. She was pleased when he stayed for a chat around the table, all of them sweaty and tired.

Then Fred went home and the two women made tea and toast and sat down again and chatted away some more. The tall trees gave a dappled light to the yard and it was such a nice place to sit.

When they heard a knock at the front door some time later, Odette thought it must be Fred again and she went inside to let him in, and Benny sat back with her feet up on the wooden table, cupping her tea in both hands. She was covered in dirt and had some sunburn on her shoulders. The gloves had got wet so she'd taken them off and her fingernails were black with earth.

She could hear Odette talking at the front door, and then a man's voice was speaking.

Benny put her tea down and got up, and entered the kitchen to see Odette leading a man down the hallway. A policeman. Benny could tell in an instant by his shirt and tie and navy name badge.

'Come through to the garden,' said Odette, and the tall man followed, glancing about at the house.

Benny walked back out to the garden and stood there awkwardly, not knowing if she should sit down or not, wondering, as she always did when she saw a policeman, if she had done something wrong.

●

Detective Sergeant Tony Simmons followed along behind the graceful woman he knew to be Odette Fisher. His mother knew Odette quite well, and Tony had met her a few times over the years. She used to be in the book club and now she lived up in the bush on the mountain. He knew she owned this house that he had once slept in as a boy.

The hallway had a long rug that ran up it—it was exotic-looking with red and brown patterns—and under that were polished floorboards. Tony felt the wood creak under his weight as he walked past the first bedroom on the right—there was an unmade bed and a lamp on a small bedside table—and then the bathroom with the pink tiles and the big bath with a showerhead over it. He looked in quickly and a flash of memory came: Viv in the shower, beclouded by steam, water rushing over her perfect body.

'Benny's just out the back,' said Odette, and Simmons walked past the last bedroom on the right—the one he had slept in. He stopped in the doorway and looked at the little single bed.

'Just out here,' Odette said, and he turned and said, 'Right,' and soon he was standing in the yard, hands on his hips, looking around the garden, which was clearly in the midst of some kind of transformation.

'Nice place you got here,' he said meaninglessly as Odette stood there, waiting for him to explain his presence.

'This is Benny,' said Odette. 'Benny, this is Tony. Would you like a cup of tea, Tony?'

Simmons said, 'No thanks, just a quick chat,' and the girl called Benny sat down slowly at the table, and then Odette and Simmons sat down, too. And when the three of them were sitting there around the outdoor setting, Odette asked after Elsie, and Simmons gave a brief appraisal of his mother's health.

Benny sat, self-consciously, and Simmons noticed her redden when he turned to her and said, 'Your mother's name has come up as part of an ongoing investigation and I wanted to ask you a couple of questions.'

Well, that was not what Odette Fisher had been expecting him to say.

'Vivian?' said Odette. 'What investigation?'

'Just an ongoing investigation,' said Simmons, and he coughed loudly as if to halt any further questions from Odette Fisher.

It had been a few hours since Tony Simmons and Jimmy Hall had spoken to Cora Franks at Curios. They had returned to the station and held a sit rep with Franklin, and then Simmons had got on the phone to make some enquiries into Vivian Moon, her death, and her most recent living arrangements.

Franklin had said, 'So this Vivian woman stole the comb from Curios and at some point she gave it to our guy?'

'That's a theory,' said Simmons.

'So the comb is the gift?' said Franklin. 'That's what the note meant?'

Simmons shrugged his shoulders.

'It could be,' said Hall, as Simmons sat there looking over his notes about Vivian Moon, who in December 1971 had left Cedar Valley and returned to Sydney, where she lived with a man called Frank Miller—currently not answering his phone—and, in 1972, gave birth to Benita Miller.

After that, the thin trail grew cold.

It seemed that Vivian Moon had travelled in and out of the country a fair amount over the past twenty or so years, and it was clear she was not really part of 'the system'. She kept a passport and a driver's licence, but no credit cards or memberships or insurance policies. She wasn't on the electoral roll, he was yet to uncover any bank accounts, and the telephone at the house she had lived in at the time of her death was unlisted—a silent number.

Now Benny Miller was living here in Cedar Valley, in the very same house that Vivian Moon had lived in, and a quick call to Tom Boyd confirmed what Simmons had suspected: that Benny Miller had arrived in Cedar Valley the same day that the unknown gentleman in a vintage suit had sat down against the window of Curios and died.

And now, here was Simmons: sitting in the backyard of the cottage, looking at this reserved and somehow defiant young woman, who sat as stiff as a board and had a face to match the otherworldly beauty of her mother.

'So, Benny,' said Simmons, 'I'm curious as to whether you can shed some light on your mother's general whereabouts. Where did she live when you were growing up?'

'I don't know,' said Benny.

'What about when you were older? A teenager?'

'I don't know,' said Benny.

Simmons asked Benny if she had been in touch with her mother recently, before she died, and the answer was no. He asked her if she understood the circumstances of her death, and Benny, without so much as flinching, said she did. Odette Fisher flinched, though, Simmons saw it and noted it in his mind as he continued on.

He asked Benny if her father was in regular contact with Vivian and she said, again, that she didn't know. She didn't know her mother's occupation. She didn't know her qualifications, her financial situation. She didn't know any of her acquaintances or friends—apart from Odette Fisher—and she did not know her boyfriends. She had no knowledge of an antique silver comb that may or may not have once been in the possession of Vivian Alice Moon.

'I think we've established that she didn't know her mother very well!' said Odette, who was visibly distressed by this wretchedly monotone interaction—as distressed as Benny was indifferent.

'Do you have anything of hers we could take a look at?' asked Simmons. 'I understand she lived here permanently for a time in 1971. I know it's a while ago, but it looks like the house hasn't changed much. Did she leave any personal effects?'

Odette, who looked at that point like a lion whose cub was in danger, said: 'Tony, I don't know why on earth you would care about Vivian's things, but if it's important to you I have some of her letters at home. If you want them I'll bring them to the station tomorrow, and then I'll have them back when you're finished. Right now I think Benny has said all she can say.'

So Simmons nodded and cleared his throat and said, 'I would like to see those letters,' and he got up from his chair.

Odette stood too, furious as hell.

'I'm, ah, very sorry about your mother passing,' said Detective Sergeant Simmons to Benny, who looked up at him with no emotion.

'Thank you,' she said.

Then she looked briefly at Odette, as if to apologise, before extending a long arm towards the end of the garden. 'There's a box of my mother's books in that shed. You can take them all away. I don't want them back.'

58

As the surrounding shops were just swinging open their doors on Thursday morning, the Cedar Valley Public Hall—a Federation era brick building on Valley Road—had been long awake with activity.

The service for the unknown man was to be held that afternoon at five-thirty, and Betsy and Fran had gone all-out in the arrangements. Considering they had their own establishments to tend to during working hours, the women had arrived at six-thirty in the morning to prepare. Chairs were brought out from back rooms and set in long rows. They felt it prudent to plan for low attendance, so they spread them out in a manner designed to give the impression of fullness, and they set up the lectern and arranged a small table for flowers. A simple brochure had been printed, with Betsy presiding over the design.

In lieu of any photos taken of the man while he was alive, the front cover of the brochure was the police-issued sketch—they'd cut it out from the newspaper. *Cedar Valley's Unknown Man* was printed in a serif font and underneath that: *? – 1 December 1993.*

Fran had consulted with Carol and John Hargraves regarding a suitable verse. Carol had suggested a short piece by Nancy Byrd Turner called 'Death is a Door', because of its optimism, and because Betsy Dell had been very strict about not wanting any mention of God or heaven. It was probably due to the fact that Fran was so well liked that the library had agreed to print the brochures free of charge.

The wake was to be held at the Royal Tavern after the service, and Tom Boyd had seemed slightly amused by the idea, in his unexcitable fashion. Fran had promised to provide two platters of party pies for guests, while acknowledging repeatedly that this was not a party at all.

●

At the Cedar Valley police station, Detective Sergeant Anthony Simmons had finally spoken to the woman in Sydney who ran the small hotel near Central Station.

She rasped at him down the line in a voice like a cornhusk, elaborating slightly on what she had told Hall. She recalled the man well enough. He'd checked in around seven in the evening on the last day of November with regular clothes on—a button-down shirt as she remembered it—and a suit-case. No, it wasn't a vintage number, just a modern zip-up thing that you'd see circling around on any airport carousel. The man had spoken so little, and the woman was no expert in accents, but she was sure that he had one, and she guessed it was European. He had paid cash, and the name he gave was T. Keane. She would send a fax to the station—a copy of the guestbook where he had signed in. She had no idea as to his night-time activities, nor if he'd received any visitors in his room.

He checked out early in the morning of December 1st and left his room spotless. 'Cleaner than when he arrived, that's for sure,' she said, and she cracked up laughing at the hilarious joke that was, apparently, her hotel's low standard in housekeeping.

But the main reason the woman remembered him at all was that he left wearing a thick brown suit, with a jumper underneath on the first day of summer. Not a cloud in the sky, a top of almost thirty expected, and the man was dressed for a wartime winter social.

It was on a hunch that, on hanging up from the hotel lady, Simmons placed a call to the German consulate in Sydney to issue a description: he had an unknown male with a European accent and a German-made comb in his pocket.

The dry man on the other end of the phone seemed entirely dubious.

'So he's German because of a comb,' he said.

'Would you humour me?' said Simmons, realising as he said it that humour was something this man did not do.

'I will undertake to fulfil your request,' said the man in a German accent, and he reluctantly provided a fax number so Simmons could send over the sketch, which he reluctantly agreed to circulate within the appropriate divisions.

Simmons had spent about three minutes looking through the box of books belonging to Vivian Moon. The novels he had set aside, but the travel guides and phrasebooks were of slightly more interest. He flipped through photographs of the Eiffel Tower and the Champs-Elysees, but it only made him feel bothered by how much Jenny longed to go to Paris and how much he did not.

But Vivian Moon's well-read copy of *The Rubaiyat of Omar Khayyam*? Well, that was something.

Simmons found it near the top—the books were shoved in every which way, like whoever had packed them was in a hurry—and there it was, a small volume with a green cover and gold letters. He held it in both of his big hands before he flipped through, astounded by the amount of notes this woman—Viv—had written in there, and entirely thrown by the language.

But here it was: a link. Something to substantiate Cora Franks's story that Vivian Moon had stolen the very comb that they had found in the dead man's pocket. Now he had Vivian Moon's meaningfully marked-up copy of the book made infamous by the Somerton Man. What did it all mean?

'It means it's circumstantial, doesn't it? That would be circumstantial evidence,' said Hall, who was leaning forward in his chair, elbows on his thighs, a picture of judicious enthusiasm.

Simmons raised his eyebrows.

'I mean, substantially circumstantial,' said Hall.

'Are we going to fucking court tomorrow, Jimmy?' said Simmons. 'We have the comb and we have the book. Are you telling me that's a coincidence? There is no such thing as a coincidence.'

Hall nodded, frowning, and glanced over at Gussy Franklin, who was sprawled in his chair with a look of amusement on his face.

'I've got dead ends everywhere with the blonde, hey,' said Gussy Franklin. 'I got no one who's seen if she had a car. We assume she did, but no one's seen it. Jimmy checked back with the bus service to make sure, but no one reckons they picked her up. It doesn't seem that she ate in town or bought anything except for the pills. Ed Johnson acted kind of cagey about the whole thing, but Ed acts cagey about everything. I think he just wants attention.'

Simmons made a noise: a grumble. His back pained him, and a headache—a swelling between his ears—was forming. He opened his drawer and found the Panadol there under his sweat towel. The whole blister pack was empty, and he closed the drawer again with some force.

'I'm thinking she killed him,' said Franklin.

'Who, the blonde?' asked Simmons, looking up, unable to tell if Gussy Franklin was serious or not.

'What else have we got, boss?' Franklin said. 'He had to get the poison in him somehow. And she's done a good job of disappearing, hasn't she? Getting in and out of town, taking a call at a payphone. Leaving without a trace.'

Hall was still frowning.

'She's obviously a bloody spy, too,' said Franklin. He grinned at Simmons. 'That's what Lil Chapman thinks. Barry's had his KGB books out.'

Simmons hooted at the thought of it. Lil and Barry Chapman, reading their spy stories, having a crack at a theory. Lil Chapman of all people, such a pasty woman.

'Wait, because we think our guy's a spy?' said Hall. 'But we don't even know if the Somerton Man was a spy.'

'They're all spies!' said Simmons, giggling now, his huge frame vibrating with amusement. 'German spies!'

Franklin slapped his trunk of a thigh and Hall smiled nervously, realising that he should be laughing. So, tentatively, he laughed. And then the three of them were having a grand old time, laughing loudly and carrying on—right up until Simmons sensed a presence.

Odette Fisher was standing in the doorway.

Simmons looked up, startled, and there she was in a dark-coloured dress, her grey hair long to her shoulders, as dignified a woman as had ever set foot in the Cedar Valley police station.

'Odette,' he said, standing. 'Hello.'

'Hello, Tony,' Odette said coolly. She held out a thick wad of envelopes. 'I have these for you. They're Vivian's letters.'

59

Cora Franks, dressed in a pink floral robe, stood in front of her vanity mirror, practising out loud her oration for the funeral.

She'd been up late fixing it. Rewriting sections. Adding a few personal anecdotes and then taking them out again. She longed to make a good impression on the audience, and she felt in the very depths of her that she wouldn't.

Using one of her several watches, she timed the final version so she could give Fran an estimate. It was four minutes. Was that too short—to commemorate the entire life of a human being? But what more was she to say, given she didn't know him in the slightest?

She wandered through the house to find Fred, who was cleaning his fishing reels, and she quietly explained her dilemma—just very softly, almost in a whisper, because she could hear busy sounds coming from Odette's cottage next door, and she knew Benny Miller was out there working in the garden, and Cora didn't want Benny, or anyone, to overhear.

•

Over the fence, on her hands and knees in the sun-dappled yard, Benny Miller had very much committed herself to the task of gardening. She had risen early and made the bed, sliding her hand over the quilt to flatten it evenly, folding the sheet over at the top. The python announced its presence with a heaving sound from the ceiling, and Benny was almost pleased to hear it. Standing in the shower, among the pink tiles, she scrubbed her body down with the stiff loofa until her skin went red. Her breakfast was a cheese jaffle and she ate it at the outdoor setting to the sound of the bush noise and Fred Franks whistling and working away on something next door.

From the gardening magazines that were in the shed, Benny had been learning about the benefits of pruning. She applied a pair of Odette's old secateurs to the rosemary and what she now knew was correa. Later, still outside, she wrote three brief letters to friends in Sydney, and a particularly warm letter to Jules Cowrie, asking how he was and telling him a little about her days. It was almost as an afterthought that she wrote one more letter—just a few lines really—to her father.

Perhaps a part of her did miss him?

She wondered this as she addressed the envelopes and put the stamps on, and then she went about tidying the kitchen while the radio played the Christian music station.

Benny Miller busied herself all morning, and it was only for a brief moment that she allowed herself to sit still on the front verandah, watching the slow activity of the street. She sat, thinking, and found herself thinking mainly of Odette Fisher.

Does she like me? Benny wondered this. Even though Odette had given every indication that she did—that she liked her very much—Benny wondered if it could really be true. What an embarrassment it was, to be thinking like this, and Benny knew that. But she couldn't help it. She sat there, watching a man across the street who was taking a long time attaching a camper trailer to the back of his car, and she wondered: was it possible that a woman such as Odette Fisher could truly like her? Or was she just being kind—dutiful— and, all the while, searching for an excuse to withdraw?

•

Odette arrived, as planned, in the early afternoon.

'It really looks good, doesn't it?' said Odette as they walked out to admire their work in the garden, and Benny thought Odette looked beautiful in her linen dress and leather shoes. She wore a long silver necklace with a turquoise stone.

Odette sat down at the kitchen table and Benny put the kettle on, but Odette said, 'Since we're off to a funeral I thought we should have a proper drink,' and she produced a longneck in a paper bag from her handbag. Benny grinned and fetched two glasses from the dresser.

She poured the beer into glasses, and the two of them discussed the garden for only a few minutes before Odette said, 'I went by the police station to drop off Vivian's letters'—and Benny looked across at Odette, saw her grave expression, and realised then that the occasion of their beer was not in preparation for a strange funeral, but a preparation for difficult news.

Benny took a sip and swallowed.

'I think it's time I told you about some of the things Vivian wrote in them,' said Odette.

'Okay,' said Benny, and a cold sensation swept across her, like swimming under the water at the river.

Odette sat back in her chair and took a sip of the beer. And then she began to explain to Benny—slowly, thought-fully—that the more she thought about it, the more she felt that Tony Simmons, the tall policeman, would find Vivian's letters of interest. She had hated the thought of giving them to him, but a part of her was relieved by the act of handing them over. For Odette had read them all again, these past couple of days, poring over them and then lying sleepless in her bed, with Bessel snoring on the mat beside her. She had churned with the information and what it meant. There were so many things that she knew already—and had long forgotten—or that she had not really thought over at the time. And all these things felt relevant now, in ways she would never have expected.

Vivian Moon was a passionate person. Heady and restless, she was forever chasing stimulation. She was a fool for it. And Odette could see that now: just how searching Vivian was, and how unmoored.

At the time, Odette didn't think much about the man Vivian met in Europe. A letter had announced their first encounter—at a bookstore in West Berlin, 'under the shadow of the Wall', as Vivian had written. Odette had loved this kind of phrase, never knowing if it was literal or metaphoric.

Vivian and this man had struck up a conversation in the bookshop's cafe over a book Vivian had just purchased—a German translation of *The Rubaiyat of Omar Khayyam*—and Vivian, who found the man very handsome, had invited him to sit. The book had led directly to the topic of the Somerton Man: an obscure unsolved mystery from Adelaide, Australia, just after the war.

The man in the cafe was instantly intrigued. His English was very good—with a strong German accent—and Vivian found him curious, charming. More than that, he was enigmatic, and the one thing Vivian Moon loved was a mystery.

Their first official date was at a hotel bar and she had told him briefly of her childhood years in Adelaide, her interest in philosophy, her most recent travels. The man, on the other hand, tended to avoid self-revelation. He smiled and shrugged his shoulders in a way that she found almost conspiratorial. Vivian Moon was fascinated by his constant deflections and unusual manner.

Over several letters to Odette, Vivian described the ongoing courtship. It was clear to Odette that Vivian was in love, or at least infatuated. On their third date, she had given the man the *Rubaiyat* as a gift, and he had looked around the hotel bar and put it immediately in his pocket, as if they were being watched. He whispered to her: *Danke, mein Shatz.*

Vivian wrote: 'Oh Odie, you would laugh! I wrote a quote in the front of the book, just like Jestyn! And he does act so strangely, I find him fascinating. Now of course I am dreaming that he has some secret life, fighting the Stasi, and we will have to flee to South America together to escape a charge of treason. Now tell me—how are you, my dearest? How have you found the move to Cedar Valley?'

Odette had stopped and read over that letter again in the lamplight in her farmhouse, and had shaken her head at the absurdity of it. The harmless absurdity of Vivian and her intrigues, and the way things seemed to have turned out in the end. Although that was the thing—Odette was only speculating, at that point, how they had turned out at all.

Benny sat there at the kitchen table, listening to Odette, considering this man in Berlin who her mother had fallen in love with, and her mind went to the box of books she had given to the tall policeman—Tony Simmons—and, in particular, Vivian's copy of the *Rubaiyat*, with all its fragrant quotes about drinking and impermanence and 'True Light, Kindle to Love'.

Now with the New Year reviving old desires, the thoughtful soul to solitude retires. Vivian had underlined this, and then copied it out again inside the back cover.

Benny sat, worrying the table with her hands, and allowed herself to dwell, just for a moment, on Vivian's death. On the very manner of it. And the stupid book, it echoed around inside her. *We must beneath the couch of earth descend.*

'What happened to the man?' Benny asked.

'I don't know,' said Odette. 'She was so enthralled by him, and then she just stopped talking about him. She came back to Australia and was living in Sydney, and then she moved here—and I can't remember hearing anything more about the man. I know there was someone. I've always known that. I knew that was the reason she left Frank the first time and came here to figure it all out. Benny, Frank wasn't the one for Vivian. I mean, you know that already. But I did know there was someone else—someone that she kept to herself. I don't know why she didn't tell me, because she told me everything. At least, I thought she told me everything. But I don't know what happened to that man she met in Berlin—or if he's even relevant now. And I imagine that's what Tony Simmons is wondering too.'

The two of them sipped their beer, and Benny understood what Odette was saying. She understood—and the disquiet was so strong in her that she got up and went to the dresser and put some cashews in a bowl, just to be doing something, and she set the bowl on the table and felt that her hand was shaking with the effort.

'What was his name?' asked Benny. 'The man in the bookstore?'

'His name was Oskar,' said Odette. 'Oskar Konig.'

Benny sat down again in her chair—her chest full of an acute anger—thinking directly now of one particular thing that Vivian had written in the *Rubaiyat*. Among all the quotes of poetry, and those little drawings, Benny had read one line and knew it was not Persian poetry. It bothered her right from the start: the girlishness of it, in neat red writing with a love heart drawn beneath it.

Everything now is O.K.

But of course it hadn't meant that everything was all right, as Benny had thought, because it wasn't. It wasn't all right, or okay, and maybe Vivian never had been either. Those letters were initials: the name of some fabled man, who caught the fancy of her mother to such an extent that she'd never acted like her mother at all. Benny could see that now, but still she couldn't shake the terrible feeling she kept inside her always: that everything about Vivian's leaving was somehow her fault.

Odette looked over at her and her mouth closed in a sad smile. 'Oh, honey,' she said, as two thin tears went down Benny's cheeks.

But ever the stoic, Benny Miller wiped them away with her shirtsleeve, took a sip of beer and said, 'I'm fine. I should get changed.'

Odette sat still, looking at the younger woman across the table; looking at her and seeing her. And she said, 'Vivian was so full of shame for leaving you. I know she was. She was so ashamed that she could never face me again. I see that now. It's why she disappeared out of my life and avoided me all those years, and sent me those photos, pretending she was there with you. I wish I could explain her. But I can't. I mean, I have my hunches as to where her mind was at, but I can't explain her. I just want you to know, Benny, that even knowing you for a short time, I can't begin to understand it. If it were me—if *I* had been your mother—I could never have done that. Do you understand?' Her eyes were glistening. 'I could never have left you, Benny.'

60

At first it was just a few people mingling outside the Public Hall a little after 5 pm. Many of the shopkeepers had closed up and didn't want to go home and then come back to town again, so they gathered a little early to talk among themselves. There were two long benches outside the white building, and by quarter past five the benches were full and at least twenty others were standing around in small groups.

It was a clear evening—December-warm—and Betsy Dell opened the door of the hall a crack and stuck her head out to see how it was looking.

'Good turnout!' she yelled to Fran when she came back in, and Fran smiled and said, 'I should think so,' and put the finishing touches to their display: a little table had a vase of white lilies on it and a framed photocopy of the police sketch of the unknown man. Next to that were some newspaper clippings about the case, cut out from the *Gather Region Advocate*—'to give mourners some context,' as Betsy put it.

And to the left was a framed photo of the Curios shopfront from 1978, on loan from Cora Franks, just because.

When the doors opened at 5.25 pm, even Fran was bowled over at the number of people who streamed in. Keith Hand, from Cedar Valley Brake & Clutch, helped them fetch every remaining chair from the storage room, and even then it was standing room only at the back.

'He's struck a chord, hasn't he,' said Maureen Robinson as she joined Odette and Benny at their spot, halfway down on the side.

Odette nodded, and Benny looked about the room, astounded by the number of people. Some women were dressed in formal attire, and others as if they'd just got off the couch from watching the soaps. Two men in council work wear sat on Benny's right. In front was an elderly couple, holding hands.

But to say the mood was sombre would be incorrect. Most people seemed simply curious; some slightly amused; and others were perhaps there for reasons they did not quite understand, driven by a kind of existential enquiry. They sat, introspective, questioning, as if the death of this unknown man on the main road of the town had thrown the nature of their own lives into sharp focus.

Fran took her place at the podium—a simple black dress highlighting her doughy loveliness—and gave a brief introduction.

She thanked the room; she thanked Betsy and others who had contributed.

'He drew his last breath in our town,' said Fran. 'All we know is he was a decent-looking person. He was exceptionally dressed. We may never know what he was here for, but we do know that he was here. And we honour his memory as we should, as we would anyone who draws their last breath in our community.'

A song played: 'Stand by Me' by Ben E. King. That had been Fran's choice, as she found it both positive and profound.

When it was time for Cora to stand, she did so self-consciously, and Benny Miller could hear that Cora's voice was stung with nerves.

'Thank you all for coming,' she said, rather shakily. 'I do think he—whoever he was—would so appreciate all of you being here to farewell him. And haven't we all just taken stock a bit in the last week, and had a good think about ourselves?'

•

Cora was struggling. She was sure there had been a percept-ible shift in the attitude of the audience with her rise to the podium. Why don't they warm to me as they do to Fran? She briefly pondered this.

'I, for one,' said Cora, 'have felt shaken up by it. I said to my husband Fred, I said, "Fred, if it's that easy to pop off then maybe we should do that trip to Bali like we've always wanted,"' and she gave a nervous laugh.

And then a man with a booming voice said from up the back, 'We might join you!' and after that everybody laughed, and Cora beamed and began to relax a bit and she managed to speak quite well.

'As many of you know, Lil Chapman and I were the ones to discover the unknown man last Wednesday. Lil's here in the front. Give a wave, Lil. And while it was not the best circumstances to meet someone—when they're already dead—he has certainly made an impression.' Cora carried on with increasing confidence—Fred Franks, watching from the front row, lit with pride—and when she was finished she sat down again between Fred and Lil, and felt a rush of pleasure at how well it had gone.

Another song played. This time it was 'My Way' by Frank Sinatra, and a surprising number of people sang along.

Cora Franks smiled as she looked about the room, clasping the funeral brochure in her hand. She really felt very good. Betsy Dell glanced over and gave her an approving nod. Cora couldn't believe the amount of people present and the cheery feeling in the room. She could see every shopkeeper on Valley Road, and so many people she knew from around town. And given the man had died outside Curios, Cora Franks couldn't help but feel that, in some small way, all of this was a little bit about her; that all these people were somehow here to support *her* and her establishment—a Cedar Valley institution—as well as the dead man in the suit.

Yes, Cora could see *almost* every shopkeeper, but not every one. She couldn't see Dieter Bernbaum, the chemist from across the road, for instance. But he was such a strange man, his absence from community events was hardly surprising.

She looked down at the printed brochure, at the sketch of the man on the front. It was a terrific likeness—some people could draw so well—and as Cora stared into the man's sketched eyes, that same feeling came over her as when she had seen him in real life—or in death, as it were—and she'd sensed some hint of recognition. She blinked and, maddeningly, the sense dissolved. If only she'd gone out and spoken to him. If only Therese hadn't been so upset that day and Cora hadn't been so distracted by her—and it was then that it occurred to Cora that Therese wasn't there at the funeral. Cora had been so nervous she hadn't even noticed.

Her 'friend' Therese, who simply didn't care an inch about the man who'd died in the street, or about anyone really. She acted like her life was a long stream of misfortunes when it wasn't at all, going on and on about Ed all the time—and Cora noted that Ed was nowhere to be seen either.

Therese should have been there. It was an affront to Betsy and Fran that she wasn't. Betsy was supposed to be Therese's friend, and Fran was too. Fran was Therese's neighbour! No,

365

Cora Franks was appalled. She was absolutely appalled by Therese's absence.

And yet: what was this marvellous sense of freedom?

Cora was struck by it. By the sudden and unusual feeling that she could just be, amid all those people, *herself*. Even more than appalled, Cora Franks was so very pleased, so deeply and powerfully relieved that, for once, Therese Johnson was, blessedly, not there.

61

'I think it's probably beyond irrelevant, but you boys should still head down.' Detective Sergeant Anthony Simmons was leaning on the edge of Hall's desk in the common area.

'Good to show a police presence,' said Hall from his chair.

'Whatever,' said Simmons. 'Just hang up the back. Imagine if our blonde woman showed up to pay her respects? Wouldn't that be convenient?'

Gussy Franklin, one desk along, said, 'Can we go to the wake too? It's catered.'

And Tony Simmons chuckled at Gussy—he loved that guy—and he went back into his office, a little cooler now that an afternoon breeze was coming in the window.

Jenny was taking the girls to the service. The ridiculous service. She'd called earlier and suggested she pick up Elsie on the way, but Tony had objected.

'She's too frail,' he said, and he hated saying it. But Elsie Simmons was so bent over and slow and it was always such an ordeal getting her in and out of the house. Besides, it irritated Simmons enough already that Jenny wanted to attend.

Tony had spent the afternoon reading through Vivian Moon's letters to Odette Fisher. There was a thick wad of them and Odette had kept them in chronological order, which had made things easier for Simmons.

The handwriting was consistent with the notes inside Vivian's old copy of the *Rubaiyat* (Simmons had looked over that again too, briefly; who knew what those little poems were banging on about?) and by four-thirty he'd got to the end of Vivian's communications, which ceased in June 1969. The last letter Odette had provided stated that Vivian was returning to Australia. It was sudden, and no reason was given. She was planning to settle in Sydney and find work. In that final letter Vivian seemed, given her earlier flourishes, oddly restrained.

He heard the boys out in the common area, saying cheerio to the others, and Simmons thought to himself that the funeral was the type of event that exemplified why he'd prefer to live in Clarke. This kind of thing would never happen in Clarke, Simmons thought, as he lined photocopies of four letters alongside each other, all of them from Vivian's time in West Berlin, and applied a highlighter to certain sections.

The pen was raised in his hand when the phone rang—a call from the austere man from the German consulate.

'I have some information,' said the man.

'Did someone recognise him?' asked Simmons.

The man said that yes, someone had.

The German consulate had circulated the sketch and the description to its Australian offices, and to the Federal Criminal Police Office in Germany, also known as the BKA. The BKA had a database of unidentified bodies and missing persons, and the sketch and description Simmons had provided was matched to a photograph and description from Berlin, where a Mrs Klein had lodged a claim.

'Who's she?' asked Simmons.

'The wife,' said the man on the other end of the line.

'The wife of Oskar Konig?' asked Simmons, the name that was highlighted before him on one of Vivian's long and flowery letters.

'No,' said the man. 'The wife of Oskar *Klein*.'

62

By the time the party pies arrived at the wake, the drinking had long started and the boisterous noise from the Royal Tavern spilled out onto Valley Road.

The service itself was supposed to run for half an hour, but the difficulty of it was that there was only so much Cora and Fran could say about a person they had never met, and popular songs tend to be brief. At ten to six the congregation was heading out the doors of the Public Hall and walking up the street to the Royal, where Tom had Gary and Ern working with him behind the bar in anticipation of a crowd.

The pub was as busy as Benny had ever seen it. It was as busy as most people had ever seen it, and the mood was surprisingly buoyant. Benny waited in a long queue at the bar to buy herself and Odette a drink. And when Tom Boyd finally got around to serving her, he said, 'Benny, you should've come around and helped yourself,' and Benny Miller felt a warm rush of belonging, which only expanded within her when

Tom, smiling, dismissed her as she held out her money, as if it were a preposterous notion that she should pay.

Odette certainly knew a lot of people, and she introduced Benny around. There were members of her book club present, and her writer friend, Arden Cleary—who talked to Benny kindly about local geology. Odette seemed to have deep resources for being social.

The party pies provided by Fran were gone in minutes, and Fran walked around with an empty platter apologising for underestimating the numbers. Benny saw the two policemen that had been there on the evening the man had died—they were standing by the pool table now in their uniforms, talking with some locals. And she noticed Cora Franks, too, sitting at a table in the bistro with Fred and Betsy and several other people who Benny recognised from behind the shop counters on Valley Road.

It was at least an hour later, perhaps more, when the crowd at the bar thinned and more people relocated to the bistro for dinner. Benny was returning from the bathroom to the table next to the window, where Odette was sitting with a small group of people, all of them eating chips from a basket, and Benny saw Odette break into a broad grin when a woman appeared beside her—a beautiful woman with wide, dark eyes.

'There you are!' said Odette, and the two women hugged before embarking on a rapid conversation, chattering away as Benny took her stool again, about a book this woman had just finished reading for book club. Carol Hargraves joined in—the book was about a man in a war hospital, burnt beyond recognition and unable to remember his own name—and Benny sat on her stool and listened and helped herself to more chips.

'And then you start thinking he's some kind of German collaborator, which is all a bit too relevant,' said the woman, whose dark curly hair was grey at the temples, and Benny realised this woman was Annie Boyd. Tom was over at the bar working away, and Benny looked across at him and then back to this woman and thought: of course.

'Oh yes,' said Odette, turning to Benny with a look that was almost apologetic.

'Relevant how?' asked Carol.

'Well, because of what Elsie says about this Adelaide connection,' said Annie Boyd.

'We'd better save this discussion for book club; I think Maureen will have a lot to say,' said Odette. 'Benny, this is Annie Boyd.'

Benny sat stiffly on her stool. She felt about as young as a seed. 'Hello,' she said to Annie.

'Oh, *you're* Benny,' said Annie Boyd, and Benny felt quietly humiliated by her own jealous sentiments. How absurd she was to feel herself in competition with this bright and intimidating woman. Benny just nodded meekly as Annie went on with the kind of unwavering confidence Benny was so drawn to; the kind of confidence she was certain to never possess: 'Well, it's so nice to finally meet you. I was just saying to Tom last night that we should have you and Odie up to the house for a meal. You can meet the girls. They're at that age now where they just *love* older girls; they get a bit starstruck, you know. What about next weekend? How does that sound to you, Benny?'

•

And all the while, as Benny was enjoying herself more than she would have expected, Gussy Franklin and James Hall were mingling with the locals and drinking lemon, lime and bitters, and then commiserating with Fran over the shortage of pies.

'At least Tom will be happy,' she said. 'Everyone's had to eat at the bistro.'

'Ed will be run off his feet,' Gussy Franklin said, and Fran asked after Gussy's mum, and Jimmy's mum, and the progress of their investigation.

'We've got a couple of leads,' said Franklin. 'We're still looking into a few things.'

Hall nodded, he finished the last of his drink and set the empty glass on the edge of the pool table. 'We haven't had any luck finding that blonde woman we were asking about the other day,' he said. 'But we're looking. It's a shame you weren't in town when it all happened, Fran. I reckon you'd make a good witness.'

Fran went *Hmmm* and gave an odd kind of smile. Then she cleared her throat and said, 'You know, boys, I don't think you should spend too much time on that one.'

'Why do you say that, Fran?' asked Gussy Franklin.

'Oh, well, look,' said Fran, and she sighed and seemed to deliberate a moment before she spoke. 'I don't want to start gossip, so I'll just say this: Ed's an old friend of mine. A very old friend. We went to primary school together, for goodness sake. And I'm not saying I approve, but he's a friend.'

'And what?' asked Gussy.

'And do you need me to spell it out for you, Gussy?' said Fran. 'That poor woman is not going to solve your case. I wasn't going to say this to you boys when you came in the shop asking in front of everyone, but I'll say it to you now, *off* the record. I live two doors up from Ed Johnson and I've seen a few things over the years that I did not need nor want to see. And all I'm going to say about last Wednesday evening is that it's lucky Therese was up at Curios having a drink. I don't know what Ed thinks he's doing. Probably making promises he can't keep, from what I can gather, and that kind of thing can send people crazy. Do you understand what I'm saying? You boys are barking up the wrong tree.'

63

M rs Renate Klein was weary with sleep as she told Detective Sergeant Anthony Simmons, in a thick German accent, down an echoing telephone line from Berlin, that she had been waiting for his call and was just rising to a wintry day.

'Hot and late in Australia, I am sure, but here, cold and early,' she said brusquely.

Simmons, holding the receiver in one hand and a pen in the other, stared down at the notepad where he had written this woman's name—Renate Klein, wife of Oskar Klein—and her extensive telephone number with its required international prefixes.

Thanks to the man at the German consulate, Simmons had acquired some very basic information. Mrs Renate Klein was an English teacher in a high school in Berlin. She'd married the man she knew as Oskar Klein in 1962 and they had four grown children, three of who were married with children of their own.

Mrs Klein had notified police immediately when her husband went missing. He had been gone for twelve days now, and she was certain he would not return. She had already emptied the wardrobe of his clothes and donated them to charity. Concern was growing among local German police as to her patent lack of distress.

As the man at the consulate explained, Renate Klein was expecting a call from Australia; she had been alerted late last night Berlin time that a body had been found, and she very much wanted to be called.

'The sketch—it looks like my husband,' she said to Simmons.

'You're sure?' asked Simmons, and because of the echoing connection he heard his own voice repeated, most disconcerting.

'No, I'm not sure. It's a drawing. But I would say I am ninety-five per cent sure. And he's not here, so he must be somewhere.'

'I'm sorry you have to go through this,' said Simmons.

'I'm not,' said Mrs Renate Klein.

Tony Simmons, surrounded by the photocopied letters, yellow highlighter illuminating Vivian's scrawls, couldn't quite put it all together.

Mrs Klein told him, matter-of-factly, as if she'd been saying the words verbatim for years, that she had not loved her husband for a very long time. He was still her husband, but that was only because she was Roman Catholic. Or, as

Renate put it succinctly to Simmons: 'We are only married because we are not divorced.'

'Will you be coming out to identify the body?' he said.

'No thank you,' said Renate.

All Renate wanted was for the death to be established, and a certificate issued in the name of her husband—Oskar Klein—so she could carry on disposing of his things without arousing such bothersome suspicion. Her children might miss their father, perhaps, but she would not miss her husband and no tears would she shed.

It astonished Simmons that Renate Klein did not ask how this man who looked just like her husband had died. And when Simmons explained it—in all its peculiar detail—she said nothing. She had no idea about the vintage suit. She had never seen any silver comb. Nothing rang a bell about a man who had died in Adelaide in 1948.

And why did Vivian's letters refer to an Oskar Konig, when this woman was speaking about an Oskar Klein? Simmons was perplexed.

'Have you ever heard the name Oskar Konig?' he asked Renate Klein.

'No,' she said. 'But I know about that Australian woman. I know all about her.' Her voice was thick with disgust.

'Which woman are you referring to?' said Simmons.

'I am sure you know who I am referring to: the one he had holed up over here in that apartment all those times,' she said.

'Are you referring to an Australian woman called Vivian Moon?'

'Is that her name?' said Renate Klein. 'Why would I want to know her name?'

Simmons closed his eyes. He was disoriented by the conversation and the difficulty of the connection—his own voice swimming around in a soup of telephonic distance. 'Mrs Klein,' he said, 'I'm going to have to make some calls and come back to you again tomorrow morning our time, which will be later tonight your time.'

'Hmmm,' she said.

'Just for my records, what did your husband do?'

'He was a teacher,' she said. 'Like me. He taught at a high school. Just a boring old chemistry teacher. I like being a teacher, but not Oskar, oh no. That was not good enough for Oskar. He wanted to be so special, the way he used to carry on, going on his mysterious trips, acting so important, making an ape of himself. I could not stand it. I have known about your Australian woman for so many years and I do not care. He can do what he likes. I really do not care.'

Simmons said, 'Right.' He said, 'I'll make those calls.'

'It looks just like my husband,' said Renate Klein. 'He has to be somewhere, doesn't he? So, it is him. I know it's him. And do you know what else I know? I know that he is tremendously full of shit.'

64

A thin moon was high in the pale sky when Cora Franks knocked on the screen door of Elsie Simmons's yellow house, where a Christmas wreath was stuck fast to the flyscreen.

A call from Elsie sounded from inside: 'Come in!'

'It's just me, Els,' said Cora as she went along the hallway and into the living room, where Elsie was sitting in lamplight with the radio playing softly.

'Oh, Cor, you came,' said Elsie. 'You didn't have to come.'

'I did,' said Cora. 'It's a day for company.' And she put her bag down and sat on the small armchair next to Elsie.

Cora had come directly from the wake. Fred was having a wonderful time sitting in the bistro at the big shop table. Gosh, he was so good at being Fred: the man who everyone liked talking to because he was so easy and fun and good.

Fran and Betsy were in their element too, and Cora had felt very included—appreciated—and the whole evening had been a tonic for her. She was in a lovely frame of mind. But she knew what the day meant for Elsie too, so she'd picked up her bag and told Fred to stay, and she'd walked in the twilight. It was the anniversary of the death of Neville Simmons, Elsie's husband, and something of a tradition for them to spend it together.

'Shall I pour us a glass?' asked Cora.

'You'd better,' said Elsie, and Cora went over to the cabinet and brought out the brandy. She emptied a generous measure into two crystal glasses and gave one of them to Elsie as she sat down again.

'To Neville,' said Cora.

'To Neville,' said Elsie, and they clinked their glasses and drank.

'The best mayor the Gather Region ever had,' said Cora, with a wry smile.

'And the worst husband,' said Elsie Simmons, and the two of them nodded silently.

'I've got a lot to tell you, Els,' said Cora. 'Tony came into the shop yesterday, asking about—you're not going to believe this—about that silver comb Vivian Moon stole from me all those years ago.'

'*No*,' said Elsie. 'What's that about? Did the daughter have it? What's her name again?'

Cora shook her head. 'Benny,' she said. 'And I don't know. Maybe. You know, I have a funny feeling it has something to do with the man who died—even though I don't see how it could. I just came from his funeral up at the Public Hall. Did you hear about that?'

'Oh yes,' said Elsie. 'That was a funny thing for them to do.'

'It was really very nice,' said Cora, and she told Elsie a bit about it, and how her speech had gone very well. Fran and Betsy had put a lot of effort in, and so many people had come. It was really just an excuse for a get-together for some people, but others seemed quite moved by it. She reached into her handbag and pulled out the funeral brochure they'd printed, with the sketch of the man on the cover, and she handed it to Elsie.

Elsie peered at it. She blinked a few times, very deliberately, and looked some more.

'My eyes, Cor,' she said. 'I get these floaters in my eyes.' But Elsie kept on looking at it, blinking and looking, and then she turned her head to the side. 'That's the man who died?' she asked.

'That's him,' said Cora. 'It's a good likeness.'

Elsie stared at the picture intently now, and then she looked up at Cora and said, 'He's familiar.'

Cora looked back at Elsie with such surprise. Her wonderful friend, Elsie Simmons, who was fading so much with age, she still had the light in her. Every so often she still shone so brightly.

'He's familiar, Cor, and you know the first thing I think of when I look at that face is that time Viv looked after Tony.

Do you remember that? There was a man hanging around, and I didn't like it one bit. Remember? The way Viv went about with men; it wasn't proper. And when I look at this face, it just makes me think of that time. Remember that man, Cor? The one who was hanging around?'

Cora said, '*No*,' and she held her hand out for the brochure and Elsie gave it back.

'We saw him knocking one time when Viv wasn't home and he was acting like he wasn't sure if he had the right house. Then, when you asked him what he was up to, he kind of ran away. He was a strange sort of fellow. Definitely not from around here.'

And Cora Franks, who had indeed looked at that dead man at Curios with some spark of recognition—a spark that kept dying out as soon as she'd sensed its flash—looked at the sketch then and, while she couldn't remember the man, she could remember herself *saying* to a man, outside the cottage on Wiyanga Crescent however many moons ago, in a tone of particular disapproval, something along the lines of: 'Excuse me, *sir*, who are you looking for? Can I help you with anything? Sir, why are you walking away?'

65

Simmons stayed on at the station after the phone call with Mrs Renate Klein, his mind swimming around in currents of information.

He went out to the kitchenette—he was the only one left at the station—and he made a cup of coffee and took a few biscuits from the tin to eat at his desk.

The light was beginning to fade outside and he switched on his desk lamp, which lit up the pile of letters, the highlighted sections of Vivian's handwriting, her copy of *The Rubaiyat of Omar Khayyam*.

Jenny had taken the girls straight home after the funeral and they would be waiting for him. And now, having borne witness to the bitterness of Renate Klein, he felt a rare desire to be with Jenny, to be with the girls, all four of them together in the house.

Simmons picked up the *Rubaiyat* and flicked through it again, stopping to read an underlined poem about love, then he carried on flicking until he reached the very back page, where there was a lot of writing in different coloured pens. He'd missed it earlier, this back page. There were several blank pages at the end of the book, and then this: the final page and the inside of the back cover, which was covered in Vivian's writing.

There were quotes he had already read inside the book written out again—they may as well have been in actual Persian for all he understood them. But in red pen Vivian had written *Everything now is O.K.* with a love heart below it, and Simmons nodded to himself, understanding immediately what she had meant. O.K. for Oskar Konig. Or was it Oskar Klein? Whoever he was, it was the little symbols Viv had drawn there underneath that really caused him to focus.

She had drawn, in black pen, a crescent moon and a crown. Simmons smiled.

The silver comb, sitting in the clear plastic bag, was in his drawer and he got it out for comparison. The crescent moon and a crown hallmarked on the silver; Vivian had copied them down exactly. And it was in a flash that Simmons stood up and went over to the box of Vivian's books that sat on the floor near his desk.

He bent down and rummaged through them until he found what he was after. Then he went back to his desk, and opened Vivian Moon's German–English dictionary.

Simmons thumbed through the German section, searching, until he found K, and he raced along, his finger tracing down the page to settle on the word *konig*.

The English translation was written alongside it.

It was *king*.

Simmons cleared his throat, the sound of it reverberating in the small office. Excitement had built in him, just with the game of it, because it was certainly a game. It had been a strange game all along, and of course Simmons had had no choice but to play. And if a man with some imagination—with aspirations to great importance—wanted to be someone else, well then he may as well make himself a king. 'He wanted to be so special,' Renate Klein had said. He was desperate to be mysterious and interesting, desperate to impress, thought Simmons, in life and in death.

He looked down at the *Rubaiyat* once more, at the copied symbols, the quotes, all of them so pathetically hopeful.

Vivian Moon and Oskar Konig: a crescent moon and a king's crown.

What a romantic pair, thought Simmons with some disdain, what an odd tribute this all was, and he made a clicking sound with his mouth—thinking, thinking—and it was before the thought had even formed that he thumbed backwards in the dictionary—a big chunk of pages—until he got to the G's, and ran his finger down the page.

A big wide smile came over his face when he found the word he was looking for and saw its meaning. He shook his head and laughed to himself, just a little, out loud in the office.

'Very good,' he said.

Gift was the German word.

Poison was the English translation.

66

Driving up to Odette's house the following morning, rain started to fall lightly on the dirty windscreen of Benny's car.

She put the wipers on but the rain was so light they only smudged the dirt on the screen, and so she drove along watching an indistinct road, glad that she knew it a little by now and was ready for the turn.

She rolled along the unsealed section towards Odette's house—tiny stones flinging about from her tyres—thinking about the night before, and how she had spent a long time talking with Annie and Odette, and how good it had felt to be a part of their conversation.

Benny had slept in that morning, unusually tired. She'd made a coffee and drunk it at the kitchen table. The day was so grey and she'd really only done one thing before leaving the house: she made a call to her father. It was something she hadn't expected to do, and from the surprise in Frank Miller's voice he hadn't expected her to do it either.

'It's really good to hear from you, Ben,' he said. 'Really good.' And she thought about their brief conversation then, driving along the rough road, and she herself was surprised by how good it had felt to hear his familiar voice. He had told her a longish story about a sideboard and she'd been almost pleased to listen; and even though a part of her wanted to ask him so many questions, she simply didn't.

As she came through the main gate, she saw Odette standing next to the long fence with the cows, emptying a bucket of feed for them in the misty rain. She turned and waved as Benny pulled up. Then they went inside, Bessel running ahead, and Odette took her raincoat off and hung it on the coat stand and there was music playing in the house, like always.

'You're tired,' Odette said.

'I am,' said Benny.

'So am I,' said Odette, smiling, and she told Benny that a lot of people would be a little under the weather today after the wake, and that the gathering had continued after close. Annie and Tom had shut the doors and a few of them had carried on. Betsy Dell and Fred Franks were two of the most entertaining people in Cedar Valley and Odette had had a wonderful time.

The rain got heavier while they were talking in the farm-house kitchen and it was loud on the tin roof. Odette made coffee, and she fried Benny two eggs in butter and Benny ate them quickly. After a little while they were both lying down on opposite couches, assessing the funeral service and how strange and good they'd found it, especially Cora's oration, which had been surprisingly touching.

They talked a while like that—in the easy way Odette always made a conversation—both of them avoiding anything to do with Vivian Moon, and they decided on watching a video since the weather was so lousy, but first Benny suggested they go outside and watch the rain from the verandah; it had got so thick and heavy. So they went out and the air was cool and the cows were just standing there getting wet. Odette sat down on the rocking chair and Benny on a low stool, her back against the house.

'This is nice,' said Odette as they watched the paddock, and the atmosphere out there was different—somehow contemplative with the rain—and perhaps that was why Odette ventured after a spell to say, 'You know, I've been wanting to ask you something, but I've been worried to ask it.'

'What is it?' asked Benny, the wood of the farmhouse hard against her back.

'How did Vivian die?'

'How do you think she died?'

'I think she killed herself,' said Odette plainly, and she looked out at the sodden cows, who chewed away at their pile of feed and didn't seem to notice the weather.

'Yes, she did,' said Benny, and her voice wavered a little, like there was wind blowing against it. It was hard, very hard, to say those words aloud to another person. Yet some relief came after she had said them. 'She was living back near Adelaide, in a town called Hahndorf. I looked at it on a map. It's just a dot.' Then, sensing that Odette wanted more of an explanation, she added: 'They think she took pills.'

It was true.

Vivian had been living alone. She didn't leave a note. Frank had said that Nola Moon was too old to deal with anything and that Vivian's brother was helping to clear out her apartment. In accordance with Nola's wishes, there'd been no funeral.

Odette rocked back and forth slowly in her chair and said, 'Right,' and then they were quiet together, with Bessel there too, resting on his long belly, his paws hanging over the edge of the wooden boards.

The cows had finished their food and the little white birds were standing next to them on the grass, and when Benny looked at the cows, the cows stared back. The two of them, with such intensity, they bored a hole in the house with their eyes, as if demanding Odette return with another bucketful, and then, for no good reason, one of them startled and turned, galloping back into the paddock. The other did the same, it turned and bolted, hooves louder than the rain, and the white birds flapped up, flying off in different directions, and

Benny had never seen cows run before and was astounded by their speed.

Bessel, unconcerned, squinted out towards the paddock, and Benny gave a surprised laugh. It was just a little laugh—at the fast cows and the nonchalant dog and the beautiful look of the paddock and the bush in the rain.

Odette let out a sob.

It was so unexpected to Benny, that sob, but she understood it, and it didn't last long at all, only a moment.

'You have this way about you, Benny, like you think you're responsible for it somehow, but you're not,' said Odette. 'It's not your fault that she left—or any of it. None of it's your fault.'

She rocked in the chair and looked out at the paddock, at the sheets of rain coming down, and she didn't speak again for a while, until her voice was composed and her body, the sturdy form of her, was at ease again. 'I invited Betsy over for Christmas lunch last night. Arden's coming too. Would you like to come? We could invite Frank, if you like. I don't know if that's something you'd want to do, but he'd be more than welcome.'

Benny Miller nodded and blinked. The rain was coming down in bucketfuls on the farmhouse, streaming over the tin roof, drenching the grass, soaking the quiet earth, and Benny blinked and nodded some more.

Acknowledgements

Thank you to Annette Barlow, Ali Lavau, and to all at Allen & Unwin who helped to bring this book into the world.

Thank you to booksellers, for the wonderful work you do.

I am indebted to Professor Derek Abbott at the University of Adelaide and former SA police officer Gerry Feltus, whose extensive research on the Somerton Man was extremely helpful. For further reading, I would suggest Prof Abbott's collection of online resource material and Gerry's book, *The Unknown Man: A suspicious death at Somerton Beach*.

For advice on police procedure, thank you to former NSW Detective Sargeant Bob Wells; and to former Detective and Assistant Commissioner of the NSW police Clive Small. Any potential errors in this area are my own.

For inspiration on old houses next to the bush, thank you to Carlie Lopez; and thanks to my mum, Margaret Throsby, for advice on various matters.

Thank you always to my family: Zoë, Alvy and Jones.

Most of all I give thanks to my mentor and friend Richard Walsh for such generous, wise, and good-humoured counsel.